S. R.

Surrogate

Sign up to the S. R. Durham newsletter to receive his first novel, Prey, for free: http://eepurl.com/hPtVSv

First edition

This book was professionally typeset on Reedsy. Find out more at reedsy.com

Contents

1

Maddie stared into the empty bedroom, mesmerised by the pulsating blackness and the distant sound of the shower spraying against Tony's back. The echoing claps each time he wrung out his hair. It seemed like he'd been in there for hours. Like he was hiding.

She looked over at the bedside table and was able to make out the curvature of their wine glasses side by side; the way they warped the light that spilled from the gap in the bathroom door. Tony's glass still had a small reservoir of red at the bottom while hers had been drained. She considered hugging the bedclothes up under her armpits and shuffling downstairs to refill the glasses, but then the shower cut off and the doors juddered open. She slumped back against the headboard to wait, the silk cold against her skin.

Tony emerged and the room was flooded with steam and searing fluorescent light. He was still towelling his hair as he lowered himself onto his side of the bed, strands of grey now visible in amongst the once lustrous black. Although the 18 years between them hadn't been as obvious when they first got together, Tony was now starting to pull away into middle age, leaving Maddie behind with her youth, fading by the day as it was.

Tony looked round at her and puffed out his cheeks in relief.

"Good?" Maddie said.

"Yeah," he said. "Needed it. Feel like a new man."

He finished drying his hair and began giving his beard the same rough treatment, then balled up the towel and bowled it into the bamboo clothes hamper on the other side of the room. They sat beside one another in the near dark, total silence. Maddie could feel the heat emanating from him, like sitting next to a radiator.

"I thought you said you were coming off the pill?" he said eventually, more of a question than a statement. The secret troubles he'd been mulling over in the shower were beginning to take shape in Maddie's mind. "Thought you said it was messing with your skin or something?"

"I have," she said. "It was."

"What, and you're still off it now?"

Maddie dropped her head slightly and sighed.

"Yeah. Have been for weeks now."

Tony sighed and turned back to face the bathroom.

"If you are, then why did we just do that?"

"You started it," she said, shoving him playfully with her foot.

"Don't Maddie."

"What's wrong with you? I thought you knew... I wouldn't have said-"

"Are you serious?" Tony said, cutting her off. He let out an exasperated laugh and shook his head. "So, I leave you three days ago and you're fine, now I'm back and you're basically telling me you want to get pregnant?"

Maddie's smile faded. She struggled for the right words, but her mind was blank, frozen by the embarrassment.

"Can you answer the question please, Maddie?" he said, sounding like a schoolteacher. "You can't just change your mind on something like that and not tell me, you know. It's not that simple, it's... When we were talking about getting married, even the week before, you promised me you weren't gonna to do this. More than once. I don't understand how you've just-"

"I've not 'just' anything," she said, finally finding the fight she knew she had inside her. "People are allowed to change their minds. Do you realise all I do is shuffle around here all day, useless? I need something else, Tony. Something-"

"You don't have a kid because you're bored, Maddie."

"That's not what I said! It's not because I'm bored. It's because I'm fucking... empty."

Water continued to drip sporadically from the showerhead, punctuating the otherwise pervasive quiet. Tony moved first. He stood and walked over to the wardrobe, then took out some clean boxer shorts and a dressing gown. He pulled them on and slid the wardrobe door closed and went to leave the room.

"Where are you going?" Maddie said.

"To get some water... then to the spare room."

"So that's it?" Maddie said. "You just get what you want and now you're leaving me again?"

"What I want?" he said, his voice beginning to crack. "How is this 'what I want'? I've only just got back and you're on this fucking baby stuff again. I'm 53, Maddie... I got out of that game years ago."

"Well I'm not," she said. "And I didn't. And don't fucking swear at me."

"I'm sorry."

"Forget it."

Maddie bundled up the covers and shuffled across to Tony's

4

side of the bed, then stood and slapped the bathroom light off and sat back down. As she curled up to try and will herself to sleep, she could feel that he was still hovering by the doorframe.

"Just go," she said. "You've said your piece."

He didn't reply, but he didn't move either. She heard him sigh and knew that he'd be massaging his eyes with his thumb and forefinger, like he always did when they reached this point in an argument. He was building up to something, to the delivery of the last word. Sometimes it was consoling, other times it was devastating. She bit her lip as she waited for it to come.

"Maddie," he said eventually. "I don't want to upset you. I'm sorry. You just... you know how I feel about all this. There's nothing I can do to change that."

Maddie screwed her eyes shut and kneaded her head further into the pillow.

"I was going to tell you later but... Al phoned me yesterday. He's still really down about his brother and all that and-"

"What are you saying?" Maddie said, though she was already sure of what he was preparing her for. She'd heard it enough times, recognised the rhythm of the conversation. It was like listening to an old crooner singing a familiar song; she was just waiting for the big finish.

"I'm gonna go away... see him for a couple of days," he said quietly. "To Brecon. Just hiking, fishing, pubs, probably. Make sure he's ok."

"When?" she said.

His made a glottal noise, as if he was about to speak but cut himself off before the sound became a word. This time he'd be looking up at the ceiling, she imagined. All she could hear was her own breath quickening against the pillow.

"When?" she said again.

"Tomorrow. First thing."

She heard him take a step towards the bed.

"I'm honestly really sorry. I should have said as soon as I got in. It was just with-"

"Just get out Tony. Leave me alone."

The rage had already burned itself out and she could feel wine on top of champagne on top of her, weighing her down. It was disorientating her, shrinking her perception. She pressed her foetal form into the mattress and cowered. She felt fragile, helpless. Like a doll in a matchstick bed, trapped inside the jaws of a tightening vice.

A tear rolled down her cheek, and she whispered: "It's what you're best at."

. . .

Maddie got up for her run at 6am to make sure there was no chance of bumping into Tony while she was still fuzzy headed. Her plan was to go once around the block, but at a good pace. Quick enough to sweat out the alcohol and clear her mind before the inevitable confrontation.

The streets of Wilmslow were always quiet at this time, usually no more than a few Manchester-bound nine-to-fivers walking their dogs or stay-at-home mums getting a head start on the day's errands. This morning was especially quiet. No doubt the chill in the air and whipping wind was enough to make most sane people realise that they'd get more out of another half an hour tucked up in bed.

Most of them probably had someone to share that with, Maddie supposed. She struggled to remember the last time she and Tony had woken up together and had breakfast in bed, like they used to. Falling in and out of sleep, in and out of each other's arms, occasionally stirring from their hibernation for another mouthful of toast or a swig of orange juice, like restless bears.

With her lap completed, Maddie passed through the house's electric gates and crunched her way back down the gravel driveway, guided through the gloom by the solar-powered lanterns that fringed it. She almost sprinted the last 50 metres, eventually slowing as she broke through the last pair of lights like an invisible finish line. She came to a stop and doubled over, panting, her hands clasped over her wobbling knees.

Steam billowed from the reflecting pool that dominated the left-hand side of the garden and rolled across the lawn, all but obscuring the cherry trees that lined its far edge. Although it was as man-made and flawless as everything else of Tony's, it looked almost ancient in that moment. Out of place. Like a lake from some Arthurian tale snatched out of time and dropped into a 21st Century suburb.

Maddie straightened back up and took out her earbuds, then stuffed them in her jacket pocket and surveyed the house for some sign of Tony.

Although it was shielded from the road by the garden's perimeter wall, once inside it was quite easy to see what was going on, thanks to wide sections of floor-to-ceiling glass that sliced through the building's dense granite facade. All of the windows were dark, making the whole structure look like a featureless monolith against the pale morning sky.

Maddie caught her breath and wiped the sweat from her upper lip, then began crunching towards the front door. Suddenly the spare room light flicked on at the far corner of the second floor. She could see Tony's silhouette hunched over at one side of the bed, his head cradled in his hands. After a few seconds, he jerked upwards and stood, then strode into the hallway.

. . .

By the time Tony was dressed and clomping down the main staircase, his bags bumping against the bannister, Maddie was standing at the kitchen island shredding spinach and kale for her post-run smoothie. After dividing the greens into equal piles, she then got to work peeling and chopping half a mango, half a banana, and a large chunk of pineapple. Small Mason jars containing seeds, protein powders, and vitamin blends were arranged next to the chopping board, ready to be measured into the blender alongside the fresh ingredients. Everything as it should be, just the way she liked it. Like she needed it.

Tony's faithful boxer dog, Tank, was already lying in wait behind Maddie's legs, just in case she was clumsy enough to lose her grip on a piece of food; though she knew he'd be sorely disappointed when he realised that it was only fruit and vegetables up for grabs.

Maddie looked up from the board to see Tony striding towards the front door, apparently oblivious that she even existed. He fumbled his keys from his jeans pocket, fighting to control his heavy rucksack as it swung from one shoulder, then unlocked the door and stepped out into the cold morning air. Tank heaved himself to his feet and padded over to watch his master load up the car to leave him once again.

When they both came back inside, Tony was walking bent over so he could pat the animal's haunches without breaking stride. He clearly didn't want to waste any more time at home than he already had, Maddie thought.

Tank continued to hop gleefully at his master's side like a dog possessed, both of them grumbling to one another in their private language. Tony approached the island and braced himself against the opposite side, the only sound coming from Tank's paws as they clicked against the tiles with every jump.

"Has he been fed?" Tony said quietly.

Maddie remained focussed on the knife in her white-knuckle grip. Despite the fact that all of the ingredients were being thrown into the blender to be churned up together, she was intent on making sure each cube was of equal height, width, and depth. Each cut was thoughtful, as if she was pruning the leaves of a Bonsai tree.

"Is that it?" she said eventually. "Is that all you're gonna say?"

"What?"

"After last night. Is that all you're going to say? 'Has he been fed'?"

"Ah, Jesus," he said, his own knuckles flexing as his grip on the granite worktop tightened. "I said I'm sorry, and I meant it, but I can't let Al down. You know how close him and Daff were; how hard it's all been for 'em. He just needs to get into the open air and talk some stuff out, I think. He's helped me out enough times."

Although Tony and Al had gone their separate ways after three years as housemates at Cardiff University – Tony starting the business that would become Degrassi Architects with his brother, Luca, and Al settling in south Wales with his wife to-be, Ginny – the pair always made a point of staying in touch, for the first decade or so, at least. Eventually, their yearly hikes took a back seat to work and family commitments, and their contact was reduced to the odd call on birthdays or holidays.

A few years ago, not long after Tony's divorce from his first wife, Kelly, Al appeared on Facebook and the stars seemed to align. Tony spoke about the reunion as if it had given both men a new lease on life; him with a new wife in Maddie and a soon-to-be empty nest and Al apparently keen to take his first stuttering steps into the 21st Century.

According to Tony, Al and Ginny were 'hippies' who had decided to live off-grid not long after they married, setting themselves up in an old farmhouse not far from the Brecon Beacons, growing their own food and even making their own clothes. Tony often made himself laugh by claiming that they even 'knitted their own yoghurt', though Maddie was never quite sure what made that funny.

Either way, the lifestyle was a choice for Al and Ginny; isolated both geographically and ideologically from the fast-paced world that Tony had gone on to inhabit.

Maddie had always assumed that this was the reason Tony had been so keen to rekindle the relationship when his old friend reappeared. For him, Al represented an escape from the stress that had been part of his life ever since he left university to become a high-flying architect. An opportunity to spend time with someone who wasn't impressed by his money or his success, who allowed him to just be himself.

Now, however, things were different. Al's brother, Daff, had finally succumbed to the tenacious pancreatic cancer that he'd been fighting for years, and it was time for Tony to pay his dues to the man who'd so often been there for him.

"This is the last trip for ages though, I promise," Tony said as he paced back and forth. "No work stuff coming up either, I made sure of it."

Maddie continued to chop the fruit, brushing the offcuts to one side with the flat of the blade.

"Do you want any of this?" she said, ignoring his empty promises.

"Nah, I'm good ta. I'll just grab a coffee once I'm on the road."

He bent down to retrieve the bag of dog food from the cupboard, then walked over to Tank's bowl and poured him a generous portion. Maddie let out a snort and shook her head.

"I can look after a dog for three days, Tony. It's not like I don't have to do it enough as it is."

"It's not that," Tony said. "You know what he's like."

He replaced the bag, shut the door, and leant back against the worktop. After silently enduring a few more seconds of wordless chopping, he turned and headed for the front door.

"Fuck," Maddie said, sucking air in through her clenched teeth.

The knife clattered onto the glass board, a thin film of blood coating the blade where it had passed straight through her thumb.

Blood oozed down her hand, dribbling over her wrist and pattering onto worktop so freely that she froze for a couple of seconds in awe. She gripped her thumb tightly below the wound, her perfectly manicured cuticles already pooling with the sticky red liquid.

"Fuck," she said again, wheeling round to lean over and bleed into the wide Belfast sink. She swatted the tap on and eased her trembling hand into the stream of ice-cold water, which diluted the blood from its deep red to a pale coral before sending it swirling down the plughole.

Tony swore and rushed over to her, plucking a fresh tea towel from a hook on the wall as he did so.

"Here you are, just wrap this-"

"It's fine," she said over the sound of the rushing tap. "I'm fine. Just a cut. Fucking stings though."

Tony set the tea towel down next to the sink and rested his hand gently at the nape of her neck. She shrugged his hand off, finished washing the wound, then went over to the tall cupboard that contained the first aid kit. She retrieved it, then slapped it down, and began thumbing through the different sizes of plasters like a secretary flicking through a Rolodex. Tony had clearly been in it over the past few weeks, as her carefully arranged system was in complete disarray. She silently reminded herself to come and back reorganise it later.

Tony watched her open-mouthed as she tore into an alcohol wipe packet with her teeth, cleaned the cut again, and covered it with a thin strip of royal blue. She put the wrappers in the bin, then turned around and looked at Tony as if he had just teleported into the room from another dimension.

"I thought you were in a rush?" she said.

"I am..." he said, gesturing to the front door. "I just didn't want to go while you were... like that."

"I'm used to looking after myself."

"I know you are, fucking hell," he said, exasperated. "It's not that, it's just-"

"Please," she said, closing her eyes in an attempt to make him disappear. "Just go. Al's never let you down. Do what you need to do, then come back home. It's fine. We'll do something nice when you come back."

Maddie did everything she could to twitch her mouth into a smile, though it couldn't have lasted more than a second.

"You sure?" Tony said, his expression strained as if he was bracing for a right hook.

"Yeah. You're gonna have to do better than those though," she said, nodding towards the bunch of guilt roses he'd returned with the previous night.

Tony's whole body loosened up as he walked towards her, like the tension was evaporating with every step.

"I will," he said, grinning. "I'll pick all the lilies in Wales."

"Daffodils," Maddie said as they embraced.

"Oh yeah," he said with a chuckle.

"And I meant more like a week in the Maldives."

She tried another smile as he leant in and kissed her cheek, the rest of her body statue-still.

"I love you," he said.

"Love you too."

Tony turned and strode out towards the door, Tank clomping along at his master's heels all the way outside to the car.

After finishing her crime scene clean-up, Maddie binned the paper towels and went over to the front door. As she reached the threshold, Tony's Range Rover had just completed a three-point turn and was spraying gravel into the pond as it accelerated away. Tank hadn't moved an inch, still sat obediently where the driver's door had been, the warmth of his master's hand no doubt still on his forehead.

"Tank," Maddie said. "Come on. Come inside."

She wafted her hands towards the open door, like cabin crew pointing out the emergency exits, but the truth was that she had just as much chance of controlling a full-sized airliner as she did Tony's dog.

"Come on," she said again, a little more force this time.

Tank turned to regard her, saliva dripping from his jowls, and stood. Maddie cocked her head, as much in surprise as in satisfaction, and pushed away from the door frame with her shoulder. She stood back to let the dog inside, but instead he sloped off in the opposite direction.

"Tank! What are you playing at?"

He reached the lawn, oblivious to the splinters appearing in the timbre of her voice, then turned around to face her and squatted to begin forcing out a shit. His black pearl eyes never deviated from hers as he began to shake.

"Fucking dickhead," she said under her breath. "Alright... two minutes, then come inside."

She sighed and went back over to the chopping board.

After she'd blended, drank, washed, and dried; a sudden shiver caused her to stare at the still open front door. She knew the electric gates would have closed behind Tony after he left, that no one could walk into the house even if they wanted to, but something about the sight of the cold light spilling across the marble floor filled her with dread.

She was used to being alone, and she hadn't always had big granite walls to hide behind, but try as she might, she couldn't shake the feeling of vulnerability. It crawled across her skin like insect legs.

"Tank?" she said, her voice wobbly with nerves. "Tank?"

After a few more silent seconds, the dog slunk through the doorway and straight into one of the sitting rooms – the one they called 'his' sitting room – barley turning to acknowledge her.

She skittered across the tiles and slammed the door; her eyes screwed shut so she couldn't see anything outside that would tip her into full-blown paranoia. Three days, she thought. Just three days and she could relax again. Safe and sound, like a fairy tale princess in her castle of glass and stone.

2

Maddie fought her way through the day, as she so often did, by amassing an exhaustive list of errands to occupy her mind. She'd already cleaned the house from top to bottom the day before, in preparation for Tony's short-lived homecoming, as well as stocking the fridge and cupboards with enough food to endure even the most protracted of nuclear winters. As a result, most of her time was spent assessing – and subsequently buying materials for – a number of DIY projects that had been rearing their ugly heads over the preceding weeks.

She'd long since abandoned any hope that Tony would find the time to sort them out, so she decided that now was as good a time as any to tackle them.

Although she never let on to Tony, the truth was, she enjoyed it. She'd always wanted to work in interior design – even though she only ended up selling adverts for an industry magazine – but having a house as big as Tony's to play around with was like a childhood dream come true; and a far cry from the two-bed council house she'd gown up in.

Her first task was to replace one of the three external lights attached to the rear of the house. These were not your average lights, of course. Not like the little one that used to click on and off underneath her bedroom window, reassuring her that her father had managed to make it home from the pub. These were football stadium-style, LED floodlights; whose glaring range extended well beyond the raised Indian stone patio and onto the sprawling back garden, falling just short of the treeline at its rear.

Even so, the whole thing was taken care of by lunchtime thanks to the combined efforts of Dan's DIY Shop in town and a few of her most trusted YouTube experts. This little victory was followed by filling and repainting the hole in the hallway wall, which only existed thanks to another of Tank's exploits. He'd come bounding into the house with a giant branch from the woods at the bottom of the garden and punctured the plasterboard like someone driving a straw through a milkshake lid.

With these two achievements and a quick workout in the bank, Maddie decided that she'd distracted herself by natural means for long enough.

Total darkness was still an hour or so away when she finally gave in but, given the pervasive grey outside, she deemed it more than dark enough to open a bottle of wine.

When she first started coming around to Tony's house – back when she could only visit if his wife, Kelly, was away for work and the kids were out – Maddie was consistently impressed by the fact that there always seemed to be an open bottle of champagne in the fridge, quite often with a silver spoon slid nonchalantly into its neck like a calcified bud in an oversized vase. It was one of the images that stayed with her. It reminded her of exactly how it felt to be crossing that final threshold from the real world into the life she'd always aspired to.

Since then, things had changed. Now champagne was just the drink that got her started every night.

Maddie filled a flute to the brim and shuffled her way into one of the two downstairs living rooms, Tank's room. This one was smaller and – unlike most of the exposed downstairs rooms – only had a single slot window to interrupt the thick stone walls.

Tank nosed the heavy oak door open and padded over to his bed in the corner, taking the time to give Maddie a look that felt as if he was authorising her to spend the evening in his room. She curled up in the corner of the large L-shaped sofa, took the three remotes from the arm, and began the arduous process of coaxing the colossal wall-mounted screen into life.

Maddie eventually decided that the perfect accompaniment to the alcohol was some trash TV; the more insipid, the better. After finishing the third episode of *Stenhouse & Radley: We Sell Haunted Houses* and her fourth glass of champagne, Maddie left the TV on the home screen and began scrolling through her various social media accounts. Facebook yielded little of interest, neither did Instagram, but when she opened her Twitter and began to dig, it wasn't long before her suspicions began to gather.

She'd intentionally spent the evening avoiding all social media, and Twitter most of all, as that was where Tony was most active. She stopped the page as she flew past one of his Tweets from the day before, presumably written at the airport after he'd left the conference he'd been attending.

The post was innocuous in itself – thanking the organisers for their hospitality and the attendees for their attention – but when Maddie began following the hashtags he'd included at the bottom, she quickly stumbled into a conversation that she was never meant to see. A woman, practically a girl by the looks of her, had posted a picture from what appeared to be some kind of drinks reception at the conference. She and Tony were both grinning broadly, and each had a glass of champagne in the hand that wasn't draped over the other's shoulder. The lighting was perfect; Tony's white teeth and dark skin making him look like a film star compared to the sullen middle-aged man that had trudged out of the door that morning.

Maddie's eyes drifted down towards the caption:

Such an inspiring time at @tedxgoteburg thanks to @mrtony-degrassi for his amazing closing speech! #ideaswortspreading #gettinspired #newworkhusbnd

The spelling mistakes suggested it had been more than just one drink they'd had together, which unsettled Maddie slightly, but it was the last hashtag that made her stomach lurch like she was in an aeroplane dropping for a rough landing.

Her hand trembled with rage, and she felt her nose begin to tingle like it did before a sneeze or a cascade of tears. She slapped the phone, face down, onto the glass coffee table and stared at the frozen television screen.

"What the fuck," she said, her voice muffled by her fingers. "What the actual fuck."

The picture was chaste enough, but she knew the subtext that often underpinned a post like that. This girl was carefree, and clearly enjoying the attention of someone she thought she admired. She was having a good time and she wanted the world to know about it. She didn't know anything about Tony's faceless, maybe even nameless wife, and neither did she care about offending her.

Maddie knew all of these feelings well, because she'd already felt all of them herself. Only now *she* was the nameless wife. *She* was the one who was isolated, oblivious to the events that led up to that 'innocent' photograph. And totally unaware of what happened in the hours that followed.

Her mind began racing through a thousand different per-mutations. Every possibility, however sordid or unlikely. Mutated memories of her formative experiences with Tony, with another girl's face and body in place of her own. When she couldn't take any more, she wrenched her hands from her lips and stood.

"No way. No way," she said to herself.

Tank raised his head slightly to acknowledge her leaving the room, then plopped it back onto his paws and closed his eyes.

Maddie stopped by the kitchen to throw a fistful of ice and a generous portion of vodka into a glass tumbler, then trudged up the stairs. She checked her phone as she walked. Tony's name was still conspicuously absent from her received messages. No sign of him on WhatsApp since 17:32.

It was out of character. Alarmingly so, in fact, given how attached he was to his phone most of the time. Even on weekends or holidays, he'd make sure he stayed in touch with colleagues and clients, if only to keep them under pressure to do the same.

She retreated to the darkness of her bedroom, the safety of her bed, and checked WhatsApp again:

Tony x
  last seen today at 17:32

"Fuck it," she whispered, taking a fortifying gulp of vodka before she stabbed the call button with her thumb.

The earpiece let out a few seconds of bubbling static, then cut straight to Tony's answerphone. She hung up and dropped the phone into her lap, her fingers instinctively pressing to her lips as her stomach churned acid. She illuminated the phone to see that midnight was fast approaching. Almost six hours since he was last online.

Although she was hamstrung by alcohol, Maddie did her best to stumble through every conceivable scenario of where he could be, why his phone would be off. None of them seemed familiar enough to be plausible.

He always travelled with power bricks, always booked into places with reliable Wi-Fi. There was no way he'd be off his phone for six whole hours, even in Brecon.

Further still, it was him in the wrong after springing the trip on her at the last minute. Even if he was callous enough to ignore her on a normal trip – he wasn't – but even if he was, he would have still sent a cursory, "made it safe and sound". He always did.

Maddie tried his number again and was again greeted by the patronising gatekeeper of his answerphone.

She placed her phone on the bedside table and retrieved her glass, the ice slush and vodka swilling around and crackling inside it like a snow globe-sized scene of a choppy Arctic Ocean. She half expected to see a couple of tiny polar bears jumping from cube to cube, their homes shrinking by the second.

She let out a flickering breath and sipped her drink and waited.

One more minute, and she'd allow herself to try again.

3

Maddie was awoken by what she first mistook to be an angle grinder carving through the back of her skull. She winced and buried her face deeper into the pillow until the noise stopped, then let out a muffled sigh of relief. Just as she was beginning to fall back to sleep, the buzzing started up again, this time in frantic, staccato bursts.

She pressed both hands into the mattress and arched her back, craning her head around to face the glow of a wall-mounted LED tablet. Her vision was impaired slightly by the blonde bird's nest that her hair had tangled itself into, but on the screen, she could see the frowning face of her ex-colleague and current confidant, Helen, jabbing her finger at something off camera.

Maddie flopped back down, then slithered her legs from beneath the covers and levered herself to her feet. She didn't remember getting naked, but her clothes became an obstacle course on the way to the tablet, bra straps like snares and sleek activewear like tiny oil slicks. The sawing sound continued as she shambled towards the screen, only relenting as she shakily tapped the green phone icon in the bottom corner. She ran her tongue over her bottom lip as she examined her friend's image, then spoke in a crackling whisper.

"Hello?"

"Maddie? Hey, it's me," Helen said, tilting her ear towards the camera for some reason.

"Yeah, I can see you."

"Oh, sorry," she said, stifling her laugh with a gloved hand. "Hiiii."

She looked into the camera and gave her best goofy wave, before she appeared to remember why she had called in the first place.

"Sorry, babe, were you in bed? I just wanted to see if you were ok."

Her voice was distant, distorted. Maddie looked at the clock in the top corner of the screen and was taken aback to discover it was closer to midday than morning.

"It's fine, don't worry," Maddie said. "Come in. Here you are."

She touched the key icon that unlocked the front gates, saw Helen's expression change as she heard them clunk ajar and begin to motor apart.

"Oh there we go," she said. "Ok, see you in a sec."

Maddie watched as Helen replaced her sunglasses and hopped down from the step towards her waiting car.

Maddie shut off the monitor, turned to look at the tsunami of bedclothes and the empty vodka glass on the bedside table. The very sight of it caused her stomach to lurch, first with sickness, then with something like embarrassment at the memory of how she had sat there and called Tony's answer phone every minute without fail until she passed out against the headboard.

She wanted nothing more than to shower. To wash away the alcohol and the sickly sweat and the fear.

The doorbell shook Maddie from her malaise, and she snatched a dressing gown from the back of the door and headed down to let Helen in. The echo of Tank's bark slapped from glass to marble to granite, accompanying the doorbell to create a powerful disharmony.

As soon as Maddie opened the door, the dog shoved past her and was only stopped from pawing at Helen's coat by the two fingers Maddie shot through his collar. The women muttered nervously as Maddie apologised and Helen slinked inside past Tank's frothing jaws. With the introductions out of the way, Maddie released her grip and nudged Tank outside with her knee.

"Five minutes, I mean it," she shouted, and shut the door

behind him.

She turned to her friend, who was waiting patiently on the spot where Tank had tried to maul her, a small handbag clutched in front of her.

"I'm so sorry," Maddie said, tucking her hair behind her ear. "He's such a dick, he just doesn't listen to me."

"It's ok," Helen said. "Honestly, it's fine. My mum's is exactly the same."

As they both caught their breath, Helen cocked her head as she examined her friend. Maddie had managed to synch up her gown but was still attempting to tame her hair back into its ponytail.

"Come here," Helen said, lunging towards her with arms outstretched. "I've been so worried... been calling you all morning."

They locked into a firm hug and Maddie closed her eyes, at peace for the first time in days.

When she'd first met her, Maddie had mistaken Helen's middle-class inflection for an air of condescension, though the truth was she was just the victim of a good upbringing.

Helen made enough money to have her own flat and dress fashionably at all times, but she'd underachieved quite spectacularly over the years, given the start she'd had. Her childhood was spent at an all-girls boarding school, after which she studied business at a red brick university. Despite these marks on her CV, and perhaps because of an extended period travelling around South America, she eventually found herself alongside Maddie selling adverts together for an interior design trade magazine.

They met in the middle, they used to say. The only difference was that Helen stayed there, forced to watch while her working-class friend moved past her, onwards and upwards, ultimately enthralling Tony, who was the co-owner of one of the largest and most ground-breaking architecture firms of the time.

With a final squeeze, the women parted, Helen's heels reverberating like a pair of judge's gavels on the marble as she stepped backwards. Maddie looked around the cavernous hallway then at Helen, who didn't seem to be enjoying the soothing gloom nearly as much.

"Right, first thing's first," Helen said. "Where's the coffee?"

. . .

Maddie perched on one of the wooden bar stools and slumped over the kitchen island while she coached Helen in the use of the barista style coffee machine. Although it looked intimidating with its dials and steam wand and brushed stainless steel, it was simple enough to make a pair of oat milk flat whites, thanks in part to Maddie's mumbled instructions. After Maddie rinsed the components and loaded them into the dishwasher, they took their coffees and went into the larger of the two sitting rooms, or The Lodge as Tony called it, only semi-facetiously.

Rather than being pointed at a television, the furniture in this room was arranged around a monolithic granite fireplace, which was raised on a three foot tall hearthstone and open on all four sides. When fully stocked with wood and roaring on a dark winter's night, it was easy to believe that you had taken a sofa and dropped it beside Stonehenge to observe an ancient druid fire ritual.

The bleached skull of a fallow deer was mounted on the stone chimney breast, its splayed antlers almost matching the width of the meteorite chunk of a mantlepiece below. This rustic touch was evident throughout the room in faux animal skin throws and a pair of antler chandeliers suspended from the high ceiling. It was a stark but admittedly cosy departure from the floor-to-ceiling glass, metal, and marble that ran throughout the ground floor.

Helen slipped off her coat, scarf, and shoes, and curled up beside Maddie on another large L-shaped sofa. They both sat in silence for a few moments, blowing gently over the rims of their steaming mugs.

"So," Helen said with a sigh. "What happened?"

"What do you mean?"

"Last night… your message."

Maddie's stomach began to lurch again, and her hand instinctively pressed against her dressing gown pocket for her phone. It was empty. She looked straight ahead, her mouth gaping, as if the memory was to be found somewhere in her friend's dark eyes.

"Do you not remember?"

Maddie shook her head and took a sip of the coffee, if only to obscure part of her face from Helen's thoughtful gaze.

"Sorry, I... I got a bit carried away," she said, forcing a nervous laugh. "I wasn't ranting at you, was I?"

Helen mirrored her smile and put a hand on her shoulder. "No, no, don't be silly," she said. "I just got a voice message about 11pm saying that Tony wasn't answering his phone and you were worried he might be-"

"Sorry," Maddie said, not wanting to be reminded of how frantic she had been. "I can't even remember calling. Sorry, you-"

"Stop saying sorry, it's fine. What was the matter? Is he not back yet?"

Maddie sniffed and took another sip while she thought. "He got back from Sweden the night before last, then left again yesterday morning."

"Again? Where?"

"Wales, with his friend Al. Al's brother died not long ago, so he just wanted to, I don't know… It's just for a few days apparently."

"Christ," said Helen, looking off into the kitchen. Maddie could practically hear the cogs whirring in her head.

"So that's why you were upset?" she said, looking back at Maddie.

"No, not exactly. I can't get hold of him, haven't heard anything since he walked out the door. No sign of him online… phone's off. Or it was last night. His phone's never off."

"Do you have Al's number?" Helen said.

Maddie shook her head and took another tentative slurp of her coffee.

Helen fell silent, the steam from her mug almost veiling her puzzled expression.

"I saw a picture, on Twitter," Maddie said eventually. "Of him and some girl, no idea who it was. Someone from the conference he was at."

"A picture of what?"

"Nothing, really… them together, looking happy. Just set me off. Stupid, I suppose."

"I wouldn't say that, given... well, you know... what happened with you two," Helen said. "You've every right to be suspicious, I think."

They both sat quietly for a moment, before Helen said: "Do you know for a fact that's where he's gone? Wales I mean... Are you sure that's who he's away with?"

"What do you mean?"

"Well, you know," Helen said. "Have you seen anything? Bookings or whatever? He tell you the name of the place he's staying?"

Maddie shook her head, then looked down into her empty mug. She stared at the sandy scum at the bottom, trying her best to find an answer in the bubbles like a mystic with her tea leaves.

"Well... you know his passwords, don't you?" said Helen.

"His emails?"

"Yeah, the logins and stuff. Surely, if he's booked somewhere, there will be some kind of confirmation or something? I mean, I know he might not have booked it, but it's worth a try."

"Fucking hell," Maddie said, placing her mug on the oak coffee table and rubbing her temples. "That's asking for trouble, isn't it?"

"Maybe... but at least you'll know. I'm not trying to fuck your head up or anything, I just think... that's what I'd do."

Maddie puffed out her cheeks, closed her eyes, and continued to massage her throbbing forehead. If she was mildly suspicious before, Helen's words had pushed her closer towards the paranoia she'd been fighting since Tony had left. She thought of the computer in his office upstairs. She already knew the password from times when Tony had called up needing her to send things from his desktop to his work email. One of the many perks he enjoyed as a result of having nudged her towards becoming a stay-at-home wife, she often reminded him.

She racked her brain. Did she have to put in a password to send those things to him, or was his mail always open on there? Either way, she thought it was worth a try; if only to give her mind something else to do than imagining Tony and some girl in a seedy hotel room.

. . .

In bare feet, they snuck up to the office like children. Maddie's breathing was shallow, and her chest was tight, her limbs pumping lactic acid. Even the few steps from the landing to the office door had felt like running a marathon through peanut butter.

"Can't fucking believe I'm doing this," she said as the glass door complained against the carpet.

"You're doing nothing wrong," Helen said. "They're facts

aren't they. You're just checking facts."

Maddie said nothing as she rounded the desk and plopped into the padded leather chair in front of the computer. Although she'd used it sporadically before, the very sight of the Apple logo at the base of the screen was enough to make her grimace.

It was an aversion that had taken many years to form, most likely stemming from the fact that it was representative of all the handsets that she could never afford. All those sideways looks when she was forced to use someone else's iPhone and didn't even know how to open the dialler. It was the same look she'd had throughout her teenage years, like when she was forced to reveal that she hadn't read Harry Potter, or been to Spain, or had a Tamagotchi. That seemingly innocuous kind of otherness that she always suspected stood in place of something more upsetting.

Even as her financial situation improved after a few months working at the magazine, that bitter taste remained, eventually festering into outright stubbornness when she realised that Tony owned Apple everything; from the computers, to the watch, to the tablets, and, more recently, the TV. He even had a box in his wardrobe exclusively dedicated to outdated Apple products, just in case he needed them. To Maddie, all that his Apple graveyard proved was how quickly those things became obsolete.

As a result of this aversion, she was basically clueless when it came to using them. While this was merely annoying at times, there were others – like trying to spy on Tony's emails

– where it was almost completely immobilising.

She tapped the spacebar with her thumb to shock the machine into life, then puffed out her cheeks and hammered in the password. After a few seconds an Alpine vista appeared; the majesty of the which was marred by the dozens of documents and folders strewn haphazardly across it. Red, circular notifications piled up at the corners of most of the icons along the bottom. Numerous open windows were minimised alongside them.

"That's killing you isn't it," Helen said as she leant against back of the chair. She'd always seemed to get a kick out of Maddie's compulsive tidiness, particularly as she was one of the least organised people Maddie had ever met.

"It's absolutely outrageous," Maddie said. "And the least surprising thing ever. The fuck is... is it this one?"

Maddie's eyes darted around for the logo that would serve as the portal into his personal emails, but the sheer chaos in front of her was paralysing. Helen reached over her shoulder and pointed towards a blue postage stamp at the bottom, depicting an eagle.

"That's emails, isn't it? There."

Maddie dragged the cursor over to the icon and clicked it, causing the inbox to warp up from the right-hand corner of the screen. It was already open.

Maddie exhaled loudly again, then began skimming the pre-viewed text for clues. The third unread message from the top – an email from a company called Red Dragon Cottages – was only a day old.

"The Old Cottage at Stone's Reach," said Maddie, reading the email aloud. "Dear Mr Degrassi, blah blah, thank you for choosing our Brecon hideaway. Check in... there, that's yesterday's date. So he is in Wales, at least."

Helen leant forwards and squinted at the screen; her head now parallel with Maddie's. They both read together in silence, before Maddie began scrolling through the emails again in search of any more correspondence with the company.

"There's no thread or VAT receipt or anything, just this... whatever this is," Maddie said, waving at the computer screen.

After another few minutes of fruitless keyword searches and scrolling in blind panic, she pushed herself out from under the desk and barged past Helen.

"Sorry, can I just... I'm gonna go and find my phone."

She breezed out of the office in the direction of the bedroom, her dressing gown billowing behind her like a runaway bride. Once inside, she slapped on the main light and began scaveng-ing madly through the piles of her discarded clothes. With no sign of the phone, she then attacked the bed, rifling through the sheets and pillows with increasing ferocity.

"Fuck's sake," she panted.

She stood back and closed her eyes and listened to her breathing, the blood thundering through her ears. She opened her
eyes again and stared at Tony's bedside table. Even though
she could see the black glass was empty, she ran her hand
over it in a circular motion, as if to glean the memory from its
surface. Just then something clicked, and she levered herself
forward to peer into the chasm between the back of the table
and the wall.

"You alright?" Helen said from the doorway.

"Yeah," Maddie said. "Think it could be..."

She flashed an awkward smile Helen's way as she contorted
herself into the right position to dig around behind the table.
After a few seconds of clattering, her hand emerged clutching
the slim black handset.

Maddie unlocked the screen and scrolled straight to Tony's
name in the phonebook and hit the call button. She slumped
on the bed with the phone to her ear, her eyes locked with
Helen's as she listened to ring after ring without end. Finally,
the network's voicemail service cut in. She cut off the call,
clenched her jaw, and dialled again.

"Still nothing?" Helen said as Maddie listened to the third set
of rings.

She shook her head and hung up, then stood and walked

around the bed towards the door.

"It's ringing now... but still no answer."

"Maybe he's just... Maybe he ran out of battery or something," said Helen. "If they were out all day, then went to the pub or something. Maybe forgot to put it on charge..."

She trailed off. Maddie stared at the phone, at the picture of her and Tony she'd chosen as her home screen, hand-in-hand off the coast of Bali on the bow of a rented yacht. Blue sky and blue sea and the white of distant sands. She searched Tony's bronzed face for an answer, but he gave her nothing.

She brushed past Helen again and headed back to the office. Once back in the chair, she scrolled back up to the email from Red Dragon Cottages, found the contact number and tapped it into her phone.

Two rings sounded, then came the clacking of an old plastic landline being unhooked and put to someone's ear.

"Red Dragon Cottages," said a husky woman's voice. She sounded tired and was most definitely local, judging by the way she rolled the first letter. "Hello?"

"Sorry, hi... My name's Maddie... Maddie Degrassi."

Even after two years of marriage, it still felt strange to say Degrassi instead of Duggan, though she didn't quite know why. Perhaps, she thought, it was common for any married person to go through a period of adjustment; even the shift from saying 'boyfriend' to 'husband' was an unnatural one for her. Many of her married friends reassured her this was normal, but part of her worried that it was rooted in something deeper. A hangover from her father's folk superstitions; that she should never marry a man whose surname started with the same initial as hers. If he was still alive, her father would have warned her that it could only lead to bad luck in the future.

"I see," the woman on the phone said, shaking Maddie from her malaise. "Well, what can I do for you love?"

"Sorry, yeah... so my husband Tony is supposed to be booked in at one of your properties," she said. "The Old Cottage at Stone's Reach?"

"Ah right. Hang on, love."

Maddie listened intently as paper rustled in the background. Helen appeared at the office door and queried her with a wide-eyed thumbs up. Maddie nodded and looked back at the computer.

"Mr Degrassi, yes," the woman said eventually. "Anthony. He was supposed to check in yesterday actually, but we never heard from him. Tried to get hold of him last night, left him a message and everything but... yeah, no news so far. Was on my list for this morning, tell you the truth. Bit of a late start, you know."

Maddie's stomach rolled again, gastric acid churning around

inside it like a raffle drum filled with toxic waste. She shakily pressed her hand to her mouth, stifling the vomit that was bubbling up into her throat.

"Are you sure," she said through her fingers. "Did he-"

She was interrupted by the muffled sound of a man's voice yelling something about plant pots and his van on the other end of the line.

"Did he what, love? Sorry, one second, hang on."

The phone crackled as the woman attempted to cover the mouthpiece, though it did little to muffle the barrage of obscenities she unleashed on the man shouting in the background, who seemed to be her son or grandson. Maddie swallowed, taking a second to catch up with her racing mind.

"Just give me a minute alright?" said the woman. "I'm still on the phone. Bloody numpty..."

Maddie heard more rustling, and the woman's voice was clear again.

"Sorry love. Yeah so, your husband. Basically, he didn't say that he was, you know, cancelling the booking or going somewhere else or anything. I emailed yesterday but there was no reply or anything. Not that it needed it."

"Yeah, I've just seen," Maddie said, her chin dipping to rest on her collarbone. "So, he's not checked in?"

"He hasn't, no."

"And you've heard nothing from him? At all?"

"That's right, love."

"Right, ok... Did you..."

"Did I what, love?"

"Sorry, I don't know. It's fine, don't worry. Thanks for your help. Sorry to-"

"It's alright love. You take care now."

The receiver clapped back into place before Maddie had chance to reply, leaving only the disorientating drone of a flatlining dial tone.

4

With the cacophony of the Red Dragon office still ringing in Maddie's ears, the yawning silence of the house began to envelop her once again. Helen was perched on the edge of the desk, chewing on the corners of her manicured nails. All Maddie could do was gawp at the computer screen, longing for the ignorance that was still intact when she first sat down in front of it.

"He never checked in," she said eventually. "Never even called them."

Helen said nothing, most likely because there was nothing she could possibly say. As far as Maddie was concerned, this meant one of two things; either the booking was some kind of red herring left by Tony to cover his adulterous tracks, or something very bad had happened. As much as she thought about it, she still couldn't decide which one she'd prefer.

In an attempt to break the tension, Helen stood and came around the desk and crouched next to the chair. She put one hand on the leather armrest, and the other gently on Maddie's knee.

"What do you want to do? Just tell me, and we can do it. Anything."

"Like what?" Maddie said vacantly. "I don't even know how to feel. Like, is he in bed with someone else or dead in a ditch?"

"Don't say that," Helen said, rubbing her hand on Maddie's leg like she was petting a dog. "It'll just be some kind of mix up... you know what he's like. Probably just decided on something else, spur of the moment."

"It was spur of the moment anyway," Maddie said. "Why would he change his plans again? It doesn't make any sense."

They both fell quiet. Maddie checked her phone again for any sign of Tony, then tried to call him again.

"Welcome to the O2 voicemai-"

"Fuck's sake," Maddie said, slapping the phone down onto the desk. She leant forwards and began sobbing quietly, driving the heels of her palms into her eye sockets until she could see coloured amoebas swimming through the black.

She felt Helen's hand move from the armrest onto the top of her back as she stood. As her cries intensified, she squeaked the chair around to face her friend and looped her arms around her waist and leant into her stomach.

"It's going to be alright, Mads, honestly. You'll be alright."

The two women remained in this embrace until Maddie's shuddering slowed and they separated, Helen squatting back down to meet her friend's eyes. Maddie sniffed and wiped her eyes and nose with the sleeve of her dressing gown, then took hold of Helen's outstretched hands.

"Not helping the fucking hangover, all this," Maddie said. They both laughed weakly.

"Look, why don't you get in the shower and get ready, and we'll make a plan? We'll try and figure something out... ok?" said Helen.

"Ok," Maddie said, still unable to meet her friend's eyes for fear of breaking down again.

Helen helped her to her feet, and they walked arm in arm towards the hall. Just as the glass door was about to close behind them, the sound of Maddie's phone rumbling across the desk stopped them dead. They turned sharply, instinctively, towards one another, then looked back into the office.

The phone buzzed again, rattling past the keyboard on its way to the carpet. Maddie spun and darted into the room and dropped to her knees in front of the glowing screen. She snatched it up, then held it out to face Helen.

"Says it's an unknown number," Maddie said.

"Answer it."

Maddie tapped the green phone icon and pressed the handset to her ear.

"Hell... Hello?"

"Hello, is that Mrs Degrassi?" said a man's voice. "Madeline Degrassi?"

His accent was soft, and hard to place. The cold authority in his tone was immediately unsettling.

"It is, yeah. Maddie," she said. "What's the... who is this?"

"My name is Inspector Clark, Dyfed–Powys Police."

"Police? What's happened? Is it Tony?"

Helen tucked her hair behind her ear and knelt down next to Maddie, taking hold of her free hand.

"Mrs Degrassi," the man said. "We have reason to believe that your husband, Anthony, may have been involved in a road traffic collision."

"Reason to believe... what do you mean? Has he, or hasn't he?"

"I apologise Mrs Degrassi, but I can only speak to the information we have at the moment."

"Which is what?" Maddie said, her voice cracking.

The policeman cleared his throat and began to recite the information like he was listing the pools results.

"Last night at around nineteen-hundred hours, your husband's vehicle – a black Land Rover Range Rover, license plate ME18 TL1 – was found upturned at the side of the road near Hay Bluff with one male still inside; a Mr Aled Rowlands."

Maddie could feel sweat collecting on the small of her back, the back of her neck. She clutched the lapels of her dressing gown together as the man continued, feeling her chest heaving beneath her fingers.

"Due to the injuries he's sustained, Mr Rowlands has had to be heavily sedated. As a result, we've not had the opportunity to question him about the collision itself, or the situat-"

"I don't understand," Maddie said. "Where's Tony? Is he in trouble?"

"That's just it, Mrs Degrassi," he said. "At present, we're not entirely sure where your husband is. There's been no sign of him."

5

The rest of the conversation had become such a blur that Maddie had been forced to hand the phone over to Helen, so she could deal with the technicalities. Helen scribbled contact details onto a loose sheet of paper and Maddie stayed where she was; sat on the floor next to the desk with her feet curled forlornly underneath her. There was a strange kind of serenity to the grief she felt, like the world had ceased its spinning, just for a moment, to allow her to process the madness that was rising all around her.

At least she was closer to one of her two possible answers now, she thought. There was some kind of relief in that, though the once unthinkable idea of a world without Tony was now becoming more and more plausible by the second.

The policeman, Clark, had done his best to alleviate that fear. He told Helen that the entire area had been combed thoroughly, first by the fire crew and local police units, then for a hundred metre radius by a drone outfitted with a thermal imaging camera. According to him, even if Tony had managed to stumble away injured, he couldn't have gone far; not without leaving some kind of trail, at least. 'Inconclusive' was the word he used to describe their efforts overall, but he apparently sounded quite optimistic, nonetheless.

While this information did help to dispel the image of Tony's mangled body lying in a nearby field from her mind's eye, Maddie was still struggling to conjure up a suitable emotion.

"What are we supposed to do now then, just wait?" she said to Helen after she'd finished the call.

"He said they'd call again when they knew more."

"Well, we can't just do nothing," Maddie said, her cold shock gradually warming into anger. "It's ridiculous. What are people supposed to do when this happens, just... sit around?"

"I don't know," Helen said. "Maybe..."

Helen walked over to the window and looked out into the garden. Her shoulders were high and tight, like she was seeing how long she could hold her breath.

"What is it?" Maddie said. Helen finally exhaled and turned back around to face Maddie, tears veiling her eyes too.

"What if we went down there? To Brecon, you and me?" Helen said. "We could help look for him... or at least we'd be there if anything happens?"

Maddie's gaze drifted stared around the room as she thought, eventually coming to rest on the picture of Tony and her that hung next to the door.

"I can't ask you to do that," Maddie said.

"You didn't ask, I offered. Work can wait. Everything can wait. This is important... the most important thing there is."

Maddie smiled weakly, then took Helen's outstretched hands and allowed herself to be pulled to her feet. They left Tony's office, arm in arm, and shuffled downstairs to the smaller of the two living rooms, stopping briefly to heed Tank's fevered paws at the front door.

Although a change of scenery helped initially, after a while the new room proved to be just as evocative as his office. Tony's gigantic TV on the wall and the ostentatious sound bar underneath it, the sleek black beer fridge and optics full of high-end spirits in the far corner. Everything necessary to bring the football terrace to him on match days. It all served to remind her of him.

It was his house, after all, not hers. She just lived in it.

"Do you think I should phone Kelly? And the kids?" Maddie said through the steam from her untouched coffee.

"I don't see why not," Helen said after a few seconds of thought. "But only if you feel up to it. I can do it if you want?"

"No... No, I need to do it."

She glanced up and noticed a look of disappointment flicker across Helen's face.

"But thank you," she added. "You've been amazing today. I've been... I'm such a mess."

"Don't," Helen said. "You've had a crap few days already... and now all this. It's awful. There's no right way to deal with it. And you're doing the best thing... I think, anyway. You just need to remember I'm here, whatever you need."

Maddie strained her lips into a smile, then let it fall and picked up her phone from the sofa arm. She clicked it open, instinctively checked Tony's WhatsApp, then minimised the app and scrolled to his ex-wife's name in her phone book.

Despite the animosity that could be expected between the first wife and the 'other woman', Kelly had always treated Maddie with something like civility. Harsh words had been exchanged in the early days – which was to be expected, given the circumstances – but then again, Kelly was a harsh woman in general; the kind of powerhouse woman who was either a badass or a bitch, depending on which side of the fence you were on. Either way, over the six years she and Maddie had been forced to communicate with one another – usually about the kids – a workable, albeit relatively frosty, relationship had formed between them.

Maddie set her coffee down, pushed call, and cuddled herself back into the corner of the sofa. The first ring had barely sounded when Kelly's voice came blaring into the stillness of the living room, car horns and clopping heels and bustle all around her.

"Hello?"

"Hi Kelly, it's Maddie."

She could barely manage more than a whisper.

"Sorry what? Who is it? I'm not in the office so I can't-"

"No Kelly, it's me, Maddie."

"Oh," Kelly said. "Hi... what's up?"

After an initial burst of interest, her tone had become clipped, preoccupied. It was like she'd been told she had a winning lottery ticket, only to find out that the prize was £10.

"Sorry, can you hear me?" Maddie said.

"Yeah, it's fine, I'm just about to get on the tube, so you'll have to... What's up?"

"I... I don't know how to say this but... I don't."

Kelly exhaled, sending the sound of static fuzzing into Maddie's ear. "Spit it out Maddie, come on. What's happened?"

"It's Tony," she said. "He... well he went away with Al yesterday, to Wales. To Brecon. Near Hay Bluff. And he's...

there's been an accident."

The line went silent, save for the waves of distortion that came with each gust of wind.

"So what's happened? Is he hurt?" Kelly said finally, her voice more solemn having dropped at least one octave.

Maddie frowned at her choice of words. Why ask if he was hurt? Why not 'is he ok'? She shook it off and continued.

"They don't know," she said. "They can't... they don't know where he is. He's missing."

"Missing? Well, what's he... what are they doing?"

"I'm not sure. They're looking for him still, but I don't know what I'm going to do. I might go down there or something... see if we can help."

Kelly fell silent again, though the sound of her strides clopping against the pavement continued. Whenever she was going, she was determined to get there in good time.

"Kelly," Maddie said. "Do you want me to call the kids? To tell them?"

"No," she said. "It's fine, I'll do it. I've got a minute before this thing anyway. Thanks, Maddie."

"It's ok. If you want to co-"

The line went dead before Maddie could finish.

6

It took Maddie forty-three minutes to move from the sofa to the shower, then the best part of an hour to get out, pack a week's worth of clothes and supplies, and get into Helen's car. They dropped Tank off with Anna – a young Czech girl who had become one of the neighbourhood's most trusted dog walkers – and headed to Helen's flat in the centre of Manchester so she could collect a few things of her own.

While Maddie had been pulling herself together upstairs in the house, Helen had called Red Dragon Cottages again to ask if they could make use of Tony's reservation while they were in the area.

Maddie had told Helen not to mention why they were following him down there or what had allegedly happened, and perhaps because of the hefty rate attached to the Old Cottage at Stone's Reach – and its minimum stay of four nights – the old woman clearly wasn't in the mood for asking any more questions than were necessary. She probably just wanted the money Tony's disappearance had cost her.

Despite Maddie's misgivings about the truth of Tony's decision to rent a cottage in the mountains just for him and Al, it hadn't taken her long to decide that it was as good a place as any to use as their base in the area during this time.

It was situated right in the heart of the Brecon Beacons, not far from the site of Tony's apparent accident and, according to the Red Dragon Cottages website, it was opposite a larger, newer property that could accommodate any other family members who might want to come down and wait for news on the situation.

While Maddie was sure that Kelly had no interest whatsoever in joining them in the middle of nowhere, she guessed that at least two of Tony's three children – his youngest, Ella, and his middle son, Luke – might.

Ella doted on her globetrotting father whenever she was back from university and he happened to be around, and Luke was even closer to him, given their almost daily interaction at the office. He was only twenty-two years old but had inherited his father's ambition and he had the boundless energy to back it up.

Tony would often share his worries with Maddie of an evening; the pair of them sipping wine beside an open fire in their glass and granite castle like a latter-day version of the Macbeths. Whether the concerns he aired were about business or money or politics, it was rare that Luke's name would remain unsaid for the duration of them. It was a familiar conversation, and one in which Maddie quite often had to avoid revealing her true feelings.

Luke had a much easier start in life than Tony, and a fully formed and successful company to walk straight into, but that didn't make it any easier to trust him. If anything, it made him even more insatiable, more convinced that the world owed him the same success as his father.

"He's not coming, is he? That little turd?" said Helen as she drove, bristling at the mention of Luke's name.

"I'm not sure," said Maddie. Her eyes were glued to the phone in her lap, oblivious of the bleak farmland whipping past her windows on both sides as they barrelled down the A483 towards South Wales.

"Kelly says she's spoken to them all... suppose I'll just wait for them to text me if they want to. I told her where we're staying. I don't wanna pressure them... still not a hundred percent sure if what we're doing makes any sense, to be honest."

"Anything that helps you cope is what makes sense," said Helen, both hands firmly gripping the wheel of her MINI Cooper. "You just have to get through this in whatever way you can... and you will."

Helen reached over with her left hand and began patting blindly at Maddie's thigh, eventually prizing Maddie's trembling fingers away from her phone and taking them in her own.

They carried on in this way for a while, not another word said between them, until they were forced to stop at a petrol station to use the toilet and remind the sat nav on Maddie's ailing phone where they were headed. Although the address given to them by the old woman at Red Dragon Cottages appeared on the map straightaway, it seemed to be completely alone for at least two miles in every direction. Even in the relatively fine weather, the pair worried about what standard of road could have been built to serve nothing more than a couple of cottages, and what state it would be in when they arrived.

As the Brecon Beacons rose up all around them, the traffic began to thin along with the roads. Untidy dry-stone walls hemmed the car in on one side, and sheer drops yawned away on the other, beckoning them to their doom with glimpses of rushing water and unspoiled woodland.

Maddie involuntarily held her breath each time they passed a car or motorcycle, each whoosh causing her to ball the sleeves of her hoody in white-knuckled fists like a baby with its blanket.

As the car rumbled on, the Black Mountains began to appear, dull and dark in the distance. To Maddie, it looked like some great wave that had reached its crest and been baked into hard stone and dry earth by an ancient sun. Petrified and entrusted to loom there for thousands of years, watching over the fledgling foothills in its wake.

She sat back into the soft leather and closed her eyes, though the weight and grandeur of the mountains remained just as tangible. She could feel them, the power they seemed to silently radiate, like the sunbeams that warmed her cheek through the windscreen. A smile, almost like one of content-ment, spread across her face.

The mountains didn't care about one tiny piece of carbon feeling hard done-to by another. Just like they didn't under-stand ambition or frustration or longing. They didn't even understand loneliness, despite the fact that they'd been on their own under the same old sky for millennia. It just didn't matter to them, nothing did.

Maddie continued to smile as she pondered this, basking in the recognition of her own insignificance like a cat stretching out on sun-scorched flagstones.

. . .

The soft sound of Helen's voice jolted Maddie awake, and she suddenly became aware that the car was no longer moving. She looked around in confusion to see the summit of Hay Bluff looming over Helen's shoulder, and a large stone cottage and outbuilding behind her own. Her friend was smiling as she undid her seatbelt and leant through to retrieve her coat from the back seat.

"You feel any better?" she said.

"Just weird," Maddie said. "Didn't even realise I was that tired."

She rubbed her eyes with the heel of her hands, then arched her back and re-scraped her hair into its customary neat ponytail.

They stepped out of the car onto a wide gravel driveway and looked over at the cottage, taking care to pull on their gilets to protect against the biting wind.

Both of the buildings were oddly shaped, with steep wooden roofs perched awkwardly atop grey stone and mortar. In the half-light, they looked like rock giants who'd been buried up to their necks and, in a kind of ritual humiliation, outfitted with crudely woven witches' hats. Fossils of some primeval execution.

The larger of the two structures, which looked to be the main house, was bearded with ivy on one side and had a bright red door at its centre, with a large iron badger's head as the knocker.

While the property itself sat on a natural plateau, it was only accessible by a steep country lane, enclosed by a clutch of oak trees on one side and a rough-looking paddock on the other. The escarpment behind the house rose sharply as well, eventually leading up to the wide, flat summit of Hay Bluff itself.

As she looked over to the newer cottage opposite, she realised the drive was actually more like a courtyard, closed off on three sides by the three buildings. The New Cottage, as it was so creatively named, looked to have been built in the last few years, despite the designers having done their level best to make it look as rustic as its opposite number.

A pair of faux Victorian coach lanterns flanked a solid oak front door, while each of the four window frames were encased by heavy stone lintels. The building even had its own cast iron post box set firmly in the brickwork; a testament to the property's seclusion. A wooden gate off to the left-hand side of the house led around to a high-walled back garden brimming with wildflowers.

"We should have booked that one," Maddie said, turning back to see Helen taking their overnight bags out of the car's boot. "Was it still free, when we looked?"

Helen placed the bags next to each other on the drive, then said: "I didn't ask, to be honest."

"Never mind," said Maddie, crunching back over the gravel to the car. "This one looks fine, not really Tony's style though... Did she say what time she was coming, the cottage woman?"

"She didn't. I just said we'd be here by about half five and it's..." Helen slipped her phone out of her jeans pocket and illuminated the screen. "Quarter to six."

Although the sky was still a chalky shade of pastel blue, Maddie noticed that an imposing full moon was already revealing itself above the cottage. The car had been greenhouse cosy on the journey down, but every minute they stood outside in the open air made them more aware of how inappropriately they were dressed. Leggings, a hoody, and a gilet might have cut it for an evening walk in the suburbs, but the rules were different at this altitude.

Maddie initially thought it was completely silent, thanks to the absence of cars or trains or people, but the longer she stood and listened, the louder the sounds of the wild became. The ambient hum of grasshoppers became the drone that allowed each soloist to come forward in turn; first a nightingale as it swooped overhead, then a solitary owl hooting in the distance. Every sound caused them to turn slightly towards it, so as not to have their back to any potential threat.

Suddenly, from one of the oak trees on the other side of the lane, there erupted a murder of crows, all cawing and flapping and they burst up into the twilight to become a pulsing cloud of black against the pale sky. Maddie and Helen both jumped like the town mice they were, their hands shooting out to find each other in the near darkness.

They both swore and laughed, stepped awkwardly towards the relative safety of the car. Just as they were discussing whether to get back in, headlights flashed through the trees from further down the lane, flickering on and off as the vehicle sped past the hedges and trees and crumbling battlements of dry-stone wall. Its engine groaned like an injured animal, throaty and tired. A perpetual death rattle from a vehicle that stubbornly refused to accept its fate.

As the vehicle finally lurched through the open gate and onto the drive, Maddie noticed it was not the old woman she expected behind the wheel, but a rugged-looking man in his early twenties. The van – a wine-coloured, rust-scabbed Toyota Hilux – ground to a halt, flicking stray gravel towards the sparkling green paint of Helen's MINI. Loud music pulsated from inside the van. It sounded, to Maddie's ears, like a recording of some unholy creature screaming over the thumping percussion of a machine gun. After a few seconds of bathing in the noise, the man shut off the stereo and stepped out, then shambled over as if he was surprised to see them.

"Sorry I'm late," he said in a gruff Welsh accent. "Set off with the wrong bloody keys didn't I."

Maddie and Helen waved away his apologies and he grinned back at them, baring a mouthful of small teeth stained yellow and brown, and framed by coarse black stubble.

"I'm Wil, by the way."

"I'm Helen... and this is Maddie," she said. She spoke as slowly and deliberately, as if she was greeting the spokesperson of an untouched Amazonian tribe. It was a strange habit that Maddie knew her friend often slipped into whenever she was required to make conversation with anyone she branded, however subconsciously, as being from a 'lower' class. She'd even done it to Maddie for a while when they first met.

Wil bowed slightly in acknowledgement, his greasy black hair brushing the collar of his lumberjack shirt as he did so. He wore the shirt open, exposing a black t-shirt beneath that depicted a cartoonishly grotesque scene; three naked bodies impaled on large wooden stakes in front of the gable end of an

American-style barn, a blood red pentagram carved into the ground around them for good measure. Although the lettering above the image was highly stylised, it looked to say the word *Aborted.* Perhaps the name of some kind of heavy metal band, Maddie thought.

"Not a fan, I take it?" he said, catching Maddie frowning at the picture on his shirt.

She let out a sheepish laugh and turned to pick up her bag, then followed him to the front door. Helen joined her on the porch, and they waited patiently as he sifted through various bunches of keys. He started mumbling to himself, becoming more and more agitated each time he tried and failed to open the door.

"Everything ok?" said Helen.

"Yeah," he said, still transferring different sets of keys from one hand to the other, then to the front pocket of his grease-stained jeans. "How many bloody keys does one woman need?"

He chuckled at himself, then looked up at them while he fidgeted.

"I'm sure I 'ad 'em, you know... my nan put 'em right in my bloody hand, I swear. It's like trying to find a black cat in a coal cellar... Tell you what, if I have to go back there a third time, she'll have my fucking pants down! Hang on Just a tick."

Struck by some kind of inspiration, he shoved the last bunch of keys into his shirt pocket and slid between Maddie and Helen and jogged away towards the van. The faint smell of cannabis and cigarette smoke whirled around in his wake, and the women shared a quizzical glance. Helen opened her eyes wide and popped out her bottom lip, causing Maddie to snort.

"The fuck are we doing here?" she said, shaking her head.

"It'll be fine," said Helen. "If we ever get inside."

Maddie followed Helen's gaze as she looked back at Wil, then at the front door. After a moment of contemplating the snarling badger's head knocker, her attention was taken by the horseshoe that had been nailed into the stone arch above it. It was as old as anything on the building, trails of rust bleeding from each of the nails that held it in place.

"I've always wondered what those were for," Helen said. "Like… is it just for good luck for the house or something? A horseshoe's good luck isn't it?"

"When it's up that way it is," Maddie said, stepping forward so they were side by side. "But it's a bit more specific than that I think."

"What do you mean?" Helen said, turning to look blankly at Maddie as if she had started speaking in a different language.

"Can be for good luck, but my dad used to say people did things like to ward off bad spirits or whatever… They don't like iron, apparently. He said that's why you always had iron fences around churchyards; to keep the dead inside. The fact there's seven nails in there isn't an accident either, I don't think."

"Jesus," Helen said absently. "Where did he get that from? Is that an Irish thing or something?"

"Welsh too, by the looks of it," Maddie said, nodding towards the horseshoe. Talking about something other than Tony for the first time in hours was like a lungful of fresh air, she could almost feel the energy coming back into her tired limbs as she spoke.

"I think it had a Christian update at some point as well," she said. "Something about a blacksmith nailing one to the Devil's foot... like he tricked him and made him promise never to enter a house with a horseshoe nailed over the door, I think... I dunno, it's all the same isn't it. Irish, Welsh... Christian, Jewish. They've all got their own stories and superstitions... most of them pretty similar when it comes down to it."

"Maybe there's something in it," said Helen dreamily. "Was he into all that stuff then, your dad?"

"Yeah, just 'cause of his upbringing, I suppose... he always had some kind of mad explanation for everything. Like the cross on top of the soda bread wasn't to make it cook more evenly, it was to let the Devil out. And if the first person we saw after leaving the house had red hair then we had to go back home and start again."

They laughed, then Maddie looked down at her shoes.

"It's a shame they didn't have conspiracy podcasts or top ten scary lists on YouTube when he was about," she said. "Might have spent less time in the pub."

Wil came striding back towards them, smiling triumphantly and waving a small bunch of keys with a wooden owl fob hanging from the ring.

"Knew it was somewhere," he said. "Put it in the bloody glove box for safe keeping didn't I. God knows what all these other ones are."

Maddie attempted to smile as she let him past but talk of her father had invited an old spectre to come and stand beside the newer ones that were gathering at her back. Wil unlocked the door and strode inside and began turning on lights, leaving them stood outside in the cold. Maddie shuddered and turned to Helen.

"I really appreciate this, you know," she said, taking her friend's shivering hands in hers.

"Coming to mine today... driving us down here and sorting it all out. I don't know what I would've done if I'd been alone when that call came through... I..."

"Well you weren't," Helen said, squeezing Maddie's fingers back. "And you won't be through any of this... I promise. Not until Tony's safe and sound and we can all get back to normal."

They parted, then picked up their bags and followed Wil into the main house.

The whole ground floor of the cottage looked to be open plan, with a cluttered kitchen to the left and a sitting room on the right, complete with a small log burner. The two areas were separated by a narrow staircase that led up to the first floor.

Despite the wide floor space downstairs, the small windows and low ceilings made it feel dark and cave-like, almost oppressive in its cosiness. It reminded Maddie of the kind of crooked, little pubs that she and Tony would seek out when they were away in the Cotswolds or Cornwall.

It looked so much more real to Maddie than her own home. Instead of sleek, processed hardwood, the floor was warped and uneven, as if the timbers had simply been thrown down and slathered in varnish where they fell. Crazy eyed woodpeckers perched on shelves across from rabid squirrels, while a haggard badger, frozen mid-stalk and encased in glass, presided over the long oak dinner table. The musty authenticity of these animals made a mockery of Tony's bleached and manicured deer antlers, as did the log burner of his ostentatious fireplace.

Helen stepped inside and teased her fingers over a bunch of walking sticks that sprouted from a stand next to the door; the varnished branches like a floral analogue to the stuffed fauna that infested the cottage. Maddie did the same, then walked over to the sitting room and rested her bag against the back of the sofa, while Wil pushed through a door that was tucked away at the back of the room and flicked on the light. From where it was located in the room, Maddie guessed that it led through to the secondary building that was connected to the side of the main house.

"Alright," said Wil from within. "Can I borrow you for a second?"

They followed his voice and stepped down into the next building, and Maddie was immediately hit by the cold air and musty smell. It put her in mind of the unctuous mud that glues moss onto wet rocks. The floors and walls were all bare grey stone, filmed with damp. The skeleton of a staircase cobbled together from slats of mismatched wood led up to a partially finished second level, though it was blocked off by a few strips of red and white barrier tape.

There were no open doors or windows, in fact there were no windows at all, and the room was cluttered with lengths of chain and wheels of copper wire, boxes overflowing with screws and nails, metal tables and drawers piled sideways on top of each other like windswept electricity pylons. Various engine components were gathering dust on a disused workbench, next to a handful other pieces that looked like miniature iron accordions.

Wil was still assessing a digital boiler and the adjacent breaker box as they approached.

"Ok," he said, turning towards them. "So, the heating and hot water's here if you have any problems. It's on and it should be fine, but... you know, just in case. Same goes for your power over here. It does go from time to time, but you just have to flick it back on here and you're laughing."

The pair of them nodded in unison, though it wasn't long before Maddie's gaze was drawn back to the chaos that took up the majority of the room.

"Is this all your stuff?"

"Nah," he said with a chuckle. "The previous owner... this was his workshop. He fixed things for the local farmers, machinery and tools, mostly. He messed around making bits of jewellery and little figures too, you know? I saw it myself, bloody weird stuff, most of it. All came with the house when he... well, when my nan bought it off him. Been sat on the to-do list ever since."

"How long ago did she buy it?" said Helen.

"Seventeen bloody years ago," he said with a snort. "It's fine though. We tend to try and keep people out of here, you know. I'm sure my nan will have told you already. It's just kind of a big boiler room; this is all you have to worry about."

He tapped on the boiler with grease-blackened knuckles.

"Fair enough," Maddie said. "What's up there?"

"There?" Wil said, pointing at the staircase. "That's just another room, a loft space. Worse than it is down here, if you ask me. That cowboy flooring job is an absolute death

70

trap. Went up for a look around a few years back and almost broke my bloody leg. You see that hole in the ceiling there? That had my Doc Marten peeping though it not long ago!"

The three of them shared an awkward chuckle.

"Best just to stay out of here altogether, if you can help it," he said, Maddie and Helen nodding along. "God knows how we'd afford it if you did yourself a mischief and ended up suing us or something – my nan would have to dust off her old stilettos and get down to Newport docks!"

Wil stood and enjoyed the sound of his own laugh for a moment, before gesturing for them to move back into the main house.

"Ok, our numbers are in the book next to the landline if you need anything," he said as he closed the garage door and bolted it behind him. "As you've probably realised, the signal is total shit up here so sometimes that's your best bet, if you want to... well, I dunno really. Takeaways and taxis act like this is fucking Mordor so you'll have no chance with them... just for emergencies, I suppose."

Maddie made a mental note to ensure that Inspector Clark had the cottage's phone number next time she called him for an update. No sense letting unreliable phone signal strongarm its way onto the long list of worries she already had, she thought.

"There is Wi-Fi, believe it or not – my idea, actually," Wil said, a proud smile flashing across his lips. "Password's in the book as well. I would give you a tour, but basically this is downstairs, and upstairs is the bedrooms and a bathroom. That's it really."

He squinted at Maddie and Helen with suspicion as he rolled his sleeves back down and approached them.

"It... just you two staying here then?" he said. "Or you... expecting anyone else?"

Maddie bunched the sleeves of her hoody in her fists as she replied.

"Just us for now," she said quietly.

"Well," he said with a smile. "Like I said, anything you need, just let one of us know."

He began to rock on his heels as if he was waiting for a bus. Maddie studied him for a second, then noticed that the awkward look on his face was actually an expectant one.

"Oh, course, yeah," she said with a gasp. "Sorry."

She fumbled in her bag for her purse, then fished out a bundle of notes and held them out towards in his stubby, outstretched fingers.

"Ta," he said with another toothy grin. "It's my nan, you see. She's old school. I can write you out a paper receipt or something, if you need one?"

"No, no,' Maddie said. "It's fine. I totally understand."

She attempted to smile back, though it never reached her eyes. She felt Helen's reassuring hand on her shoulder as Wil manoeuvred past them and their bags and strode towards the front door. As he was about to reach the threshold, he stopped abruptly as if one of them had shouted his name. He turned slowly back around, though his eyes were cast down nervously at the floorboards.

"Everything ok?" said Helen, careful not to break contact with her friend as she faced him.

"Yeah," he said, rubbing the back of his neck. "Just... Look, I dunno if this is like, not appropriate to say, or whatever, but I just wanted to say something."

Maddie's blood ran cold as she anticipated his condolences. Did he know about Tony's disappearance? Or had he heard some piece of gossip somewhere that morning? She imagined every possible way he could have found out, then every clumsy thing he might try to say to reassure her. Without looking she entwined her fingers in Helen's and braced herself.

"Basically," he said. "I just wanted to say that... on my life... I think youse two are the best-looking dykes I ever seen. Like, on the internet or in real life... Anywhere. Usually, it's buzz cuts and dad jeans and faces like a bulldog's arse, but... Really like... you know. Just lovely, both of you."

He touched his thumb and forefinger together as he said the

last word, like a chef satisfied with his latest creation. Maddie and Helen turned to face one another, their open mouths and furrowed brows like a mirror image in blonde and brunette. It wasn't apparent from Wil's reaction whether that was what he expected, but he lingered for a moment longer before muttering his goodbyes.

"Ok, yeah, so…. Any probs with that boiler or anything else, just give us a shout. I'm only down the hill. Alright, have a good night, good stay and all that. See ya laters."

The door slammed behind him and a few seconds later the Toyota's engine groaned back into life, closely followed by the sound of pounding drums and shrill, distorted guitars. It took a while for the noise to fade completely, but when it did, the resultant silence seemed to fill the room like sand into the bottom chamber of an hourglass.

7

Perhaps because of the air of strangeness that still lingered as a result of Wil's backhanded compliments, Maddie had persuaded Helen that they should stay together, if only for the first night. She was used to sleeping alone, but their misguided tour of the house had done little to settle her nerves.

Both of the bedrooms were decorated in a similar style to the floor below them. The majority of the drawers and dressers were topped with white lace doilies that served as placemats for even more taxidermy, while pinned butterflies were on display in large picture frames, and faded oil paintings lined the walls. Most of them depicted mountaineers and their faithful pets under ashen skies, all looking stoically out over the Beacons, while others showed grotesque anthropomorphised animals standing around in hunting tweeds or sitting down to afternoon tea. The plaster on the ceilings was discoloured and beginning to bloat in the corners, sagging behind white textured wallpaper. Tired hooks had been hammered into the walls and wooden beams, straining to hold the weight of ceramic jugs and large brass plates that looked like oversized sovereigns.

All of this wasn't exactly to Maddie's taste when it came to interior décor, and it unsettled her to think that it certainly wasn't Tony's either. Of course, he had a desire to rough it from time to time, but he still preferred to do so in a certain style. Nothing about the cottage added up for her. Even its proximity to the Beacons didn't justify him choosing somewhere so unashamedly shabby.

Maddie and Helen eventually dumped their bags in the least cluttered of the two rooms and – after being attacked by a particularly vicious moth – fled back downstairs to light the fire and get ready for a night of pestering the police, calling Tony's answerphone, and attempting not to drink the wine they'd brought along in the car.

Although it had caused some debate as they were preparing to leave Maddie's house that afternoon, she'd ultimately been able to persuade Helen that taking at least a few bottles was acceptable, just as long as they made sure at least one of them would be capable of driving safely at all times. It was the same look she'd used on Helen countless times before, just to stay for one more drink, one last song. Whether or not Helen believed that the wine was purely medicinal in this instance, the bottles went into the car and there they remained while Helen boiled the kettle and Maddie curled up on the sofa with her phone.

As she was staring blankly into it, her tired reflection barely visible in the dim light from the kitchen, a message from Ella suddenly illuminated the screen.

"Shit," she said, loud enough to make Helen to look up from the tea she was stirring.

"What's up? Everything alright?"

"Yeah, it's... It's Ella, Tony's daughter. She says she's coming here. Tomorrow."

"Seriously?"

"Sounds like it," said Maddie, still scrutinising the message like a jeweller inspecting a suspect gemstone. "They've booked into that cottage on the other side, her and Luke. Fucking hell."

"That's good, isn't it? That way everyone's here if there's any news," said Helen as she glided over, steaming mugs in hand. "When there's news, I mean."

"I suppose, just a bit surprised," Maddie said, taking one of the mugs without looking up. "Didn't think they'd... I dunno. Just didn't expect them to acknowledge it to be honest. Now we're all gonna be here. Together."

She unleashed a flurry of precise thumb taps against the screen of her phone, then placed it face down on the sofa arm and smiled her belated thanks to Helen. They sat and basked in the warmth from the drinks and the burgeoning fire that snapped away in the belly of the log burner.

It'd been easy enough to light with the kindling provided,

though Helen had been caked in ash when she removed the overflowing tray a little too quickly.

"Not exactly Airbnb, is it?" she'd said as she dusted herself off.

The silence settled between them as they drank, and Maddie was already starting to run through potential meals she could cook once Ella and Luke arrived. If Ella was still vegan – and this was hard to tell, given that her stance on the subject seemed to shift with the seasons – then some kind of vegetable curry or chilli would do. Warming, nutritious, comforting. Something they could all enjoy together. She would have to go into the nearest town first thing and gather supplies, she thought, maybe even some special cookware.

As she continued to brainstorm, she looked over at the dining table and locked eyes with the badger once again. She grimaced, then made a mental note to move him, along with the rest of his woodland companions, into the garage building and hide them among the clutter. Not exactly ideal dinner companions for a vegan, she thought.

Just as she was about to voice these concerns to Helen, perhaps enlisting her to do a taxidermy sweep of the ground floor, she suddenly became aware of how callous it might sound. How could she be thinking about playing the diligent stepmother to Tony's children while their father was nowhere to be found? She silently scolded herself, buried her chin in the collar of her hoody.

"How are you feeling?" said Helen, taking a shallow sip and resting the mug in her lap.

Maddie thought for a second, her red-rimmed eyes staring blankly at the flames.

"I'm not sure really," she said. "It's so strange. Everything about it. The fight we had, then this last-minute trip to this weird old cottage, then they crash and he's just... nowhere to be found. I don't get it, any of it... but at the same time it doesn't matter if I get it or not, does it?"

Helen nodded and took another sip.

"We just have to find him," Maddie said.

"And we will," Helen said. "I'm sure of it. The reason every-thing's such a mess now because it's all so new. Nothing's certain. You just have to trust that it will all make sense. And it will soon, I know it will."

Maddie nodded, but it was more in acknowledgement of the general sentiment, rather than its relevance to Tony's disappearance. While time was still on their side, she felt an emptiness in her stomach that was unmistakeable. The realisation that the last words they said to each other could have been exactly that. Her eyes began to well up.

"This won't last forever Maddie, this limbo," Helen said. "Obviously, it's a completely different thing, but I remember last year, with my mum... as bad as it sounds, it was the waiting and wondering that was the worst bit. Worse than anything after. Not that this is like that, but... you know what I mean."

It wasn't a question. It was a statement of fact, hard-learned. Maddie looked up at Helen and saw tears in her eyes too. Echoes of the tears she'd shed twelve months previously, when the two women were sat on opposite sides of a different sofa, after six years of suffering had finally come to an end for Helen's mum, Molly.

Maddie had always asked after her, helped Helen however she could. Molly even looked to be improving at first, though it wasn't long before everything seemed to stagnate. Every time Helen spoke about her or every time that she turned up somewhere late and red-eyed; it was always the same story. The same heart-breaking uncertainty and frustration. Lots of gestures from doctors; shaking heads and wringing hands and blind eyes turning. If there was one thing Helen knew about, it was waiting for a hammer to fall.

Towards the end of Molly's life, Helen had become obsessed with online forums. She told Maddie that it was a relief to be able to speak with other people whose loved ones were facing similarly desperate odds. Perhaps unsurprisingly, this led to her chasing a few of the fads and outlandish remedies that are endemic in those kinds of communities, even taking Molly to visit some of the holistic therapists she befriended, towards the end.

That night when Maddie had called around to bring flowers and a card, Helen had spoken at length about how much comfort she'd gained from just being able to share her anxieties and frustrations with like-minded people, even if they were dotted all over the country.

Maybe, if the situation became truly bleak for Maddie, she could join a support group for people with missing husbands. They must exist, she thought. How couldn't they?

"Sorry," Helen said, attempting to sniff away her tears with a laugh. "I'm supposed to be here for you, not the other way around."

"Don't be silly," said Maddie, her mouth muffled by Helen's jumper as they hugged. "We're here for each other. That's how it works."

They sat like this for a while, until Maddie slumped back onto the sofa and wiped her eyes with the sleeves of her hoody. Helen took a deep breath, then swore quietly, and stood.

"I feel disgusting," she said, brushing weakly at the few remaining smears of ash on her jeans. "I think I'm gonna have to brave the shower... are you sure you're ok?"

"Course, yeah, go," said Maddie, waving her away.

"You're sure you're sure?"

"Yes," Maddie said. She drew the word out like grumpy a teenager, playfully swatting the back of Helen's thigh as she said it. "I'm good. Do you want another brew?"

Helen bit her lip, then nodded. "Ok. Lovely. See you in a sec."

She walked around the sofa and picked up her bag and started up the stairs, when Maddie called after her.

"Hey..."

Helen stopped in her tracks and turned. "What's up?"

"Remember to watch out for moths."

Helen let out an involuntary snort, but it faded quickly, like the ripple from a disappointing firework. It was as if she felt guilty for it. Or like it was a joke that she didn't think Maddie should have been capable of making. Her smile melted into a confused frown.

"Yeah... you too," she said eventually.

She turned and carried on creaking up the stairs, leaving Maddie alone in the gloom. She sat back and watched the flames as they licked hungrily at the fresh log in the burner. Her eyes began to droop as she inhaled the faint smell of ash and smoke. It conjured comforting images. Finally entering the pub after a long, cold winter walk, sipping cabernet by the fire. The lights twinkling overhead at the Christmas markets, mulled wine and Bailey's hot chocolate. Such thoughts quickly made the idea of a cup of tea seem weak by comparison.

She thought of the bottles in the boot of Helen's car. How even just one or two glasses of red might be enough to put thoughts of Tony out of her mind long enough for sleep to take her. The pipes groaned as the shower started upstairs, and within seconds she found herself knelt on the sofa, facing the front door and Helen's car key sat on the small, round table beside it.

Maddie shuffled forwards and climbed over the back with the grace and stealth of a master cat burglar, then jammed the front half of her feet into her trainers, flattening the backs down with her heels, and took the key and quietly opened the door.

The chill in the night air was bracing as she stepped outside, the gravel crunching loudly under her makeshift slippers. She flipped up her hood, the stubby plastic car key still clutched in her left hand, and walked over to where the MINI was parked. It was little more than a silhouette in the gloaming, a series of metallic curves catching the cloud-veiled moonlight, but she it was a short enough trip through the dark that she felt happy enough to approach it without using the torch on her phone.

She looked down to find the open padlock icon on the key, then clicked it with her plastered thumb. The locks in the door clunked and the courtyard was briefly daubed in indicator orange for two clicks. As the second pulse of light faded into darkness, Maddie stopped abruptly and turned towards the entrance to the driveway.

Something had caught her eye. Nothing more than a smudge on the periphery of her vision, but a smudge out of place, nonetheless. She continued to stare at the shape. It was motionless, black against the near blackness of the lane, and partially obscured by the dry-stone perimeter wall.

Maddie clicked the key again and orange light pulsed out from the car once more. Although the glow fell just short of wall, it travelled far enough to show that the dark mass was in fact the head, broad shoulders, and torso of a person standing behind it, facing in at the cottage. At her. The stiff hood on the figure's jacket was pulled so far forward that she could only see shadows where a face should have been.

She felt a rush of cold air down her throat as she gasped and stumbled backwards, every sinew in her body tightening as one. The figure stayed completely still.

The second pulse faded and, again, the colour and shape bled from the courtyard. Still she kept her eyes glued to the figure, her feet to the gravel. This rhythm continued for another two clicks of the key; second and third opinions requested by a mind stalled in disbelief.

The whole world remained frozen solid while she pressed the button again and again – Maddie, the figure, the trees, the thin clouds hanging in the darkened sky. The only movement was the twitch of her thumb, followed by two beats of amber light, each one seemingly weaker, more tentative, than the last.

She wanted to shout over to the figure – to ask their name, what they wanted, why they were there – but her mouth was dry, her breaths too shallow to force such serious words past her trembling lips. She took her thumb away from the button, then spun on her uncovered heels and began stumbling towards the front door of the cottage.

After a few clumsy bounds, the smashed-down heel of her right trainer snagged against the drive and she fell forwards onto her hands, the impact driving the key from her grip. She wheezed in shock, then struggled up onto her knees and began scrabbling around in the gravel for the familiar feel of plastic. Her manicured nails and moisturised palms became the claws and pads of a truffle dog, her ragged breaths as loud as the huffing of a steam train's chimney in the still night air.

The possibility of abandoning the car key flashed through her mind, then she felt plastic slap against her hand and heard something skitter towards the cottage. She looked up, her pristine ponytail now a feral mane spewing from her hood, and saw the key, stark against the pale stone doorstep. She scrambled headfirst on all fours, a strange moan of desperation now spilling from her mouth, then snatched it up and lunged upwards for the door handle.

Even as she fell inside and slammed the door behind her, she could feel the invisible eyes of the hooded figure at her back. That void from within the hood fixed on her through an inch of solid oak. A secret, silent scream.

8

Maddie was finally spared from her restless night by the rumble of Helen sliding a coffee cup onto her bedside table, which was closely followed by a small plate piled high with buttered white toast slathered in jam. Maddie blinked hard a couple of times to unstick her heavy eyelids, until she could see the steam rising from the cup, thick and white against the golden haze pouring in through the open window. She smiled at Helen's silhouette and pushed herself onto one elbow, then looked at the plaster on her thumb. She peeled it back to inspect the knife wound, which had already begun to scab. It was surrounded by puffy, pale skin wrinkled by overnight sweat. With a wince she removed the plaster, folded it carefully, and placed it on the table next to the mug.

The cut throbbed as she took the weight of the coffee cup, the fresh scrapes on her palms sensitive against the heat from within.

The marks are real then, she thought. Just like the figure at the end of the drive had been real. She'd hoped, in some childish part of her brain, that the new day would bring with it reassurance. Confirmation that the whole incident had never happened or had at least not been as frantic as she remembered it to be. She was hoping for that same feeling she'd had as a teenager at the carnival; emerging from the ghost house into the light of day, laughing at how she could have possibly thought any of it was really frightening.

But the scrapes reminded her of that fevered scramble to the front door, the feeling of being scrutinised, of being toyed with like prey. It was all real.

Last night, after the urge to vomit out the adrenaline had passed, Maddie hauled herself to her feet and scrambled up the staircase, then pounded on the bathroom door without mercy until Helen emerged, clouds of steam billowing behind her like she was taking to the stage on *Stars in Their Eyes*. From then on Maddie had babbled at her without so much as taking a breath.

"It was a man, I think. A person... well, I don't know but it looked like a man in a hood and he was just staring, not moving at all just staring at me. I couldn't see his face or his eyes, but I know, I just know that he was staring at me. He didn't say anything or move or anything, he just watched me... the whole time just watching until I got back inside. Then I came up here and-"

"Look Maddie," Helen had said, sitting Maddie down on the edge of the bed. "I know this is such a hard time for you, so it's totally understandable that you're stressed. The brain's a weird thing, isn't it? Like sometimes it can make you see things, even think things that you might not-"

"He was real, Helen. I promise you; I swear on Tony's life... he was real. He's probably still out there now."

He wasn't, of course. Helen had confirmed that for herself, after calmly towelling her hair and slipping on her pyjamas.

"It could have just been a dog walker, or someone coming back from a hike," she'd said, taking Maddie's hand in hers as if she was explaining to a child that the bogeyman was not, in fact, hiding in her wardrobe.

All Maddie could do was repeat herself, over and over, like a mantra: "I swear to you, Helen, he was weird, and he was there. He was watching me. Honestly, he was right there."

All through the night she'd had to remind herself that she should be worrying about Tony instead. Her own husband was missing, no one even certain enough to presume him dead, and all she could think about was the hooded figure at the end of the drive.

She and Helen had shared the same bed, but it was as if they'd been existing on entirely different planes of reality. Occasionally they communicated through the squeeze of a hand or pacifying touch on the back, but neither seemed to sleep for more than a few minutes at a time.

As they sipped their morning coffee, sat up in bed side by side, Maddie did her best to deflect Helen's compliments, well-meaning as they were. She'd begun with small talk, explaining how difficult it had been to toast the bread using the Aga's crusty grill, then inadvertently brought up the very thing Maddie had spent all night trying to forget.

"I'm really proud of you, you know."

"Me? What for?" Maddie said tentatively.

"Well everything actually. But I mean last night. Not drinking. Must have been really hard to keep a clear head with every-thing going on. Just shows how strong you are. How you're gonna get through all of this, whatever happens."

The truth was Maddie had simply been interrupted. After all, she'd strode out to retrieve the wine in such a rush that she couldn't wait to put her shoes on properly. It was the watcher who had kept her away from the car and the rest of the evening she'd been too shaken to even think about anything as trivial as alcohol. She'd even felt the need to lie to Helen about why she was outside in the first place, blurting out that she intended to get her hairband from the car.

"Thanks for this," Maddie said, nibbling the corner of the piece of toast she'd forced upon herself. "It's really good."

"It's fine," said Helen. "Was all in the welcome pack."

She made little air quotes as she said this and smiled. The basket of goods provided by Red Dragon Cottages, while paltry, had already proven useful in the few hours since they'd arrived.

As well as the jam to go with their service station bread, there was a selection of fruit, tea and coffee, and even fresh milk and butter in the fridge.

Maddie's appetite had begun to wane long before Tony's disappearance, but Helen had taken it upon herself to force food onto her at every opportunity. It was strange, Maddie thought, this notion of 'keeping your strength up' in trying times like this. What did she need this strength for, exactly? Would she be called on to free Tony from underneath a giant boulder with her own bare hands, or trek from mountain to mountain in search of his footprints? It didn't seem likely.

. . .

She had given up calling Tony, now that it was going straight to answerphone, so the only thing left to do, as far as she was concerned, was to try and speak with Al. He was the last person to see Tony, and the only one who knew the real context behind this strange, last-minute holiday to a beat-up shack in the middle of nowhere.

After they finished their food and took turns in the cacophonous shower, Maddie and Helen got into the car and set off to Nevill Hall Hospital, on the outskirts of Abergavenny.

According to the dreary Inspector Clark, Al was stable in the hospital's accident and emergency ward, though he hastened to add that he thought any visits would be a bad idea.

While Maddie had originally agreed with the policy of letting severely injured dogs lie, the knowledge that Al was sitting only a few miles away with potentially important information unsaid was too much to take. Ella had already texted Maddie overnight to say that she and Luke wouldn't arrive until early afternoon, so the least she could do was welcome them with a fuller picture of what had happened to their father. Maybe it would even make them happy to see her, she thought, though that might be too much of a stretch.

Maddie and Helen arrived at the hospital after the best part of an hour on mostly uninhabited roads, the car's interior pleasantly warmed by the morning sun all of the way. The building itself was a brutalist slab of concrete that was neither bright nor beautiful, despite standing in the shadow of Alexander's famous 'purple-headed mountain', Blorenge.

After circling the car parks twice in vain, Maddie decided to get out and send Helen to wait at a coffee shop they'd passed on the way. It would most likely mean a boring couple of hours for her, but Maddie could sense Helen's relief at the realisation that she wouldn't have to go inside. Of course, it wasn't the same building that she'd helped her mother in and out of on so many occasions, but every hospital seemed to emit that same menacing indifference to her. Like the Black Mountains that had felt so powerful to Maddie the day before, these places seemed just as immovable, just as unflinching; and in the face of so much suffering and death. If there was any way she could have avoided entering the place too, she certainly would have.

Maddie walked in through the main sliding doors and was directed into the lift by black and white signs stacked on the walls.

She reached the third floor and the doors clunked open. As she stepped into the corridor, linoleum floors and fluorescent light stretched out uniformly in both directions like a hall of mirrors. There were no patients – or even any rooms – in sight, but the hum of a dozen jumbled conversations echoed all around her. The corridor itself was decorated in varying shades of green, lightening from the moss-coloured floor tiles to the mint green walls to the high ceilings that were almost white.

Maddie approached the end of the hall and the reverberations increased in volume, accompanied by the high-pitched whine of monitors and alarms like the sound of some robotic orchestra all tuning their instruments all at once. As she walked towards the noise, she entered a cloud of sterile smells. Freshly opened needles and antiseptic wipes and plastic aprons. No wonder Helen was so relieved to avoid coming in here, she thought. It was all too familiar.

She rounded the corner and was confronted by another, equally green, corridor. Its left-hand wall was punctuated by double-wide doorways every ten feet or so, and a bulging desk around halfway up that looked to be a nurses station.

Maddie came to a stop in front of the desk and waited for the nurse – a lean, straw-haired woman in her forties – who was furiously typing at a bulky computer. After a few seconds, she jabbed the return key triumphantly and fixed a smile to her face.

"Hello love," she said with an involuntary sigh. "And what

can I do for you?"

"Hi, sorry... My name's Maddie. Maddie Degrassi. I'm here to see a friend, Al... Aled Rowlands."

"Ah," she said, glancing up the corridor. "Well, to be honest, Mr Rowlands isn't in the best shape at the moment. If you're not a family member then I'd probably advise you to come back another time."

"Another time? What do you mean?"

The nurse readjusted the stethoscope around her neck, then placed both hands flat on the desk. There was compassion in her tired eyes, but not for Maddie. She was like a protective mother making excuses for why her son wasn't allowed to come out and play.

"His wife's with him now. Basically, he's still very banged up from the accident so he's heavily sedated. You might just be better off coming to say hello a bit later on in the week, when he's had chance to rest."

"I'm not here t-" Maddie stopped in the hope that her trembling voice would steady. She closed her eyes and inhaled deeply through her nose.

"Sorry," she said. "It's just... I'm not here to say hello. I need to speak to him about something personal, something very important. I've driven down a long way to see him..."

The nurse dipped her head to try and catch Maddie's eyes, which were pointed firmly at the desk's faux wooden surface.

"Look love," the nurse said. "I'm sorry. If you want, you can leave your name and we'll let him know you-"

"No," Maddie said, forcing herself to look back at the woman. "No, I can't do that, I have to see him today. It really can't wait. I just need five minutes; if he's asleep I'll leave straight away, I promise. I just need to know."

The nurse stared at her for a moment, scrutinising the shimmer of her tear-glazed eyes in the fluorescent light. She looked back up the corridor.

"Ok," she sighed, checking the tiny watch that hung from her top pocket. "Five minutes. But please just remember that he's been through a lot, alright? He doesn't need any undue stress or... excitement."

"I know, I know. It's fine... I'm fine. I just need to see him."

"Alright. Well it's up there," the nurse said, pointing down the corridor to her right. "Room Four, last bed on the right. I can take you."

She fidgeted with her stethoscope again and stood to move around the desk.

"No, no, it's ok, I'll find him," Maddie said, already edging away, her arms folded across her stomach. "Thank you."

She turned and followed the corridor, her ponytail swishing behind her. As she walked, she looked down at the different lines painted on the floor. They were like colour-coded road markings leading towards, then into each room. She wondered what each colour represented. Were they simply there to mark some kind of traffic system for the doctors and nurses? Or was there something more sinister going on?

She was suddenly reminded of a conversation with an old schoolfriend who she'd seen working as Emirates cabin crew on a flight to Dubai a few years ago. They'd met for drinks on the Marina later that night and, after a few glasses of wine, she'd begun telling Maddie about all the private games, secret codes, and disgusting details that were only known to those of her ilk. Like the fact that any flight attendant heard talking about 'HR' on the plane's intercom was not discussing 'human resources', but human remains in the cargo hold. Or the additional fact that the boxes containing those very same remains could occasionally leak onto other passengers' luggage.

Did these tracks mean something just as sinister, Maddie wondered? Some kind of special code. Did the red line lead to the patients who were more likely to die? Had those in the green ward been labelled as timewasters who didn't deserve to be there? Which colour would Tony be classed as, if he was there? Maddie was shaken from these dark thoughts as the nurse scurried up behind her and pointed to the next room along.

"He's just in there," she said. "At the back on the right-hand side."

Maddie thanked her again and stood and watched until she was back at her station, then entered Room Four. It had been designated as blue, whatever that meant.

There were four beds on either side of the room, all of which had their curtains pulled shut, presumably to shield the modesty of the injured or ailing people within. Aside from the pale yellow that was filtering through the smeared glass at the end of the ward, the only light came from tall adjustable lamps that loomed over the top of each bed like microscopes above their specimens.

As she approached, she saw through a gap in the curtain that one of Al's legs was in plaster, his ankle suspended by a wire sling like an injured cartoon character.

Maddie pushed the crumpled material aside, mimicking a nurse's shallow smile as she entered.

Aside from his leg, both of Al's arms were bandaged from elbow to shoulder, a faded tattoo peeking from beneath the right one. Matching black eyes suggested a severely broken nose. He looked forlorn, shackled into his sling with his face swollen into a fixed grimace.

Al's wife, Ginny, was perched on the edge of a plastic chair by the side of the bed. One of her hands was cradling his, while the other massaged a palm-sized worry stone; pale white marbled with gold and orange and black. From behind, all that could be seen of her was a shock of bright red hair atop multiple layers of tie-dye, patchwork, and floral prints.

Maddie entered, and the sound of the rings clinking along the curtain rail shocked Ginny from her daydream.

She tried to smile, then stood and lurched forward and pulled Maddie in for an awkward hug. Ginny leant back and cradled Maddie's cheek with her right hand and smiled, like a proud grandmother to her bonny grandchild. Her multiple necklaces clinked as she shook her head, all manner of protective symbols and charms. The two women muttered condolences to each other, then Ginny sniffed away her tears and retook her seat, her hand automatically seeking out the stone she'd left at Al's side.

Next to the bed, on a sad-looking grey MDF cabinet, sat a cloudy glass bowl filled with multicoloured tumble stones; jade and opal and polished tiger's eye. Next to it was the cross-section of a geode, its outer layer of smooth dark stone a stark contrast to the crystalline amethyst within, like a fossilised piece of rotten fruit. The requisite scented candles and incense had clearly not been permitted.

"When did you get down here?" Ginny said, her Welsh accent soft and musical.

"Last night. We're staying in Brecon."

"We?"

"I'm with Helen, a friend of mine."

Maddie considered telling her that they'd hijacked Tony and Al's reservation, but wanted to avoid any unnecessary conversations about the place or its shadowy visitor. She shuddered at the very thought of the cottage, of scrambling towards that red door like a wounded animal.

"Have you been here long?" Maddie said, her voice cracking under the pressure of the flashback.

"Since they let me come back," Ginny said. "Got one of the young girls looking after the shop."

Branwen's Emporium in Abergavenny was Ginny's pride and joy; a hole-in-the-wall shop selling all manner of allegedly mystical trinkets, charms, and alternative medicines that only stayed afloat thanks to the continued support of a handful of the region's kookiest residents. Maddie had popped in once – at Tony's behest – when they visited the area so Tony could ask Al to be his best man. She'd been forced to feign interest as she browsed through fairy statues and multicoloured candles and divining rods. When she tried to leave, she was forced to stand in the beaded doorway for almost five minutes, smiling politely while Ginny reeled off all of the holistic treatments that she thought would serve Al's brother better than the chemotherapy that he was undergoing at the time.

Maddie pulled a plastic chair around from the other side of the bed and sat opposite Ginny.

98

"Still nothing from the doctors?" she said.

Ginny shook her head, her crimson perm swinging from side to side like a cheerleader's pom poms.

"It's been alright really, considering," Ginny said, glancing over at her husband. "He's not in any pain or anything. Been asleep since they brought him in here. They say his brain is fine, no internal injuries."

"He's not said anything then? About what happened? Not even to the police?"

"Nothing," Ginny said, pulling a cotton handkerchief from the sleeve of her blouse and dabbing at her eyes and nose. "I can't get my head around it, Maddie. Any of it. This was supposed to be such a special time for him, for everyone. I just don't understand what could have happened..."

She trailed off and a silence began to swell as they both looked at Al's semi-mummified body. Maddie glanced over to Ginny, noticed the puffiness around her eyes, but was unsure of what to say next.

Even in the past twenty-four hours with Helen, she had felt a sense of detachment from the situation. To her, it was all so outlandish that it couldn't possibly be real, like the whole thing could still turn out to be some big misunderstanding. Like the implausible cover stories that swirled around in the lead-up to a surprise birthday party. Now, sitting across from Ginny and her broken husband; the gravity of the situation was inescapable.

"When did you last speak to him?" Maddie said, doing everything she could to keep her tone as casual as possible.

"I'm not sure," Ginny said, her fingernails scratching at the bedclothes. "He did call, in the afternoon, maybe. So, before it happened... It was just nonsense, mostly. It wasn't like a real conversation, he just kept babbling about all sorts, you know what he's like. That's probably why the police have had no luck, so far. When they take him off all this stuff, maybe some of this will start to make sense. Maybe he'll be able to help you too."

Maddie opened her mouth to speak, then hesitated. The awkwardness grew alongside the silence.

"What about you? Anything else from the police?" Ginny said, balling up the handkerchief and jingling it over her bangles into her sleeve.

"Nothing much," Maddie said. "They've been pretty useless to be honest. Think I might have to go and ask around myself, see if anyone can help. He can't have gotten far without his car... but then why would Al be in it without him? Like you say, none of it makes any sense."

"Well they don't really make sense, do they," Ginny said.

"Sorry, I don't... What don't make sense?"

"Accidents. Accidents don't make sense. They just happen. People leave the house and they have no idea what's coming. Doesn't matter whether it's just a normal day or the most important day of your life. The universe doesn't seem to notice."

Ginny turned so she was speaking directly to her husband: "People have all these plans and all this pressure. I suppose it can make you take your eye off the ball – off the road – and even a tiny distraction is enough to cost you up there, but... Oh, Al, you silly old bugger. What were you playing at?"

"He'll be back on his feet soon, hopefully," Maddie said quietly, attempting to brush off the cryptic monologue.

"He will," Ginny said. "And Tony'll turn up soon, I'm sure. When you see him again, you'll both realise how lucky you are. I'm telling you, nothing else matters if you've got each other. Just you make sure you don't forget that, don't waste any of the time you have together. Not even a minute. You never know how long you've got, until it's all over."

Ginny looked over at Maddie then and pulled her tear-slick cheeks back into a painful-looking smile.

"But he'll turn up, Maddie, sooner or later. I promise you."

"I hope you're right," Maddie said with a weak smile. "Ok, so... You two take care. I'll be around. Just let me know how he gets on."

As she turned to leave, Maddie took another look at Al, his ragged sideburns and his mop of greying hair.

"Ginny," she said. "I'm really sorry, but... can I ask you something?"

Ginny's bangles clinked together again as she shuffled around to face her.

"What is it, love?"

Conscious that her five-minute cut off was fast approaching, Maddie looked through the curtains for any sign of the nurse, then turned back to Ginny.

"I was just wondering if you'd ever heard of the place Tony booked for them, the cottage. I had a look online and it doesn't look very... Tony, if you know what I mean? I was a bit confused to be honest, so I just wondered if you knew... It's near Hay Bluff, a place ca-"

"Stone's Reach," Ginny said, a statement rather than a question. "Yes, I know it. It's a very special place. For Al... for lots of other people too I suppose. I expect he's mentioned that to Tony at some point and Tony's just booked it for him. A surprise to cheer him up maybe. He's good like that, isn't he?"

"Yeah," Maddie said with a nod. "Yeah, he is."

Ginny smiled and said: "I know they've spent a bit of time apart over the years, but Al always knew Tony would be there when he needed him. You should be very proud."

9

As they passed through the gates of Stone's Reach onto the cottage's driveway, Maddie had to will herself not to look at the spot where the watcher had stood. She didn't even know what she expected to see there – footprints, perhaps, maybe even the shape of two cloven hooves in the dust. All she was certain of was that it would do her no good to look. She had to keep her eyes closed. That way, with no material evidence forthcoming, she could continue to convince herself that it was all some kind of hallucination. A fever dream brought on by the stress of the previous few days.

It was the only way she would be able to keep her mind together; to be the person Tony needed her to be.

As the car to ground to a halt, Maddie opened her eyes to see Luke's Audi TT parked in front of the New Cottage. He was perched on the bonnet, his ankles crossed and his Ray Bans still on despite the fact that the sun had started to retreat behind the mountains almost an hour ago.

He was smart casual, as always. The collar of a white polo

neck t-shirt was peeking out from a dark designer jumper, his sleeves rolled up to display a chunky TAG Heuer watch on one wrist and a silver bracelet on the other. Even in the gathering dusk, his olive skin looked as healthy as his immaculately coiffed hair. Maddie could almost smell the Giorgio Armani just by looking at him.

He waved at the MINI, then hoisted himself up and ducked his head into the TT's open window.

"There he is, Richie Rich," said Helen.

Maddie rolled her eyes, undid her seatbelt, then stepped out onto the gravel to greet him. He walked over to them with his hands stuffed in his pockets, a shark-toothed grin on his face.

"Hiya Maddie," he said, leaning in to kiss her on both cheeks.

As endearing as it was that he'd inherited Tony's courtesy and charisma, they were still something of an awkward fit on him. There was a novelty to it all. For Maddie, it was almost like looking at a teenage boy wearing his father's suit to his first job interview. Not that Luke had ever needed to have a job interview, of course.

"You alright?" Maddie said, giving his shoulder a squeeze. "How you doing? How's Ella?"

"Not too bad," he said, raking his hair back into place. "She's alright. Bit morbid on the way down here... You know what she's like. How was the hospital? What's Al like?"

Maddie proceeded to fill him in on the day's events — or lack thereof — taking care to omit any references to Ginny's cryptic ramblings. She'd not even mentioned it to Helen on the drive back. No sense in confusing people any more than they already were, she thought; not until it could be of any use, at least.

. . .

Despite Maddie's desire to act as the matriarch of this ill-fated get-together, she accepted Luke's invitation to have dinner together in the New Cottage. Ella had brought everything to make their grandmother's penne arrabbiata; one of Tony's favourite meals. Maddie was initially reticent to eat it without him, but Ella reassured her that the reason it was on the menu was because it was the only vegan food Luke was prepared to eat with minimal complaint.

Ella was, it turned out, off animal products again, apparently "for good" this time.

As Luke opened the door to welcome them into the cottage, Maddie immediately noticed the brown glass bottle in his hand. It looked more like he was welcoming them into a cocktail party than hosting a vigil for his missing father.

The air outside had been crisp, almost painful to inhale, which made the kitchen feel like a steam room by comparison. A large, stainless steel pan full of pasta was bubbling away on one side of the hob, while the unmistakeable smells of onion, garlic, and basil wafted from another.

The room itself was high and airy, two huge skylights framing

106

the clear blackness above. With the exception of the cottage's exposed pine skeleton and matching cupboards, every surface from the floor to the walls to the spotlight-studded ceiling was some shade of white.

Luke collected the jackets Maddie and Helen had shrugged off as they entered the kitchen, then strode back towards the porch to hang them up.

"Smells amazing," said Helen. Ella briefly turned to acknowledge the compliment, then returned to chopping a huge pile of fresh tomatoes.

"Drinks in the fridge if you want one," she said absently. "I told Luke this wasn't a lads' holiday, but he said it's either watch him drink beer or listen to him moan about why there isn't any in."

"I'm alright for now, thanks," Maddie said, gesturing for Helen to go ahead if she wanted to.

"You sure?" Helen said.

"Yeah, I'm fine. Could do with keeping my head screwed on, for now. Go on."

Helen smiled and took a bottle out of the fridge and knowingly unscrewed the top. The fizz, and subsequent clink of bottle cap into bin was enough to make Maddie salivate for a moment. She walked over to stand behind Ella and put a gentle hand on her shoulder.

"Is it ok if I grab some water?"

"Tap's over there. Glasses are in that cupboard."

Ella waved the large carving knife towards one of the pine cupboards that lined the kitchen's far wall, as if it was common knowledge; her insouciance belying her tender years. It was a strange power she had, and it always seemed to intensify whenever she was fulfilling the role of house chef. Maddie had always assumed she had inherited it from Tony's mother, the kids' 'nonna'.

Although Maddie had only met her on two occasions before her death, it was enough to make an impression. She and Tony had gone to visit her in their family's ancestral home of Naples, where his parents had returned after he and his brother moved out of their Gamesley housing estate to start their business. Even then, despite her age and wizened features, it was clear that she was a powerful woman. Tony often spoke of her as being stoic yet firm, able to command respect with little more than the wiping of her hands on her apron.

Maddie smiled, both at the memory of the woman and the sound of her doppelgänger chopping away in the background. She took a heavy crystal glass from the cupboard, filled it from the tap, and took a healthy swig. It was cool and refreshing, but ultimately feeble, next to the thought of an ice-cold beer.

She took a seat opposite Helen at a surprisingly modern-looking dining table at the back of the room. Helen was staring down at the smooth wooden tabletop, teasing the corner of the beer bottle's label nervously with her thumb. If Maddie still felt like an outsider in Tony's family after six years at its centre, she guessed that Helen must have begun to feel like an even bigger imposter. She only came here to support me, Maddie thought, and now she's stranded.

"Hey," she said, getting Helen's attention with a gentle touch of her foot under the table. "Are you sure you're ok being here for all this?"

"Don't be silly, course I am. I'm here to help you, not for me."

"I know that, and you've been so amazing, but now they're here and stuff," she gestured towards Ella. "Honestly I'll be fine."

"Maddie, after last might there's no way I'm leaving you in that house on your own. What if you see that... well, whatever it was you saw? What if you see it again and I'm not there?"

Maddie closed her eyes, her head propped up by her fist, stroking the grain of the table with her injured thumb.

"I suppose. As long as you're ok with it."

"Honestly, babe, it's fine. I want to be here."

The pair of them fell silent for a while afterwards, occasionally murmuring between themselves about one aspect or another that made the New Cottage superior to theirs, until Ella hauled over the pasta, which she'd combined with the sauce in one of the huge pans.

"Always the pasta into the sauce, not the other way around," Maddie heard Tony's voice echo in her head.

"Where is he? Is he still not back?" Ella said as she returned with the cutlery.

Maddie just stared at her, unable to speak. A scared little girl again. Surely, she didn't mean Tony? Did she?

"I bet he's sat somewhere doing emails or something," Ella said, ignoring Maddie's confusion. "He's barely stopped since all this happened. Luke!" she shouted into the hallway.

Maddie exhaled in relief at a confrontation averted, while Ella shepherded Luke back into the kitchen; head bowed like an errant teenager. He slyly tucked his phone in his pocket as he walked.

"Sorry," he said, pulling out the chair opposite his younger sister. "This looks quality, El."

Maddie and Helen muttered their agreement, eyes wide and stomachs tremulous with hunger. Maddie hadn't eaten since nibbling the corner of a piece of toast that morning, such was the rush of the day, and the sight of bowls being piled high with fiery red pasta was as awe inspiring as any mountain peak or golden sunset. She peered through the veil of steam for a few seconds like a jewel thief separated from her prize by the slightest pane of glass, then picked up her tools and set

9

to work.

. . .

After the bowls were cleared and the dishwasher was loaded, the four unlikely dinner companions retired to the New Cottage's relatively cramped sitting room to try and improve on the meal's stilted conversation.

The room was more in keeping with the style of the Old Cottage, its low ceilings and uneven stone walls making Maddie think that it could also have been another one of the site's original buildings, with the modern kitchen section perhaps some kind of update or extension. All of the furniture – an armchair, a two-seater sofa, and a double-wide bean bag – was pointed towards an ornately tiled fireplace. According to Ella, neither she nor Luke had the knowledge, skill, or inclination to build and light a fire to go inside it.

Luke and Helen had decided to bring in freshly opened beers – a common interest that was apparently causing Helen to warm to the man she'd recently branded 'Richie Rich' and worse – while Maddie and Ella opted to nurse insipid-looking mugs of green tea, if only for the warmth they provided in the hand.

"Soooo," Luke said as he slumped into the armchair. "Where's Tank?"

"Anna's got him," said Maddie. "The dog walker. She's has him overnight now and again, when we go away and stuff. He'll be fine."

11

1

She sat beside Helen on the sofa, while Ella had taken the bean bag in the corner of the room. She briefly looked up from scrolling through her phone at the mention of her old dog.

"Why didn't you just bring him here?" she said.

"Well," Maddie looked first to Helen then to Luke for some kind of support. "I just thought he'd be better off there. He'd have just..."

She stopped short of saying that she thought he'd have gotten in the way. Then again, even that sounded kinder than the simple truth that she and the animal had a mutual disdain for one another, at best.

"I didn't know what he'd be like up here, that's all," she said finally. "And the long drive down and everything. Thought it was for the best."

"We're in the mountains," Ella said with a sarcastic laugh. Her eyes flitted back towards the phone screen. "He'd have loved it here."

"I just thought, you know, once things start happening... we'd be here, there, and everywhere. Probably wouldn't have time to walk him, let him out."

"*If* things start happening," Ella said. "Doesn't look good so far, does it."

The room fell silent. Maddie had the urge to go and sit next to her, to tell her everything would be fine; that no matter what, they still had each other, but she knew the damage it could cause. Ella's independence and indifference were equally formidable, but they paled into comparison to her rage, if it was properly triggered.

During the early days of Maddie and Tony's relationship, when Ella was only thirteen years old, she'd flown into fits of rage at even the slightest provocation. Once, when Ella was going through a period of refusing to visit her dad, Maddie had made the mistake of sending her a text asking her to reconsider. Sufficed to say, she didn't take it well at all; the crux of her reply being that if Maddie ever had the audacity to message her in such a way again, she'd call her older brother, Ben, back from the Army and get him to kill her.

As Maddie and Helen attempted to change the subject, Ella shuffled around on her bean bag and cut back in.

"You could've just brought Anna here as well, you know," she said. "She could've walked him, looked after him. Seems like it's an open invitation anyway, so... why not?"

The last part, fired over at Helen with a flick of her eyes, was designed to eviscerate. She really is cold steel, this girl, Maddie thought. No prisoners.

Helen laughed nervously, then excused herself, asking Luke for directions to the toilet in an attempt to spare her blushes.

"Jesus El, that was a bit harsh," he said after Helen was out of earshot.

"What you on about?" Ella said, apparently oblivious.

"You know what I mean, fucking hell," he said, waving his beer towards the door. "What's she done wrong?"

"Fine," she said with a sigh, then locked her phone and placed it gently on her lap. "I'm sorry, I just... I don't know why she's here. Do you? She's weird."

Maddie put her mug down on the coffee table and stood.

"She's here to look after me," she said. "She drove me all the way down here and she's taken time off work... all because she's a good friend, to me and to your dad."

Ella, having seemingly forgotten her grandmother's poise, rolled her eyes and snorted.

"Whatever. I'll apologise. Just thought it was odd, that's all," she stared at Maddie, her dark eyes like hypnotist's pinwheels in the flickering candlelight.

"I'm sorry, honestly," she said with a shrug. "I'm just fucking... anxious, or something. I don't know. I'll tell her."

Just then there was a heavy knock at the front door. Maddie's heart fluttered in her chest, and the three of them exchanged panicked glances.

"Think your mate's ended up locked outside," Ella said with a smirk.

Maddie ignored her barb, strode out of the room towards the second burst of knocks, which were even more pronounced this time. The brightness of the kitchen made her squint as she rushed through to the porch, encountering a confused-looking Helen on the way.

"Who's that?" Helen said, her voice little more than a distant echo to Maddie's ears.

Whether it was good or bad news about Tony on the other side of that door, she simply wanted to be free of the crippling uncertainty. That yearning for an answer had caused her to bolt from the sitting room initially, but the longer she had to wait, the more doubtful she became. Could it not just be someone like Wil or his grandmother with another basket of supplies, she thought? Or worse still, the shadowy watcher from the drive, having decided the time was right to take a closer look at her.

As Maddie approached the door, she saw movement through the diamond of frosted glass, someone loitering on the doorstep. It was a man on his own, dressed in civilian clothes. Could still be a plain clothes officer, she thought. She got closer, close enough to make out his dark hair, his olive skin. She swallowed dryly and took hold of the handle.

10

"Alright Maddie," the man said as he stooped to pick up his holdall from the driveway.

"Ben?" she said, gasping as she spoke. "Jesus, I wasn't... oh my God."

It wasn't usual for them to hug when they met, but Maddie felt compelled to step down onto the gravel in her bare feet and throw her arms around his broad shoulders. He recoiled slightly, most likely in surprise, then dropped his bag and patted her in between the shoulder blades like she was an over-zealous younger cousin. She realised how strange it felt as she rested her cheek against his jacket, but it was too late to go back. Instead she closed her eyes and smiled, the faint smell of cheap aftershave and cigarette smoke filling her nostrils.

"It's good to see you," he said as they parted. "How's everyone doing?"

"Ok, I suppose... considering," she said with a shrug. Just then she realised there was an easy, content smile on her face, and wrenched it away as quickly as she could, looking down at his shoes instead.

Maddie hadn't seen Ben since they all gathered at the house two Christmases ago, as he spent the majority of his time either at his regimental base in Cyprus or travelling elsewhere; one of the few personality traits he'd inherited from his globe-trotting father. This wanderlust meant that his complexion was even darker than Tony and Luke's. Although he shared their strong jawline, he chose to keep his hair and beard trimmed almost to the skin, even when on leave.

"More to the point, how are you?"

"Yeah, not bad," he said. "Looking forward to seeing everyone... well, you know. Almost everyone."

"Course, sorry," she said, ushering him inside. "Come in, come in. They won't believe it."

"Thanks Maddie."

He picked up the bag and stepped inside, his head bowed in reverence as if he was entering a house of worship. Before she followed, Maddie turned back to stare at the gate. The sky was clogged with thick cloud, making the space behind the wall darker than it was the night before. Even if the watcher was there again, she wasn't certain she'd be able to see him.

"What the fuck!?" Ella's voice thundered from inside the house, breaking Maddie from her trance. "What are you doing here?"

"Hey! Alright bro," Luke's own hollers cut Ben off before he could answer.

As Maddie walked in, shutting the door behind her, the three of them had become one huddle, their arms and hands all intertwined. Helen was stood to one side, her hands clasped nervously in front of her.

They separated and Ella tried again.

"I thought you said you'd have to stay over there?"

"I did," said Ben, running his palm over the stubble on his head. "My officer heard about dad and he told me to stop being daft, so I did."

"Always following orders."

"Yeah, I suppose," Ben grinned at his brother. "But, yeah, so I got on a flight this morning."

"You speak to mum?" Ella said.

"Yeah, she said you were here, so I thought I'd come down. See what was going on."

Ben paused, looked over at Maddie, who was still stood in the shadows of the hallway.

"What *is* going on?" he said.

Maddie looked around as if his question might be directed at someone standing behind her, then stepped into the blinding light of the kitchen.

"Not much, really," she said. "We've not spoken to the police all day... they've been useless anyway."

"Are they still searching?"

"They say they are... they've already done it on foot, used drones and stuff, haven't they?" she said, looking over to Helen.

"That's right," she said, nodding obediently. "I'm Helen by the way, Maddie's friend... not just some random woman in the house."

"Yeah, sorry. Hiya Helen," Ben said, apologising on behalf of his impolite siblings with a hurried handshake. He came back over to where he'd dropped his bag, picked it up, and turned to Maddie. "It ok if I dump this somewhere?"

"Oh, sorry," she said. "This isn't mine... ours. We're across the way in the older place."

"Yeah this is our digs mate," said Luke, cuffing his brother on the shoulder. "There's a spare room; first one on the left at the top of the stairs. You wanna show him El?"

"Yeah, come on," Ella said, bounding off towards the stairs before Ben had a chance to reply.

"No worries, cheers," he said, returning the gesture to his brother, although it was more of a gentle squeeze than the full-on slap he'd received. "I'll grab a shower too, if that's alright?"

"Hey, it's your place too now, go for it."

"Ta," he said, then glanced at Maddie and Helen. "Are you two staying?"

They shared a sideways look. Ella had turned back at the threshold to the stairs and was hovering there impatiently as they spoke.

"We should probably get off," said Maddie. "Leave you guys to catch up."

She and Helen were moving to leave when Ben called after them.

"Maddie?"

They both turned and checked each other over as if to make sure they'd not forgotten anything.

"You alright?" Maddie said.

"Yeah, I just... I was thinking of having a look at the crash site tomorrow, maybe going around and asking some questions. Do you want to come too? You were the last one of us to see him, that's all. You know what he had on, what he took, I'm guessing? Might be something you can help with if we find anything."

Maddie felt her cheeks flush, then stuttered for a while until a sentence formed.

"Sure," she said finally, slapping her hands against her thighs to accentuate the word. "Sounds like a plan. Just come and get me when you're ready."

Ben smiled politely at Maddie and Helen, then finally put Ella out of her misery and followed her up the stairs.

. . .

Back at the Old Cottage, Maddie and Helen had taken their make-up off together, brushed their teeth side by side, and even carried on talking while they took their turns on the toilet. It wasn't unusual practice for them – a comfort born of having shared countless hotel rooms while attending trade shows and property visits for the magazine – but Maddie had made sure of it this time. There was no way she was being left alone again; tempted by the wine in the car and apprehensive of running into the mysterious figure who could be watching over it.

Maddie was taking the throw pillows from the bed and stacking them neatly on the floral-patterned armchair in the corner of the room when the bedside lamp flickered into darkness.

"Fuck," said Helen with a chuckle. "Scared the shit out of me. Are you ok babe, you still there?"

"Yeah, fine," Maddie said, her voice little more than a whisper. "You?"

She strained to swallow the ostrich egg of a lump that had formed in her throat. Even the feel, the texture of the darkness was enough to cause her skin to start buzzing with adrenaline once again.

"Hang on, one sec," Helen swore as she bumped into the corner of the bed. After a few seconds of fumbling, her phone's torch seared Maddie's eyes, causing her to recoil and cover her face with the pillow.

"Sorry," Helen said. "I'll go and have a look now, wait there."

Maddie heard the door handle jiggle, then the creak of Helen leaving the room.

"Where are you going?"

"It'll be the breaker box," said Helen. "He said it might happen didn't he. Our friend the pervert."

She listened to Helen pad down the stairs, clutching the drab pillow to her stomach like a child with her favourite stuffed animal. As she stood staring at the faint shape of the open door, she traced the stem of an embroidered rose on the pillow's surface with her thumb, following it up and

122

over tightly stitched thorns to a head of garish pink petals, then onto the golden tassels that fringed the pillow's edge. She moved her hand back and forth, letting the thin strands cascade over her skin like a waterfall, caressing the thin wound that marred her thumb, now free of its plaster.

It reminded her of Tony, of the last memory she had of him; standing forlornly in the kitchen while she bled over the sink and gritted her teeth and swore. She wanted to close her eyes and wish that moment away, wish him into the room to protect her, but closing her eyes would mean disregarding the open door. The thought that she could open them again to see the hooded man framed there made her shudder.

She slowly placed the pillow on top of the pile, eyes still fixed on the door, then walked towards it and pushed it closed with both hands, prompting a reassuring thunk to echo around the house. As she turned to lean against the door, she found herself facing the large sash window that overlooked the back garden. The thick, check curtains were wide open, revealing oppressive darkness beyond the swollen wood and flaking white paint.

She swallowed dryly, raked a stray strand of hair behind her ear. From downstairs she heard the door to the boiler room clunk open, reminding her of the backup available if she needed it. She wasn't outside anymore, she thought. She wasn't alone. It was dark, but it was still the safest place she could possibly be, in the circumstances, at least. It was enough to steel her.

She pushed herself away from the door and edged across the room, her bare feet sinking into the heavy shag carpet as she went, over-ripe avocado and harvest gold in colour, she knew. She went through the motions in her head as if she was preparing to compete for Olympic gold. All she had to do was take hold of the curtains, yank them closed, and dart into the bed to wait for the light to come back on. It would be all over in the space of a second, as long as she resisted the temptation to peer beyond the windowpane. Somehow, the curiosity still prickled at her skin like warmth from the midday sun.

She leant forward and knelt on the padded window seat; each curtain grasped tightly like the straps of a safety harness. Her eyes adjusted from the room's near dark to the dense blackness outside, and she began to make out the outline of the path that wound all the way up to the iron perimeter fence.

The path was flanked by overgrown shrubs and explosions of wildflowers and, as she continued to stare, some of their lighter petals began to appear. The moonlight, filtered down by dense cloud, caught on the edges of the ivy leaves that crawled over the wooden arch at the end of the path.

The longer Maddie looked through the arch, the more convinced she became that a figure – *the figure* – was standing beneath it. She couldn't be sure, but the way the darkness seemed raised somehow, instead of flat black, was indicative of there being something there, rather than nothing. The shape shifted slightly, little more than a ripple among the undergrowth, then stilled once more.

124

Just then, the light burst forth from the bedside lamp, the power of its appearance like a shockwave knocking Maddie to the floor. She crouched in place, her knees buried in the thick carpet, as the sound of the phone bleeping back into life downstairs rang as loud as an air raid siren. She heard the door slam and the bolt clunk back into place, then waited for Helen to thud back upstairs and along the hall.

Even though she was ready for it, Maddie couldn't help but gasp as the door swung open to reveal a bewildered-looking Helen, her phone's torch still blazing at her side like a handheld supernova.

"Maddie, what's wrong? Are you alright?"

"Yeah... slipped. Just looking outside."

She stood and snatched the curtains shut without looking back out of the window.

Helen chuckled. "It's pitch black."

"I know, I just thought I..."

Maddie faltered; her mind consumed by the potential conse-quences of the next few words. Helen had treated her like a frightened child when she'd told her about the figure at the end of the drive. She meant to be reassuring, Maddie knew that, but it only served to make her feel weak and useless. That look of pity... it was the same kind of look Maddie had given her grandmother when she was in the nursing home. Sitting there in silence while the old woman talked about looking forward to starting a job at the stables she hadn't even set eyes on for over forty years.

With Ben's arrival, the whole mood had changed. Of course, Helen had been supportive, as she always was, but it hadn't even been ten minutes before Ben was speaking of action, of actively trying to get out into the real world and do something positive. Everyone else seemed content with just being there, like they were clocking in for a long shift. If it was up to Ben and Maddie, the last thing she needed was for Helen or one of the kids to see her encounters with the watcher as some kind of grounds for dismissal. To be frog-marched back to the house and kept there like the liability they always suspected she was. It was unthinkable.

She took a deep breath, straightened the curtains.

"It's nothing," she said.

"You sure? You look a bit peaky. Do you want some water or a brew or some-"

"Honestly, it's fine. I'm good. Just knackered."

Maddie smiled weakly. Another lie heaped onto the pile. She couldn't decide which was worse, deceiving her friend when they could both be in serious danger, or deceiving herself that there was nothing to worry about.

The snare was tightening, and she could sense it. First the

edge of the drive, now the back garden. She shuddered as she imagined what the watcher's next step might be.

"You sure you're ok?" Helen said.

"Yeah, honestly. Was just heavy day all 'round, I think."

"I know," said Helen, puffing out her cheeks. "Ella's turned into a little piece of work, hasn't she?"

"She's not that different really... I dunno. She knows her own mind, I suppose."

"Well, I'll be giving her a wide berth from now on, I know that."

11

Maddie awoke to an empty bed. No tea, no toast, and the hollow sound of cold rain drumming against the window. The sound intensified each time the wind groaned, causing the cottage to snap and creak in reply. An everlasting argument hundreds of years in the making.

After a few more minutes of listening for any sign of Helen, Maddie slunk out of bed and padded across the carpet to the large, varnished wardrobe that took up more of the room's far wall. The empty eyes of a taxidermy barn owl violated her as she changed from her nightshirt into fresh clothes, his parliamentary poise having seemingly eroded after years of voyeurism perched atop his antique dresser.

"Helen? Are you down there?"

There was no answer. Maddie edged down the stairs, keeping one hand pressed against the bare plaster wall so she could lean in and survey the ground floor before she entered. The curtains had been opened, but such was the grey outside that most of the room had been reduced to a range of dark shapes. All she could smell was the cold and a faint air of damp. No signs that Helen had made any food or drink before she vanished.

Maddie checked the sofa, then crept over to one of the front windows to look out over the courtyard. Helen's MINI was nowhere to be seen, but the skylights in the New Cottage were illuminated from within, stark against the grey like two white hot embers nestling in a heap of ash.

Maddie had decided that the only way she was going to even attempt to sleep was by keeping her phone as far away as possible, which meant leaving it to charge on the kitchen worktop. She crept over and unplugged it and clicked it into life. No missed calls from Tony, nor from the police – which was unsurprising, given how accurate Wil's comments were about the signal – though it was only just past 10am. She unlocked the handset and opened her WhatsApp to read a message from Helen, sent less than an hour earlier:

Morning babe, hope you slept well. Just going for a drive out with Ben for some more stuff. Call on here if you need me or want anything. LY xx

Maddie cocked her head as she read the message, confused as to when the pair of them even had chance to arrange it. Had Helen gotten up quietly on purpose so she could go over there at the crack of dawn? It wouldn't have been the first time Helen snuck away to meet a man, and God knows Ben was her type – he was most likely anyone's type – but the decision to pursue him now would certainly be an odd one, given the situation.

She sighed and slipped the phone into the front pocket of her hoody, then walked over and opened the front door. Although the rain had relented, the wind was still rushing around the courtyard in all directions like a rabid dog, causing Maddie to pull up her hood as she made her way across the drive to the New Cottage.

She knocked on the door and allowed herself to glance at the gate as she waited for it to be answered, though she was careful not to give the thoughts of the watcher's existence any more than a few seconds. Today was about taking action, affecting the world, not preoccupying herself with unnecessary fears.

"Morning," Luke said as he opened the door and ushered her inside.

He was already dressed in designer jeans, trainers, and a loose jumper, and his laptop was open on the dining table. She took a seat across from it, looked uneasily at the Apple logo on its back. Even seeing it was like hearing somebody shout Tony's name.

"You want a coffee?" said Luke from the kitchen.

"Only if you're making one," she said, swivelling around to face him. "Didn't think you'd be up so early, actually."

"Been up for a bit, yeah," he said over the noise of the tap blasting into the kettle. "Loads to do today."

"What, work stuff?" Maddie said.

He clicked the kettle into place, flicked it on, and came over to sit across from her. He rubbed at his jawline, his close-cropped beard fuzzing up like the duck fluff it really was.

"Kind of, yeah."

"Like what?"

"Well," he said, the nervous rubbing having now migrated to the back of his neck. "Obviously dad wouldn't have been working today anyway but we've still got to... you know, make sure everything's in place. Just rescheduling stuff, you know."

"In the event of him not being found," she said, trailing off towards the end.

"Ah no, nothing like that," he said, straightening up in his chair. "Honestly, Maddie, I'm not saying anything like that. I just mean I'm trying to keep everything ticking over until he turns up, that's all."

Maddie pulled the sleeves of her hoody down over her hands, then leant on the table and clasped them in front of her mouth, as if in prayer. She looked over at Luke, watched his eyes darting from the screen, then back to her, as the kettle bubbled away in the background.

"Ella still in bed?" said Maddie, her voice muffled by her fingers.

"Nah, she's up as well," said Luke, grasping gratefully at the change of subject like a drowning man at a life ring. "She's sat out in the back."

"In the back garden?"

"Yeah," he said, pointing past Maddie at the wall of the cottage. "Out there. Says she's doing a video or something."

"A video? What kind of video?"

"About dad," he said, as if it was a perfectly sensible thing for her to do. "For her followers and that. Better than doing nothing, she said. Obviously taken a leaf out of your book, trying to be proactive."

Maddie suppressed a rueful grin at his attempt to serve her own words back to her. Despite six years as the alleged matriarch of the family, somehow their callousness was still able to surprise her, particularly when it came from him.

"That's not exactly what I meant," she said, each word formed as carefully as she possibly could. "Is she still out there?"

He nodded. She pushed herself up to leave, the wooden chair legs complaining against the tiled floor as she slid the chair out, then back under the table.

"You still want this coffee, Maddie?" he said as she strode towards the back door.

She ignored him, opened the door, and walked outside.

. . .

The back garden, much like the one at the Old Cottage, was overgrown with all manner of weeds and wildflowers. A barely visible flagstone path cut its way through waves of waist-high ferns and nettle plants, while an old woodshed stood sentinel at the rear wall, huge clusters of pigweed piling inside it like eager children bursting into a sweet shop.

Maddie noticed Ella sat under a small wooden arbour in the back corner of the garden, her legs wrapped up in one of the patchwork blankets from the sitting room. She was holding her phone out in front of her with one hand and attempting to tame her wind-whipped hair with the other as she spoke.

Maddie approached, stopping her mid-flow and causing her to tut loudly and slap her phone down onto her thigh.

"Morning."

"Morning," she said, her greeting a few notes lower. "I was actually just in the middle of something then Maddie... did Luke not tell you?"

"He did," Maddie said, glancing back at the cottage. "I came to see... well, to ask you about it, actually."

"I was filming something. To help dad."

"Yeah he said... what are you doing, exactly?"

Maddie could feel her cheeks reddening, fury rising higher with every ragged breath.

"Just for socials, you know," Ella said, holding up the phone as if it somehow legitimised the notion. "For Instagram. I've got thousands of followers on there now... thought the more people knew, the more likely someone might be able-"

"You think telling the whole world our business is going to help us? Help your dad? We don't even know what's going on yet... what if anyone from the company sees it, or his clients, and it all turns out to be nothing? He'll be mortified..."

Ella appeared to falter. She looked as if she wanted to smirk, to laugh even, but it was like the muscles in her face had been paralysed by shame. The acerbic self-defence mechanism she had always been able to call on so easily was now stalling when she needed it most.

"Maddie, it's not like that, it's-"

"You should be ashamed of yourself," Maddie said, her voice now trembling as much as her hands. "Until we know what's happened to him, we shouldn't... It's the last thing you should be thinking of. It's like you're-"

"Is everything alright?" Luke said from the back door. "El?"

"And you're no better," Maddie said, turning her ire on him.

"Sat there making plans like you've buried him already. You didn't appreciate him when he was around, and now it's showing even more. Makes me sick. You both need to grow up, fast."

She stormed past Luke, through the kitchen and out of the front door, slamming it behind her. The cold air was bracing, the argument flashing back through her mind like half-remembered scenes from a film she'd watched while drunk. She felt as if she was waking from an out of body experience, all of her limbs turned to marmalade, her lips numb from the fury that had so easily spilled over them.

As she strode across the driveway with her arms folded across her stomach, she looked up to see Ben and Helen taking shopping bags out of the MINI's boot, chatting as easily as two old friends. Helen was dressed as if she was heading into town for a day's shopping – black jeans, heeled boots, and a burgundy leather jacket – while Ben was wrapped up in a thick check shirt and work boots, a grey beanie covering his head.

They both stopped what they were doing and looked up as she approached.

"Morning," said Helen. "How you feeling?"

"Great," she said, stone-faced. "Ben, do you mind if we have this drive out sooner, rather than later?"

"Yeah, no worries. Just let me take this stuff inside and I'll-"

"Can we not go now?"

Ben and Helen looked at each other uneasily, like they'd just been asked a particularly challenging riddle.

"There's some fridge and freezer stuff in here, that's all," Helen said.

"My keys are inside anyway," Ben said. He was already heading towards the New Cottage, a plain blue plastic bag in each hand. "Won't be a minute."

Helen waited until the front door closed behind him, then placed her bags on the drive and sidled over to Maddie, who was now staring uneasily at the front gate.

"Are you sure you're ok babe? You seem a bit..."

"Not really," Maddie said, turning to face her. "I've just had a massive bust up with those two. Don't even know what happened really, or how."

Helen pulled her into a one-sided hug. She smelled like orange blossom and water lily, elegant and feminine. Maddie hadn't washed for over twenty-four hours and was beginning to smell like it.

"Try not to worry," Helen said. "It's fair enough with all this stress, God... Just give it time until everyone's calmed down and it'll be fine. You just need to look after yourself, to make sure you're strong and well. Ready for whatever comes at you."

The hug dissolved and Maddie looked straight at Helen. She noticed her full face of makeup and became conscious of how haggard she must have looked by comparison. It was the first morning in a long time that she'd not checked at least one mirror before leaving the house. She took out her bobble and scraped her hair back into place, then re-tied it into its ponytail.

"How did you end up going out with Ben?" she said.

"What do you mean?"

"Well, there was nothing said about it last night. You only met him for all of five minutes. Next morning, I wake up and you're gone without a word."

"I messaged you, did you not-"

"You know what I mean... at the time."

"Sorry. He knocked on the door this morning, said he was going into the nearest town. You were still fast asleep and I thought we could do with some more food and drink, so I said I'd go with him. It's all tiny villages really, but we did find a Co-op, couple of other shops. Even managed to get some healthy stuff for you. Ben wanted to ask around a bit, so we stopped in a few places on the way, just talking to the staff to see if they'd seen anything."

"And?"

"Nothing. I'm sorry Maddie, honestly. I just thought you'd need the rest."

Maddie closed her eyes, took a deep breath. She was being a dick, she knew she was, but there was still something about the whole situation that made her uneasy. Like she was being left behind. Even without telling anybody about the watcher, they were beginning to think she was losing it, or that she was incapable of taking control of the situation. Now she was starting to look as shit as she felt.

"It's fine. I'm sorry, I'm just a bit wound up after all that," Maddie said, gesturing towards the New Cottage as Ben was emerging.

The stern look on his face told her that Ella and Luke had filled him in on the argument, no doubt with plenty of colourful descriptors for their so-called stepmother. Even so, it didn't worry her. Ben always seemed to be above the whole situation, immune to the toxic fallout of their parents' divorce. He was so stoic and controlled, in fact, that it often seemed that he was the family's outsider, rather than her. Able to separate emotion from every conflict, regardless of its magnitude. The fact that he was only two years Maddie's junior – despite technically being her stepson – did little to dispel this air of authority.

"Shall we go?" he said, pitching his head towards the rented Skoda parked next to Luke's Audi.

Maddie nodded, hugged Helen – both sorry and goodbye – and followed him to the car.

12

They drove in silence, Ben's eyes fixed on the narrow country road ahead. It was enclosed on both sides by steep banks of green that had been cut away to make what looked like a jungle toboggan run. The shadowy rainclouds were beginning to drift over the horizon, but only to be replaced by a lighter shade of grey.

"Luke told me about what happened," Ben said after a while, his voice barely audible over the rasp of the engine.

"I feel awful," Maddie said, her hands clasped on her lap. "I don't know what it was, it just kind of exploded out of nothing."

They slowed, then came to a stop at a wide junction partially obscured on both sides by dense hedgerows. Ben's eyes flicked from one side to the other, then to the map on his phone, which was lodged in between the speedometer and the wheel. He edged out, then accelerated away to the right, changing all the way up to fourth gear before he spoke again.

"It's gonna happen isn't it, I suppose. It'd probably happen with us lot up here for a week anyway, even without all this extra stress. Don't beat yourself up about it. We just have to stick together, try and crack on, don't we."

Maddie smiled weakly.

"I'll have a chat with them when we get back," she said. "Try and explain."

"It's up to you," he said. "I wouldn't worry about it too much; those two are probably at each other's throats over something else by now anyway."

She let out a stifled laugh, turned to see there was a smile on his face too.

"It's only just after ten 'o clock now, so we can have a quick look around here, then go into a few of the towns and ask around. Me and Helen did a few but there's loads of these little places dotted around near here. Someone in one of them must have seen him."

Ben went on to explain how, after Maddie and Helen had left the New Cottage the previous evening, he'd spent the majority of his time trawling through local news articles and cross-referencing them against Google Street View to pinpoint the approximate location of the crash.

Maddie was so proud of him, but instead of admitting how glad she was that he'd decided to come and help them, she allowed the quiet to settle as they carried on through more tunnels of greenery, occasionally breezing through a sleepy hamlet or decrepit-looking village. No more than the odd dog walker or jogger to witness their passing. The undergrowth eventually fell away to reveal rolling fields on either side, the looming presence of Hay Bluff still filling the rear-view mirror.

"Right, we're not far off now, I don't think," said Ben, squinting at his phone screen. "Keep your eyes open."

A wall of pine trees rose up in front of them as the road narrowed and curved away to the right. Although there were tyre tracks going off into the adjacent fields, they were too deep and too well-worn to be made by anything other than farm machinery.

"That's it," said Ben suddenly, slowing the car just before a series of serpentine bends. He pulled onto the grass next to a cattle fence and pointed at a set of parallel tyre burns on the apex of the first turn. They were faint, perhaps worn away by the overnight rain, but unmistakable, nevertheless.

They got out of the car and walked over to the burns, the path of Tony's car becoming evident as they drew closer. Although the vehicle itself had long been towed away, a definite Range Rover-sized chunk had been taken out of the vegetation that covered the roadside. Ben stepped off the road and inside the cavity, standing up onto his tiptoes to peer over its far edge.

"There's some more debris over there," he said, having somehow adopted an almost Inspector Clark-like level of indifference.

He turned to see Maddie frozen at the roadside. Her fists were balled inside the sleeves of her hoody and her chin was tucked down into its collar. The air outside was still, soundless except for the conversations of nesting birds in the nearby trees, but it was soon filled by the soundtrack of chaos growing inside Maddie's her head. Rubber screeching against asphalt. Flesh and bone breaking against glass and steel. Crackling fire, panic and confusion.

"Are you alright?" Ben said, stepping back towards her and stifling the sounds of imagined carnage. He wore the concern of a man all too familiar with the terror that was raging behind Maddie's motionless eyes.

"Maddie," he said bluntly.

The weight of his voice knocked her free, her eyes locking instinctively on his. He edged closer like he was approaching a cornered animal, his hand coming to rest gently on her elbow.

"Are you alright?" he said, even slower this time.

"Yeah, sorry," she said, attempting to smile. "Just wasn't expecting it to look like this. To feel like this."

"I know," he said. "It's weird, course it is. It's not something you see every day. You just have to try and ignore what it feels like, focus on the facts. Being here, seeing this, even speaking with the police... it's all just noise. At the end of the day; either my dad's walked away from this, or he wasn't in it to begin with. We know Al's gonna be fine... so maybe it looks worse than it is."

"Then where did he go?"

He sighed, let go of her arm, and straightened back up.

"I don't know, but I'm gonna have a quick look around over there," he said, frowning over at the crash site. "Do you wanna wait here? I'll only be two minutes."

"I'll come, it's fine. I'm good."

Ben hopped over the edge of the Range Rover-sized cavity, then offered a hand back to her. His skin felt rough under her own pampered flesh as he took her weight and pulled her over the crest without so much as a gritting of his teeth. She was forced to bend her knees to absorb the shock of the drop on the other side and would have toppled backwards were it not for his hand solid at her back.

They walked over to a few pieces of scattered debris; mostly small shards of black metal, broken glass in various shades of amber, white, red. The clutter was organised to an extent, suggesting it had been abandoned by the exasperated recovery crew like those last few kitchen crumbs too stubborn to be brushed into the dustpan. Flies buzzed in and out of the mess like Boxing Day shoppers.

Paper and leather and pieces of green fabric – most likely

from a rucksack or waterproof coat – were scattered among the detritus, the majority of which was covered in a strange brown liquid. Ben knelt down, produced a small lock knife from his jacket pocket, and stabbed a large piece of the fabric.

"What is that? Oil?" said Maddie.

Ben held it up to his face and sniffed it.

"No, it's sweet. Honey, maybe?"

He held the knife toward Maddie, but she backed away and held up her hands like she was declining an hors d'oeuvre at a dinner party.

"It *is* honey I think," he said, touching the flat of the blade on the tip of his tongue. "That seem weird to you?"

"Pretty weird," Maddie said. "Part of snack for the walk maybe? I dunno, Al and his wife are both into some odd stuff. Could be anything, couldn't it?"

The words were becoming harder for her to force out. Ben wiped the substance off his blade with the piece of fabric, then continued shuffling the debris around while Maddie stared on blankly, uselessly. After a few more moments of digging around, Ben heaved himself to his feet, closed the knife, and slipped it back into his pocket.

The longer she looked at the mess, the louder the screeching and smashing in her ears became.

"Sorry, I'm just gonna," she gestured towards his car.

"Course, course. No worries," he said with a brief smile. "I'm gonna have a look over there first, if you're sure you're alright?"

She nodded.

As Ben strode off to the other side of the field, Maddie walked across the road, then around the back of his car. Instead of opening the passenger door, she found herself looking towards the edge of the forest. She glanced at the crash site, trying to calculate the likelihood of a disoriented Tony staggering towards the trees instead of helping Al or waiting on the roadside to flag down a passing car. The forest was only around twenty metres away, so it was possible, even if it didn't seem likely.

He certainly wouldn't be the first person to get lost in the woods, Maddie thought. Like a character in one of her father's tall tales, he could have wandered in there by mistake and now he needed someone to go in and rescue him.

She tried to remember how long the human body could survive without food, without water. Was it two weeks? Maybe that was just food, she thought. Ben would know. But then again, with the rain, maybe he was ok for water, if he was incapacitated somewhere. He certainly wasn't up to catching or foraging his own food, even if he was fully mobile. Not unless there was some kind of woodland Deliveroo service available.

As she pondered this, Maddie caught a glimpse of a figure standing slightly behind the first layer of trees, stock-still and partially obscured by the shadows within.

She was very short, perhaps even a child, and certainly not dressed for the overcast weather. The hem of her lace dress barely came past her knees, and her pale arms were completely uncovered, almost grey with cold. Maddie shivered just looking at her. Although it was difficult to tell from the distance between them, the girl looked to be mouthing something to her.

"Hello," Maddie shouted, giving an awkward, chest-height wave. "Are you ok?"

The girl made no reply, but still looked to be saying something. With her eyes fixed on the girl, Maddie began marching towards the forest, quickly breaking into a run as the girl turned and began drifting further inside. The ground was uneven; mole hills and potholes and tufts of marsh grass combining to create an ankle sprain gauntlet.

A sudden splash, followed by a sucking sound, brought her down onto her hands and knees, but the momentum and adrenaline kept her moving forward. She managed to scramble to her feet without breaking stride, but soon realised she'd lost sight of the cold-looking girl.

Maddie's limbs were numb with panic as she came to a stop on the precipice of the forest. The sweat was slick on her face and neck and heaving chest, and her hands and leggings were smeared with mud and torn up blades of grass. She wiped her top lip with the sleeve of her hoody and peered into layer upon never-ending layer of pine.

It looked like an ancient vault constructed by some elder race, used to store precious commodities like silence and darkness, hemming them in with wood and needles and leaves away from humans and their avaricious senses. The only sound came from the pines as their trunks creaked in the gentle breeze, the occasional hoarse call of a crow in the distance.

As Maddie drank in the illicit sights and sounds, or lack thereof, her heartbeat began to slow. She inhaled the smell of damp moss and soil, noticed patches of wildflowers. Daisies smiling up at her, oblivious like children, while dew-speckled columbine loomed behind, their purple hoods bowed in quiet meditation.

She called out again. "Hello? Hello? Do you need help?"

All she heard by way of reply was the sound of her own voice reverberating from tree to tree, gradually becoming quieter like a disintegrating pinball. She stepped over the threshold, into the mulch of the forest floor, and it felt comforting, like the first pats of bare feet on wet sand.

"Hello? Are you there? Hello?"

She moved deeper, her head scanning from side to side until she noticed the glimmer of something pale amongst a nest of leaves just ahead, tucked behind the trunk of a broken tree.

She approached quietly and knelt down in front of the object, then plucked away the leaves that partially shielded its form, laying them in a pile next to her mud-soaked trainers. It was some kind of stone, not purely pink, as she first thought, but translucent. It looked like a wisp of smoke that had been encased in rosewater and polished until gemstone smooth, alien amongst the roughness of bark and bracken. If it had been half the size, it could have quite comfortably blended into the bowl of healing stones Ginny had brought to Al's bedside.

She stayed still for a while, almost content, until Ben's voice exploded into the forest like a clap of lightning.

"Maddie? Maddie?"

"I'm over here," she said absently, her eyes never deviating from the way the light rippled across the stone's surface.

She listened to his footsteps until they stopped just behind her, his voice now lowered back to its customary rumble.

"Are you alright? What's that?"

Maddie finally pulled her gaze away and stood to face him, her back to the stone like a mother shielding her young from a hungry predator. Ben's expression hadn't changed, his concern still painfully evident.

From the last time they saw each other at her and Tony's house, and in the two years that had passed since then, Maddie had come to know that Ben was a man of his word, even if that meant withholding the truth from the ones he loved the most. The simple existence of the dangerous secret they shared was enough to convince her that he'd never betray her trust, even if the things she needed to tell him sounded like the ramblings of a maniac. Like something straight out of her father's weird Celtic folktales.

She took a deep breath, looked into his eyes, and let the words, at last, tumble free.

. . .

Although the appearance of the stone may have had nothing to do with the crash or the disappearing girl, its presence at least served as an effective visual aid for Ben to glance at while Maddie made her stuttering confession.

He barely flinched when she told him about the girl, though he did begin to berate her like an overprotective father when she went on to discuss the watcher at Stone's Reach. Regardless of his bluster, the main thing for Maddie was that he seemed to believe her.

After she finished, they both stood quietly for a few minutes, transfixed by the way the stone seemed to glow like a star that had fallen straight through the canopy and come to rest in the padded brush. She could almost hear it radiating, slicing through the silence like a moistened finger slipping around the rim of an empty wine glass.

"Well, what do you want to do?" Ben said in a hushed voice.

"I don't know. We could go and look for her but... I don't know, part of me thinks she might... fucking hell, I don't know."

Ben said nothing, the corner of his jaw pulsing each time she spoke.

Maddie blew out her cheeks in frustration, as if she had forgotten how to say the words she needed. He'd humoured her politely while she told stories of cold little girls and hooded watchers, but she doubted he'd be able to do the same if she started to quote her father's old sayings and – God forbid – include talk of the fair folk.

To Maddie, the stories always seemed that little bit more plausible when they came from her father; a kind of authenticity granted by his thick Galway accent and scraggly red hair and the wry smile he always followed them up with. Whenever she'd made the mistake of repeating them to people in the past, she just came off as a naïve little girl who'd read too many fairy tales. More often than not, she was met with confusion, laughter, or – in the case of the kids at her high school – branded a 'gyppo' or a 'pikey'.

She felt insane just by thinking it, but was it so much stranger than a girl all the way out here on her own, dressed like a Victorian going to the beach, who then suddenly vanished?

"What do you think?" she said eventually.

"Well, I didn't see her, did I, so I don't know. Sounds pretty strange. She could have just wandered off from her parents I suppose, on a hike?"

"But the way she was dressed, it was too-"

"Or she could just live out here. Looking at the maps, there's a pretty big farm on the other side of the forest. Farmers can dress weird, sometimes. Out in the sticks, like this? Maybe she's from there? Could be foraging or something."

"Yeah, I suppose," Maddie said. She scolded herself for not having come up with these explanations first. Maybe she was too inclined to believe the fanciful first, as much as she thought she was better than her old man.

"You think that's hers?" Ben said, nodding towards the stone.

"Maybe," Maddie said, blatantly unconvinced. "She probably came this way... But even if she is from the farm, how can she have just vanished like that? She was right here and then... nothing."

"Look," he said with a gentle sigh. "We're already missing one Degrassi and I reckon going deeper into here with no map and no gear will probably mean two more down before the end of the day."

"I guess," she said, her voice cracking as tears began to glisten in the corners of her eyes. "But she can't have just disappeared, can she? If I start thinking I've, I don't know, made it up or something then... what about the man at the cottage? The watcher. Have I made that up as well, twice?

If Helen or your brother or sister hear me talking like this, they'll have me off to the fucking loony bin."

"Come on," Ben said, stooping to look into her eyes. "We'll go into the next town and see if we get anywhere with that, then maybe come past here on the way back and have another look. We've still got plenty of time. That ok?"

"Yeah, ok," she sniffed.

She looked at the stone and considered putting it in her pocket. After all, it could be used as evidence, either in relation to Tony or the disappearing little girl. She bit her lip and stepped forward.

"Maddie?" said Ben.

She turned back to see his outstretched hand, then smiled and decided to take it instead of the stone, clambering over a clutch of twisted roots towards him.

They headed for the road, though she continued to glance back at the stone as she trailed after him, ducking under each stray branch as he held it back for her. As soon as they were out of the forest, back into the blinding grey of the open air, it all began to seem like a distant memory, as it the stone couldn't possibly have looked as alien as she thought it did.

She tried to remember its shape, how smooth and tempting its surface had looked. She'd resisted touching it in that instant, more out of fear than good sense, but she was already fantasising about rushing back in and pocketing it.

They cleared the last line of trees and Ben glanced up at the ashen sky then back at her.

"Bloody hell," he said, "Looks like it's gonna throw it down."

Maddie muttered her agreement, though she couldn't help but scowl in confusion at just how faint the sun's light had become, especially given it was still morning.

Ben paused as he opened the driver's door, and squinted at his phone. After a few seconds, he looked over to Maddie, his gaze just skimming the roof like a pebble over still waters.

"Maddie? What time have you got?" he said.

Maddie scowled at him for a second, then slipped her phone from her pocket and clicked the screen into life.

"Shit," she said, looking up at the sky once again. "Must be something wrong, it says it's…"

She trailed off as she looked back up to see Ben holding his phone to face her. The thin white digits on his screen matched the ones on hers: *16:49.*

"What the fuck? She said. "How is that possible?"

Ben scowled.

"I think we need to get back to the house."

13

They sat around the table with their eyes cast down, surrounded by gloom but for the last dregs of grey filtering through the skylights overhead. Luke sat directly opposite Maddie at the head of the table, while Ella was slumped in the middle, her head resting in the crook of her arm like an apathetic student at the back of the classroom.

After Ben had settled his siblings in place, he removed the cigarettes and lighter from his jacket pocket and stepped into the back garden, leaving the three of them to fend off the gathering silence together.

Although the respective arguments seemed to be fresh in Luke and Ella's minds, Maddie couldn't expel the image of that cold, pale little girl. Every appliance and piece of furniture in Maddie's peripheral vision seemed to slowly morph into the girl's porcelain face, only to change back to its original form when Maddie snapped her head around to regard it.

She had the sudden urge to scream it all away, all of the eyes that had been burrowing into her since she arrived at Stone's

Reach, from the lascivious stuffed animals in the Old Cottage, to the hooded watcher, to the little girl. All of them intent on doing nothing more than staring at her, assessing her. What the fuck could they all want from her?

This increasing pressure, alongside the stress of still getting nowhere with Tony's disappearance, served to make all of this 'playing stepmother' feel so false by comparison. Maddie shifted in her seat and began to mumble, causing Luke to look up from his interlinked fingers.

"I feel like... I know none of this is ideal, but I just – and I really shouldn't have been like that with you both anyway, I know that – but..."

She sighed and swore under her breath, frustrated by the timid nonsense coming out of her mouth. She took a deep breath and continued.

"Look, my dad wasn't a very nice person... for some of the time, at least," she said. "I know your dad is away a lot – and obviously all the stuff with us and your mum didn't help – but he loves you so much. I know that for a fact. He loves you so much... and I'm pretty sure he loves me too. We're all really lucky to have someone like him around, and I think we need to..."

She trailed off, distracted by the snort that came from Ella. She paused and cocked her eyebrow, waiting for the girl's response.

"I get what you're saying, but what's it got to do with what happened this morning?" Ella said, heaving herself into a sitting position. Her thick hair was a mess, obscuring most of the right side of her face. It was as if she was doing everything she could to look disinterested, Maddie thought.

"El, come on just let her-"

"I'm sorry but I just don't get it," she said, turning her ire on her brother. "She's told us stuff about her dad before, I don't understand what it's got to-"

"Ella, please," Maddie said, her words becoming more deliberate. "I'm just trying to explain why I think I snapped at you like that. It's hard... I just think I saw you on your laptop and you outside filming and I felt... well I felt like you were being-"

"What? Ungrateful?" said Ella.

"Well," Maddie said. "Not ungrateful but maybe just..."

"What, were we not sad enough? If I remember it was you who said we need to do something."

"I know I did... and we do."

"Look, this isn't getting us anywhere," Luke said. "Can we just act like this didn't happen and get on with what we need to do?"

"No," Maddie said. "No, we need to sort this. I wanted to say

I'm sorry, 'cause I am sorry, not because I feel like I have to. I shouldn't have spoken to either of you like that."

She turned to face Luke.

"The business is everything to your dad... when he gets back, he'll be so proud to know that you were looking after it, even when you must be so confused and worried. And I don't think I understood what you were doing with those videos, Ella... but I know you were doing whatever you think was right and I'm sorry for letting my own stuff get in the way. That's what I meant. He's *your* dad at the end of the day."

"We don't want to stress you out either Mads," said Luke. "You're his wife. And I know what it must have looked like, me on the emails and that. So, yeah, I'm sorry too. We all need to be on the same team, don't we."

They shared a shallow smile, then glanced over to Ella. She raked the ropes of hair back from her face and exhaled as if she'd been asked to help move a piano. She sucked her teeth, then said: "Ok."

All three of them sighed in relief, the tension dissipating as they began to laugh.

"El's video's helped already, actually," Luke said, half standing to slide his laptop off the kitchen counter. His face was illuminated as he opened the screen, and after tapping away for a few seconds he spun it around to face Maddie like a gangster revealing a briefcase full of banknotes.

"We made a Facebook page. 'Find Tony Degrassi'," Ella said, directing Maddie's eyes to the title on the screen. "Just got a bit of an overview on there, last known location and other info stuff. I said on my Instagram video that anyone who knows anything, or might have seen him or whatever, should just post it on here. It's had loads of shares and quite a few people have posted already. One of my followers has got relatives around here, said her great aunty lives in Talgarth, which isn't far. Says she's gonna ask her if she's seen anything... look, there she is."

Maddie began to scroll, eyes unblinking in the glare of the screen. With the exception of the odd stupid comment – which Ella leant in to delete each time they appeared – they were mostly supportive. She even found a smile occasionally creeping onto her lips at a few of the more positive ones. All of the things she and Tony had said about Ella's social media obsession being useless were coming back to haunt her.

"This is all so," she hesitated, then broke free of the screen and looked at Ella, placed her hand on her outstretched forearm. "It's amazing Ella. You've done something amazing. I'm so sorry."

"It's fine. Honestly, I get it. This whole thing's fucked. Heads are all mashed aren't they... not a surprise really, is it."

The two of them stood and embraced, both bending at the waist to meet in the middle of the wooden slab of table that separated them.

"Hopefully someone can give us something to go on soon," Ella said as they sat back down.

The back door opened and Ben stooped inside, his eyebrows arched as if to ask whether the coast was clear. All three of them smiled to reassure him and he strode over to the table.

"Anyway," Ella said. "What about you two? Where've you been all day?"

14

On the drive back from the forest, Maddie and Ben had felt pressured to invent a story about why they had been so long on what was, ostensibly, a short trip out. They had debated telling the truth – that time had seemed to evaporate in that forest – but eventually decided that it would have meant telling them the full, outlandish story; a burden that no-one else needed.

The party line was that she and Ben had wandered further into the woods to look for more clues and had inadvertently gotten lost. Thanks to Ben's Army orienteering skills, they'd eventually found their bearings and the car and come straight back to the cottage. As far as Maddie was concerned, this was both a plausible and partially truthful account; the perfect kind of lie.

Helen was still at the Old Cottage alone, so Maddie messaged her to come over and join them. She knocked on the door just over thirteen minutes later; her perfectly applied make up giving a good indication as to what had held her up.

Luke came over to the table with a bunch of beer bottles held out in front of him, beaming eagerly like a new bride clutching her bouquet.

Despite the watcher and the trip to the hospital, or perhaps because of them, Maddie had been able to distract herself enough to avoid alcohol the previous evening. Now, after the addition of their strange encounter in the woods, her preoccupations were becoming her biggest problem. Luckily, she'd spent her whole life becoming an expert on the effects of alcohol on an overactive mind.

Conversation began to flow as freely as the alcohol, and it wasn't long before talk turned to one of the only things that all five of them had in common.

"I remember, when I first met him," Helen said, topping up her glass of malbec. "It was at that trade show in Amsterdam, do you remember Maddie?"

They shared a smile, then she turned back to meet Luke's expectant gaze, her confidence seeming to increase with each and every sip.

"So, yeah. It was about two or three and we'd been on the show floor since nine, hungover as shit, doing meetings and stuff for the magazine. We were already dying for a drink but nowhere was allowed to start serving until about four thirty, was it? Anyway, we came over to the Degrassi stand and your dad was there, in the same boat obviously, so we persuaded him to sneak into the back and smuggle us out some prosecco, and those little plastic cups. We ended up missing all the rest of our meetings because we were just drinking and smoking outside on those sofas, do you remember? Your uncle Luca was so pissed off when he found out."

Maddie nodded as the rest of them chuckled together, though the memory chilled her. Tony was a married man at that time, stealing away two young girls to drink and smoke in an empty beer garden, like teenagers gathered around a bench in a darkened park. It wasn't even that long ago, in the grand scheme of things, she thought. Would he still be capable of that now? Is that what he had been doing with the girl in Gothenburg?

"He's such a dick," Ella said, grinning as she sipped her beer. "He's obviously past all that now, coming to a place this boring."

At least his children had been oblivious to most of his indiscretions, Maddie thought.

"I know, the state of it," Luke agreed, tilting the neck of his bottle in the general direction of the Old Cottage. "Does it look as bad on the inside Mads?"

"Worse," said Helen, butting in again. "It's all crooked, and it's got these stuffed animals everywhere, and this dirty old room that they've still not sorted out."

"Stuffed animals? Like teddies?" Ella said.

"I doubt it El," Luke said with a snort. "You mean like real animals, don't you? Dead ones?"

Helen nodded.

"What's this old room?" Luke said, his brow furrowed.

"The creepy guy who let us in said it was like an old workshop," Helen said. "The previous owner fixed things and made jewellery or something. It's all still there, has been for years apparently. They're just too lazy to sort it out."

Just then Helen straightened up, appeared to glance sideways at Maddie as if she'd caught her saying too much.

"The guy's told us not to go in there anyway," Helen said quickly. "Said it's really dangerous in there."

"That's so gross," said Ella. "What the fuck was dad think-ing?"

"Do you mind if I go over have a look?" said Ben. He'd been leaning against the worktop, listening, his face partially obscured by shadow.

"You want to look at the workshop?" Maddie said, suddenly interested in the conversation. Ben nodded as he stepped into the light.

"Yeah. Well, all of it," he said. "But yeah that does sound a bit odd. It's probably nothing, but if we can figure out why dad came here in the first place, it might help us to find out where he's gone. Could be there's something in there."

The shallow laughter that had continued to crackle around the room following Ella's misunderstanding quickly subsided at the mention of the issue at hand. It was as if Ella, Luke, and Helen were, for their own reasons, doing everything they could to try and distract themselves from the fact that Tony was still nowhere to be found. Ben's mind, on the other hand, was like that of a hungry predator, focussed and relentless. As if nothing could sway him until he found out the truth for himself.

"I did mention it to Ginny, yesterday... Al's wife," Maddie said. "She seemed to think the cottage was kind of a special place for Al. That maybe he mentioned it to your dad and that's why he booked it. For Al."

"Yeah and the guy who showed us around said we really shouldn't be going in the older bit anyway. Said it wasn't safe," Helen said, as if no one had heard her the first time.

"Right," Ben said, taking a sip of his beer. "Well, if it's all the same I wouldn't mind looking anyway. Obviously, we can eat first and that."

"Thank fuck for that," said Luke, prompting another titter from Helen. "What vegetables are we on tonight, chef?"

Ella rolled her eyes, lolled out her tongue, and stuck her middle finger up at her brother.

166

"Hey hey," he said, holding up his hands. "I'm serious. Honestly, I won't moan. It was alright last night, that gear. What are we on?"

Ella paused, allowed her lips to curl into a sadistic smile, and said: "Tofu."

. . .

With Ella set to work chopping and boiling and the others talking quietly at the dinner table, Maddie commandeered the landline to check in with the police. It was one of the clunky, moulded plastic handsets that she had grown up with, cream in colour and tethered to the base with a tight spiral of cord. As well as serving up a heavy dose of nostalgia, it allowed her to employ a tactic she hadn't had to use since she was in high school; taking the base from its table to the foot of the stairs, then climbing as far away from prying ears as the straining cord would allow. Unfortunately, she wasn't about to whisper sweet nothings to a boy she liked; she was going to subject herself to the personification of dreariness that was Inspector Clark.

She unfurled the scrap of paper with Clark's phone number on and dialled carefully with her free hand. After being passed from a call handler to a junior officer, she was eventually put through to the man himself. He sounded as if he'd just woken up.

"Mrs Degrassi," he said by way of a greeting.

"Hi... sorry I know you're all busy, but I just wanted to see if you'd got any further since I last called?"

He sighed, making the receiver crackle with static. "We're doing everything we can at the moment, Mrs Degrassi; co-ordinating with local Mountain Rescue and other volunteer services, as well as the NCA and Missing Persons."

"And? Have you found anything?"

"Well, it's slow going, to be completely honest with you. I'm not sure why, but the searches are taking longer than expected, particularly in the wooded area near the crash site."

Maddie swallowed dryly, shivered slightly at the thought of her phone's screen reading 16:49. The sensation that the forest, or something in it, was somehow distorting time itself had seemed easier to ignore when it was just her and Ben's frazzled brains being affected.

"I've been told you've started a Facebook group?" Clark said, clearly oblivious at the chill his words had sent down Maddie's spine.

"Yeah," Maddie said, pausing to take a fortifying swig of beer. "That was Tony's daughter, Ella."

"Ah I see, that makes sense. Must be hard for all of you at the moment, especially the kids."

"Very. I guess she just wanted to feel like she had some kind of... control in all this."

"Well, whatever helps," he said. "As long as it doesn't hinder our investigations, of course."

"Sorry?"

"The hospital, yesterday. I believe you paid a visit to Mr Rowlands. Spoke with his wife?"

"He's Tony's friend," said Maddie. "I just wanted to make sure he was alr-"

"Look, Mrs Degrassi," Clark said with a sigh. "I've been in this job for a long time and I can say quite confidently that no good will come of you conducting your own investigations. A situation like this, there's a lot of parties to coordinate, a lot of interests... Anyone working independently is only going to slow things down. Course, I can't legally stop you or anyone else from doing so at present, but I can tell you this kind of thing could potentially affect our official enquiries. Obviously, that becomes a much more serious matter. Is that understood?"

She was in the headmaster's office again, only this time she had the benefit of being able to take another swig of Dutch courage before she responded.

"I wasn't conducting my own investigations; I was visiting a friend in hospital. Last time I checked that was still legal... unlike police negligence."

She took another swig with her eyes closed, braced for impact, but it never came. He simply sighed again.

"Mrs Degrassi," he said, his voice softening. "I understand that you and your family are going through a very stressful time at the moment, and me having no news for you must make things very hard, but I assure you we are doing everything we can to find your husband. We're using every available resource and the absolute depth and breadth of our networks. Mrs Degrassi, are you still there?"

"Yeah," she said her head in her hands. "I'm sorry, I shouldn't have... I was just hoping you'd have something. Anything. We're just so confused, all of us, still. None of it makes sense."

"I understand."

He didn't. Not unless his spouse had vanished off the face of the earth too, and he was stuck in a creepy old house, being stalked by hooded men and strange little girls. He didn't have a fucking clue.

"Ok," Maddie said, plodding down the stairs with the phone clamped between her ear and shoulder. "I'll call tomorrow and see if there's any news."

"That's not necessary Mrs Degrassi," he said. "If we have any developments, you can rest assured I'll contact you straight away. You're still at Stone's Reach, I expect?"

"We are. Me and the kids."

"Well, there you go," he said. "And that's exactly where you should be. Take care Mrs Degrassi, I'll speak to you soon."

15

Once again, the food was as nourishing as it was delicious, despite Luke and Ben's fake vomiting at the mention of the 'T word'. It was a melting pot of Asian cuisine, each bowl layered with Singapore noodles, pak choi, and wild mushrooms, and topped Teriyaki marinated tofu, sliced chillies, and crispy shallots. Clearly, Ella's return to the vegan corners of her vast social media network brought with it a new and very serious set of kitchen skills.

Although the majority of the day had somehow disappeared while Maddie and Ben were in the forest, she had become acutely aware of how long it had been since she'd last eaten; at the very same table the night before. The bowl warmed her hands as the food warmed her empty stomach, each forkful like an umami grenade detonating in her mouth.

Dinner conversation was slightly less stilted than it had been the night before, thanks in part to the way empty beer bottles were clinking into the recycling bin with increasing speed. Although Maddie had initially been worried about what could happen with no one sober enough to turn the other cheek if another argument erupted, the atmosphere gradually became one of reluctant, almost guilty, normality. Helen in particular had adopted a quite pronounced slur to her speech, and even appeared to be drifting in and out of sleep where she sat.

As Luke and Ben cleared the plates, Maddie gave her a gentle tap on the arm and gestured for her to lean in for a quiet word.

"You ok?" she said. "You seem like you're on the slide."

"Me?" Helen said with a snort. "Fine. Why do you say that?"

"I've been in enough hotel bars with you."

"You certainly have," she mumbled. "Do you reckon Ben will let me nick one of his fags?"

"Helen," Maddie said, trying to regain her attention.

"Sorry, yeah, what's up?"

Helen chuckled to herself, despite not having made a joke.

"Why don't you go and have a lie down in the sitting room for five minutes?" Maddie said. "These won't mind, I'm sure."

"No don't be silly, course not. That's so rude. I have to look after you, anyway. Watch out for stalkers."

She laughed again, and this time Maddie even felt the slight scratch of spite just beneath the surface of her words.

"Sorry," Helen said. "I'm only messing, babe. Sorry."

Maddie shrugged Helen's mollifying grasp from her forearm and lowered her voice even further.

"Go and have a lie down. I'll tell Ella. Go on, it's fine."

"Maybe just a cat nap. You sure you're ok, if I... You're not going in that room, are you? I don't need you getting hurt while I'm drunk sleeping."

"No, come on, don't worry about that."

"You're sure you're sure?"

Maddie nodded, then stood and shepherded Helen towards the sitting room. Once she was securely curled up and snoring on the sofa, Maddie took a thick woollen throw that was crumpled at the foot of the bean bag and laid it over Helen's bottom half.

"She's just having a lie down," Maddie said to Ella as she re-entered the kitchen.

Ella briefly looked up from her phone to acknowledge the statement, then sat back in her chair and allowed her eyes to reattach themselves to the screen.

Ben and Luke were stood at opposite sides of the cleared dining table, deep in hushed conversation. Both men were gripping the backs of their respective chairs like they were afraid they'd float away if they were left unattended. Maddie smiled with relief as she heard them both begin to snigger like teenage boys.

She sidled over and attempted to get Ben's attention with a timid wave. As far as she was concerned, the longer they stayed in the New Cottage and the more they all drank; the less likely he was to follow through on his intentions of inspecting the workshop for himself.

"Hiya," she said, trying to sound casual. Ben halted the conversation with his brother and shot an expectant look Maddie's way.

"Everything alright?" he said.

"Yeah, I just thought... Do you fancy having a look at that workshop now? Before we all turn in?"

"Erm, yeah... can do. What about your mate?" he said, gesturing towards the living room with his beer.

"She'll be fine. I'll come back and get her after."

. . .

It was dark and silent as they crossed the courtyard, the moon's light stifled by yet another thick layer of cloud. As Maddie looked up at the way they loomed overhead, they seemed somehow familiar. She even thought that they could have been the very same ones that had confronted them when they emerged from the forest earlier that day. The same crushing presence, the same indifference, like a herd of elephants watching two ants scurry around in their shadow.

Ben lit a cigarette as they walked and had somehow managed to finish it by the time they reached the front door. Maddie fumbled with the keys, her mind flooding with images of her scrambling for them on her hands and knees as the watcher's gaze burned a hole in her back.

The cottage itself was dark but for a solitary lamp Helen had left on by the staircase, and the air was thick with stale wood smoke and the mustiness of old furniture. It felt like walking into a quiet pub in early January, the entire room exhausted and uninterested in their presence.

"It's not that bad," Ben said as Maddie switched on a free-standing lamp in the corner of the room. "Cosy."

"If you say so," Maddie said as she locked eyes with the stuffed squirrel that straddled a bureau at the back of the sitting area. "So, this is all of downstairs really, then up there it's just-"

"Is that the workshop, through there?" Ben said, pointing at the clapboard door in the corner of the room.

"That's it, yeah. You want to go in there now?"

"If that's ok?"

"Course," she said. Instead of walking over to the door, she stood and blocked Ben's way.

"You alright?" he said.

"Yeah, I just... Are we not gonna talk about what happened today?"

"What do you mean?"

"The little girl? The fact that we were in that forest for all of, what, five minutes, and it turns out it was more like five hours? Or more, actually? You even don't seem-"

"I know," he said. "Course, it's... weird. And all of this with dad is getting weirder along with it but, I dunno... It's happened. There's nothing we can do about it. Neither of us have any explanation for any of it so to stand around talking about it is... I just want to try and concentrate on what we can control right now. You know what I mean?"

They stared into each other's eyes for a moment, Maddie's breath flickering as she attempted to still her heaving chest. She broke away and walked over to the door, having to jiggle the latch a few times before she shouldered the door open and tumbled through into the annex. The pitch-blackness was disorientating until Ben's phone torch painted the room in stark monochrome. She edged over to the wall and found the row of light switches; each click bringing one of the fluorescent tubes overhead buzzing into life.

"Bloody hell," Ben said as the extent of the clutter was revealed. "Can see why they've been putting it off."

"It's mental," Maddie said as she picked her way past the first heap of clutter. "I... this kind of thing just really bothers me. It's almost like they were actively trying to make it look a mess."

The last few rows of shelving had crashed into one another, either through human carelessness or the sheer weight of the boxes they supported. As a result, the bare concrete floor was scattered with nuts and bolts and screws, rolls of solder wire, and sawn-off pieces of copper pipe. A cast iron Singer treadle sewing machine, just like the kind an antique shop would sell as an objet d'art for hundreds of pounds, had been crushed under one of the shelves and left to rust.

So chaotic was the far end of the room that the taped off entrance to the staircase was almost completely blocked.

"There's another room up here, like a loft space or something, but the guy said it's too dangerous to go up. Said he almost fell through it a while ago, over there. Maybe it's rotten or something."

Ben clambered over the toppled shelves and stood next to her, his eyes never deviating from the staircase.

"We'll see," he said. He put a hand on her shoulder as he eased past and climbed over the pile of twisted metal, then ducked under the red and white tape and began climbing the stairs. With each step, the creaking became louder, more pained.

"Ben, be careful," Maddie said. "That doesn't sound good."

"It's ok. It's better than it looks."

He kept his left hand pressed against the bare stone wall as he ascended, the shadows from above gradually obscuring his head and face, then his shoulders and arms and hands. He stopped and reengaged the torch on his phone before continuing all the way until Maddie could hear his boots scraping over the boards above her.

A light came on inside the room, and she heard Ben swear under his breath.

"Maddie," he said, his usually solid voice now wavering. "Do you want to come up? You need to see this."

16

Maddie first steps upwards were tentative, each creak of the staircase teasing a total collapse that never came.

Ben was stood at the top of the stairs, the low ceiling causing him to hunch over as he stared ahead into the room. He helped Maddie up as she approached. She was about the say something to him, thank you perhaps, but the words disintegrated as soon as she followed his gaze.

Even with the naked lightbulb that hung at around chest height, the corners of the loft were thick with shadow. Maddie could clearly make out a mattress at the far end, pillows resting against the wall and a thin, floral quilt pulled tightly over it. On either side of the mattress was a set of varnished wooden drawers; one of which had a few unburned black candles on top, and the other a wooden figurine.

A crudely woven Saint Birgid's cross, much like the one Maddie's father used to keep on the shelf above their front door, was perched on top of the headboard.

While this makeshift bedsit was unsettling, it was clearly not what had caused Ben to freeze where he stood.

"What the fuck?" Maddie said.

She gestured towards the uneven floorboards as she spoke, which were covered in symbols scrawled in what appeared to be black chalk or charcoal. The markings looked almost wet, greasy, on top of the dry wood. Although the majority of the smaller symbols that ran up both side of the mattress were too intricate to be recognisable, the form of a large seven-pointed star at the foot of the bed was unmistakable, a ring of seven black candles at its centre.

Ben stepped forward and Maddie grabbed the sleeve of his jacket and hissed his name.

"It's ok, it's not going anywhere," he said, stomping the floor twice with his boot. "Whoever said this was rotten was either wrong or they were lying."

He edged closer to the star and crouched at its perimeter, touched his index and middle finger to it. Maddie moved towards him as he was turning his hand over to inspect the substance.

"This is... well, it's not old."

"What do you mean?"

"It's been done recently, look at it."

Even in the dim light from the blub hanging just in front of them, the outlines of the star and the circle that enclosed it were stark.

"How long have you been here?" he said.

"What do you mean, at the cottage?

"Yeah."

"Two nights."

"And you've only been out with me today?"

"And to the hospital with Helen the day before. But she was here all day yesterday while we were out, if that's what you're thinking. No one could have gotten in here without her knowing."

Possibilities began to flash through Maddie's mind. She walked over to the undisturbed mattress and knelt next to it, then ran her hand over one of the faded daisies that adorned the quilt.

"Could there be someone living here? Like a squatter or something?" she said. "The guy who showed us around, Wil... he was pretty odd. Really odd, actually. Blasting some horrible noise in his car and wearing this awful, violent t-shirt. Maybe it's him. Maybe all of this is his idea of... decoration."

She drew out the last word as she stared at the wooden statue.

It appeared to be some kind of deity, sat on a pile of leaves – half holly, half oak – with his cloven hooves crossed at the ankle. The figure's face was smooth and feminine, and ostensibly human but for a pair of thin horns that protruded from its forehead. Its neck was elongated and covered by what looked like piled metal rings, while two ram-headed serpents were coiled around the figure's bulging belly.

"Ugly bastard," she whispered.

She moved away from the statue, her attention taken by the small symbols that ran up the side of the bed. As much as she tried to compare them in her mind to the Arabic characters, Japanese kanji, or Thai script, or even something more angular like Norse runes, nothing seemed to add up. They certainly weren't Cyrillic or Latin, and they were too intricate to be pictorial representations of real-life animals or objects.

The marking directly next to her knee appeared to be a thin 'V' shape, ornamented with dots up each side and bars across its point, and a spiral at its centre, almost like a seashell. The V shape was ringed with single characters punctuated by dots, all of which were just as alien in their appearance as the central symbol.

This wasn't someone just drawing shapes for the sake of it. There was intent, knowledge. These symbols meant something.

"Maddie," came Ben's voice from the other corner of the room.

She half-stood and crept over to him, still paranoid that the floor could fall out from under her at any moment, despite his assurances. He was knelt in front of a flat-bottomed leather case, next to a pile of folded linen and a steel bucket, which reminded Maddie of a milking pale.

"Hang on," Ben said as he fished his phone back out of his jeans pocket.

He clicked his flashlight back on and opened the bag and shone the light inside to reveal rows of pockets, each one holding some kind of metal tool. Maddie leant in closer as Ben pulled out an elongated pair of scissors.

"What the fuck?" he said. "This is like some kind of-"

"It's a medical bag," said Maddie, reaching in to take a tarnished set of forceps. She turned and held them up against the bulb, the ridges of the surgical steel cold against her fingers.

"He strike you as a medical student, or something, this Wil?" said Ben.

"Well, no. But even if he was... this stuff is, I dunno, more like antiques, hand-me-downs."

She passed the forceps to Ben and he inspected them with the light for a second, then put them back in the bag. It was hard to tell in the gloom, but she was almost certain she caught a glimpse of worry in Ben's eyes as he turned to meet hers.

It was the first time she'd seen that look since he'd arrived, despite the gravity of the situation they were in.

"Do you recognise any of this?" he said, nodding towards the seven-pointed star.

She turned to check, as if some bolt of inspiration might strike her, but it all looked just as mystifying as it had when she first walked in. If anything, the discovery of the surgical tools gave the symbols an even more sinister aspect.

"I don't know," she said. "We need to speak to them, the cottage company. They might not even know this is here, the old woman at least. If it is someone squatting, some weirdo or something, they need to... shit."

"What? What is it?"

"Well... You don't think this could be..."

The thought made her skin crawl. Could this be where the watcher sleeps? Had he been hiding in here all along, toying with her when he could have just as easily opened the door and walked upstairs while they were in bed?

"Could be what?" Ben said, breaking her from her malaise. "This watcher?"

Maddie stood and walked over to the staircase.

"Come on, I can't stay in here. Not with... this."

"Do you not want to-"

"Ben, please. Come on, let's talk in the house."

. . .

Ben leant on the kitchen counter while Maddie paced the floor, occasionally deviating to straighten the bread bin or one of the tea towels that hung over the oven door handle.

"Is it too late to call her now?" she said. "I know she won't be in the office, but maybe there's a number on the website for emergencies or whatever."

She didn't wait for Ben's reply, fumbling her phone from her pocket and tapping '*Red Dragon Cottages, Wales*' into the search bar. Her phone remembered the site and offered to take her straight there.

"What the fuck?"

"What is it?"

"This site can't be reached," she said, reading from the screen. "The *www.reddragoncottages.co.uk* server IP address could not be found..."

"Did you type it in right?"

"I didn't have to; it was in my history. I visited it a couple of days ago. Now it's... gone."

Ben came to look over her shoulder at the screen; the smell of cigarette smoke and the faintest trace of supermarket body spray engulfed her. She turned to look at his reaction, though his face remained stern.

"What do you want to do?" he said. "Maybe we should give that copper a ring, tell him-"

"Tell him what?"

"Everything. We've got nothing to hide. You never know, there could be some kind of clue in all this. It could help them find out where dad is."

"They'll fucking commit me."

"They won't because you're not making it up. That's obvious now. The watcher and the girl, yeah, no one else can vouch for that, but that fucking room, the website disappearing; that's concrete evidence. What if it's got something to do with dad going missing? This could be-"

"It could be nothing," Maddie said, clasping her hands behind her head. She allowed her restless feet to walk her into the living room, weaving in and out of the battered furniture like it was a corduroy obstacle course.

"Hang on," Ben said. "Why is it *me* trying to convince *you* that something's up now?"

"Because I've already been doing this for days," Maddie hissed.

"The police are useless, and we can't find Tony until we figure out what all this means. Obviously, the room is weird but, it's not following me like the watcher or leaving weird stones for me like that creepy looking girl. It's a room, that's it. Plus, it's not like there's blood up there or anything. There's nothing incriminating. It's just weird. And the website could just be down for maintenance or it's expired or whatever. I'm starting to hear that fucking Clark's voice talking me out of stuff before I even think it. No, we need to speak to fucking Wil... first thing tomorrow, see what he really know about all this. He admitted to us that he's been up there before, maybe he knows what's up there now. Maybe it's his."

"Where do we find him?"

"He said he lived down the hill. Can't be too hard to find around here, can it? If we ask around?"

"Ok," Ben said. "Do you want me to go and get Helen or do you-"

"No," she said.

"Right... Why?"

Maddie breathed deeply and balled the sleeves of her hoody in her fists, then took a considered step towards him. She felt as if she was moving to the edge of bridge for a bungee jump, the carpet unsteady beneath her feet.

"Can you stay here tonight?" she said.

Ben looked around as if he hoped someone would answer for him.

"Look, Maddie, I'm not sure that's-"

"Please," she said, taking another step closer. "Honestly this is nothing to do with me and you. I think about what happened all the time and I feel awful, I promise you it's not that... I just can't stay here on my own."

"Well, that's why I said about Helen."

"She'll be fine over there with them," Maddie said. "She's off her head anyway. What use is she going to be if that fucking creep decides he's gonna let himself in here? First night it was the end of the drive, night after he was in the garden... what's next? It's obviously me he wants to fuck with, especially if he's got anything to do with whatever's up there."

She swept her hand in the general direction of the workshop and its sinister garret.

"In fact," she said, turning to stride over to the sofa. "Can you help me with this?"

She took hold of one arm and waited for Ben to come over and do the same. With a great deal of effort, they fought the hulking sofa over the shag carpet until it was tight against the door.

"That's a start," she said, tucking a stray hair behind her ear.

"We can put that behind the front door as well."

Ben gave her another nervous look, then sighed and walked over into the kitchen. It was like he was afraid of her.

"Look, why don't you come with me and we'll all stay there, if you're worried?"

"No," she said. "No, I don't want them to see me like this. They'll think I'm being paranoid. Please, Ben, will you just do this one thing for me?"

He cricked his neck, then scratched nervously at his beard. "Ok," he said. "If it'll make you feel better, we'll wait it out here. But we have to tell them tomorrow. This could be dangerous for all of us."

"Ok," Maddie said as she breathed out a sigh of relief. "Ok. Tomorrow. And you'll back me up, right? When they all think I'm mental."

The smile that appeared on Ben's face was a kind one. "I will."

After securing the front door and turning out the lights, they went upstairs to Maddie and Helen's bedroom, Ben trailing behind like a man being led to the gallows. She helped him remove the throw pillows from the armchair and set them up to act as a footrest for him while he watched the door. It was called being 'on stag' in the Army, he told her, and usually meant sitting on top of a compound and trying not to get shot or fall asleep. Keeping watch through the night so the rest of the platoon could rest safely below. Despite the horrors of the outside world, Maddie caught herself smiling as she hunkered down into her duvet, reassured to have him within arm's reach. There was no one on earth she'd rather have watching over her.

17 - Boxing Day 2017

It was the first time that all three of Tony's children had been together over Christmas time since he and Kelly separated. Ella was still living with Maddie and Tony back then, in her final year of college, while Luke had been in his city centre studio since the summer, so was happy to return to the lap of luxury that was their granite and glass castle in Wilmslow. Ben traditionally spent the Christmas Day itself with his mother – a show of solidarity – though Ella had managed to persuade him to give his dad a chance and make the drive up from her place in Kent for Boxing Day.

As a result of such an unprecedented occasion, no expense had been spared. Maddie ordered in a lavish roast beef dinner with all the trimmings, courtesy of the same company that had catered their wedding, and they had enough alcohol on hand to put a blue whale to sleep.

Tony had thrown a pile of logs onto his gigantic fireplace, but the thing had burned so hot that they'd been forced to eat at the second, smaller dining table in the next room; a long slab of opaque glass that sounded as if it was going to crack with every clink of cutlery.

"I just want them fixed, that's all," Ella said, tapping her front teeth with the edge of her knife. "I get stuff stuck in the gaps all the time... I've always hated them. It's not like I'm asking you for fake tits or something."

"Fucking hell, pack it in El," said Luke, choking on his food. He laid his cutlery down to give his chest a few thumps.

"Sorry, mate, but it's true," Ella said, shooting him an unsympathetic sneer. "Someone I know on Twitter has just been to Turkey to get his teeth done and they look amazing."

"Turkey?" said Tony. "I'm not so sure I like the sound of that."

"You'll end up with some bloke doing it in his mum's kitchen over there," said Luke, still blushing from his choking fit. "God knows what you'll end up with."

"It's not like that, you dickhead..."

"Ella."

"...Anyway, it doesn't have to be there. That was just one person I saw. You can get veneers done in town, it's not even that much."

"What's your mum said?" Tony again, a pile of mashed potato

193

still poised in front of his lips.

"I've not told her."

Ella looked down at her food, pushing a few slivers of creamed leeks from one side of the plate to the other as carefully as an artist putting their first stroke onto a blank canvas.

"Come on, Tony," said Maddie, taking her wine glass. "Girls are getting all sorts done nowadays, lips and nose and-"

"And their arses," said Luke.

Laughter erupted, Luke smirking as he enjoyed the sound. Ella cuffed him on the shoulder with an open hand.

"What? You can talk about tits, but I can't talk about arses? They do anyway... I bet half of your social media mates have got arses the size of beach balls."

"You're such a dick."

"Ella."

"What the fuck? He's swearing too!"

"Well... yeah, he's got a point though," said Maddie, smiling as she sipped her pinot noir. "And I don't think – if it makes you happier, you know – I don't think getting your teeth done is the same thing." She glanced over to the head of the table, where Ben sat listening in silence. "Not that it's anything to do with me," she added.

"Bloody hell," Tony said with a sigh. "Just let me have a think about it, yeah?"

Ella pushed the leeks onto her fork, smiling at her father as she ate them. Silence began to settle as everyone tucked back in, until Ella continued, her voice almost a whisper.

"Have you had yours done, Maddie?" she said without looking up from her food.

Maddie looked at Tony, then back towards Ella.

"My teeth? No, nothing. Just lucky, I suppose. I do try and take care of them."

Tony snorted, causing Maddie to abort the sip of wine she was about to take.

"Something funny?"

"Come on, Maddie," he said. "You've not had them done but you put all sorts of shit on them. Bet it costs a fortune."

He leant forward, so as to address the whole table. "I walked it once when she had this UV gumshield thing on... I thought I'd gone back in time to Hacienda and she was in there chewing on a glowstick!"

Maddie hid her eyes behind her hands as she tried to laugh

along with everyone else, but flush in her cheeks only burned hotter the longer she endured it. She shuffled her chair out from under the table and stood to leave. Tony tried to take her hand.

"Ah come on, Maddie, I'm sorry," he said. "I shouldn't have taken the... come on."

"Fuck off," she said under her breath.

As calmly as she could, she walked out of the dining room and into the cavernous foyer. She stood there for a few seconds until a whimper juddered past the hand she'd clamped over her mouth. The echo was startling and propelled her out of the front door to be alone with her shame.

The rain was lashing down once again, thundering off the roofs and the row of cars on the driveway. The sky had all but turned to black. Maddie skipped over the gravel, around the side of the house, and sheltered under the granite eaves. She pressed her back against the glass, the glow of the roaring fire at her back, and clenched her teeth.

"Fucking prick," she hissed.

She stared out at nothing for a while, hypnotised by the constant downpour and white noise, until the sound of the front door opening jolted her back into awareness. She looked at the corner and waited for Tony to appear, his head bowed like a penitent shuffling into a confessional.

A lighter clicked a few times, then a plume of blue smoke drifted past.

"Maddie?" came Ben's voice from around the corner.

"I'm round here," she said, having to raise her voice to cut through the crashing of the rain. She pulled the sleeve of her dress into her palm and used it to dab at her running mascara.

Ben kept his back to the wall as he made his way around to her refuge, though the rain was bouncing up off the ground so hard that it soaked the legs of his jeans regardless. He took another drag of his cigarette, the end glowing like a signal flare inside his cupped hand, and blew the smoke away from her, out into the chaotic night.

"Sorry, I didn't want to mither you," he said. "Just wanted to see if you were ok?"

"I'm fine," Maddie sniffed. She suddenly became conscious of the way she looked. She tucked her sodden hair, remarkably free of its customary ponytail, behind her ears, smoothed her dress against her hips.

"I should know by now, shouldn't I?" she said. "He probably didn't mean anything by it, I just... He's been away so much recently that I forget what he's like."

"It's not your fault. He needs to remember that he doesn't always have to be 'on'... taking the piss all the time like he's at one of his networking parties. Luke's the same. I don't know

197

how you ever did it."

He continued to smoke while Maddie processed this, watching the lines of his face appear in orange each time he brought the cigarette to his lips.

"What do you mean? The parties?"

"Yeah, all the bullshit. Just fake people patting each other on the back and making a load of empty promises. I can't imagine you in the middle of all that."

"I cried a fair bit back then too," she said, prompting a polite laugh to bubble up between them. "I never really liked it though, you're right. I don't think you would either. But then again, if I never worked for the mag, I wouldn't have ended up meeting your dad, or you and Ella and Luke so... you know, every cloud."

He didn't reply, continuing to stare out onto the garden as spears of rain pierced the surface of the reflecting pool. The cherry tree was doing its best to weather the onslaught, though it was little more than white limbs struggling in the gloom.

"Did you never fancy it?" Maddie said. "Working with your dad?"

He shook his head. "Nah, no chance. I always held it against him a bit, I think. Like he was always away, and obviously I felt sorry for my mum and those two when they were younger, but it wasn't just that... It was the fact he was away all the time and, for what? To make fake fancy houses for rich pricks... You know what I mean? Just all seemed pointless. That's what it is; fake. It's not real."

"Is that why you joined the Army? That's definitely real."

"Maybe," he said. "I dunno. It's not like the Army is real life either, to be fair. Think I just wanted to do something worthwhile. My uncle Tim – my mum's brother – he was an officer in the Army and I always thought he was a good bloke, you know."

"Your dad's really proud of you," Maddie said, wiping away another inky tear with her thumb. "Everyone is."

He smiled briefly, then looked back out at the garden and took another drag.

"Thanks... for coming out here I mean," Maddie said.

"It's fine, just wanted to make sure you were ok."

She opened her arms, though it took him a moment to notice.

"Oh, sorry," he said. He dropped the end of his cigarette onto the gravel and accepted the hug, hunching over to allow Maddie to reach his neck.

His shoulders felt tense, awkward, but she was comfortable in his arms. She squeezed him; the ends of her sleeves gripped tightly in her fists. He smelled of the smoke, beer, and some kind of cheap aftershave she didn't recognise. It wasn't unpleasant, just unfamiliar. Like an old acquaintance half-recognised across a busy street.

"You're so sweet," she said as she finally released him. Her cheek brushed his as she went to step back, then she stopped and spoke again, this time more of a whisper. "You're so sweet."

The last word fell away as their lips met. She couldn't be sure if it was her that went in first, or him, but neither of them resisted. She felt heat, the drive to rake her fingernails through his hair, but the sound of the front door clunking open was like ice water down the back of her dress.

"Maddie?"

It was Tony, letting his voice brave the rain while he kept himself dry.

"Ben?"

"Round here dad," Ben's eyes never left Maddie's as he spoke, she felt as if she was drowning in them. "Just having a smoke."

He stepped backwards, away from her.

"Is Maddie with you?"

"I'm coming now, Tony."

"You ok?"

"I'm fine... fine. I'll be there in a sec."

After a few more thudding heartbeats, Maddie mouthed 'I'm sorry' to Ben, and eased past him to return to her husband.

18 - Now

Maddie sat up in bed with her heart racing, the room dark but for a sliver of moonlight from between the curtains.

"Maddie?" It was Ben's voice, hoarse and hushed.

"What's happening? Where are you?"

"Over here... quiet."

She squinted across the room to see him stood tight against the door, easing it open with a yawning creak.

"What are you doing?"

He shushed her and pushed the door a little further. His rudeness was out of character and unsettling, almost as if he was speaking without thinking. She wasn't seeing Ben the man now, but Ben the soldier, just like she had at the crash site and in the sinister garret.

She slipped out of bed and crept across the carpet towards him but was stopped dead by a volley of thuds against the cottage's front door.

"Shit," she gasped. "It's him, it's the fu-"

"Maddie stay in bed," he said, holding his hand out in an attempt to push her back. The knocking on the door continued.

Her chest was tight, her pulse throbbing in her throat. She could practically hear the blood as it rushed through her ears.

"Fuck it."

Ben launched himself into the corridor and thundered down the stairs.

"Ben no! What are you doing?"

Without a second thought she scampered after him, the cold air in the hall biting at her bare legs. By the time she reached the bottom of the stairs, he was leaning against the door, the sofa they'd used to barricade it shoved to one side. He leant over and took the thickest of the varnished walking sticks out of the stand and rested it on his shoulder like it was a baseball bat. His other hand went for the keys dangling underneath the door handle and gripped them. Another four thumps on the door.

Ben turned the keys and snatched open the door and leapt sideways to wind up a haymaker swing. Maddie screamed.

"Jesus," said a man's voice as he leapt back onto the gravel. "What the fuck? What's the matter with you?"

"Fucking hell," said Ben, exasperated. He doubled over and leant on the walking stick like a bent-backed old hermit, revealing Luke's confused expression framed in the doorway.

"What's going on?" Luke said. "You nearly took my fucking head off mate, what the fuck?"

"Sorry," Ben said as he straightened up. He slid the stick back into the stand and turned to Maddie, who was sat on the bottom stair.

"Are you alright?"

She nodded; her hands still clasped over her mouth. She pushed herself to her feet as Ben turned back to his brother.

"What are you doing here? It's three in the morning..."

"Mate, you're not gonna believe it. Maddie... Maddie come here."

"What's the matter what is it? Is it Helen?"

Luke mood had shifted from shock to excitement. He looked like a child on Christmas morning, his eyes wide as dinner plates in the moonlight.

"It's dad," he said with a beaming smile. "He's back."

. . .

Maddie's stomach lurched, cold sweat beading on her upper lip.

"What are you talking about? Back where?" she said.

"Mate are you sleepwalking or something?"

"No, for fuck's sake! Maddie, look at me," Luke said, stepping inside. "Look at me. Dad is back. He's sat in our cottage right now. He's with Ella... he's fine. Why would I wind you up about this?"

"Tony... Tony is in there, now? In that cottage? And he's ok?" Maddie held a trembling finger towards the illuminated windows across the courtyard.

Luke nodded slowly, the clownish grin still on his face. "Yeah. That's what I'm saying! Come and see for yourself. Come on."

The walk across the courtyard felt like being pulled along by travelator. Maddie's entire body was numb, from her lips to her toes, the cold night air almost inconsequential to her, despite being dressed in nothing more than shorts, socks, and a one of Tony's old football shirts. The hoots of owls and clatter of crow's wings that had once sent her and Helen backing towards the car were now little more than background noise. The soundtrack to a moment she had begun to think would never arrive.

Barring some kind of sick, and uncharacteristically cruel, joke from Luke; this was happening. Tony was alive and well and sat in the same house that she was, somehow, still moving towards. It could be a dream, she thought.

In the past, whenever she'd realised that she was dreaming, she'd been able to change things. If the mood struck her, she could run and jump and soar off over the trees. If she was stuck inside the constricting walls of an exam hall, she could blow them down to reveal Elysian fields and wander out, her hands skimming over the waves of long grass. If it was a particularly unpleasant dream, she could even just make the decision to open her eyes, her real eyes, and wake up.

If this walk to see her husband really was all in her head, the last thing she wanted to do was risk anything changing before she saw him. She had to concentrate, to preserve it, just as it was, if only for the few minutes that followed. That way, even if it was a dream, she'd be able to set eyes on him one more time. To smell him, hear his voice, feel his hand at the small of her back.

They made it to the threshold of the New Cottage and Luke stood aside to show her in like the doorman at an expensive hotel. She seemed to pass him in slow-motion and, as their eyes met, he became just that; bowing too low and waving her through, top hat and brass-buttoned overcoat and pearly white smile.

It was just a hallucination, she thought. She was exhausted, after all, and in a state of shock. This was still as real as

206

anything else, it had to be. No dream she could concoct would be this cruel to her waking self, offering Tony only to take him away again.

She stepped into the blinding light of the kitchen and saw Ella sat on his knee, her bare arms wrapped around his neck.

His thick grey walking socks were sodden, as were his muddied trousers and rain jacket, the latter unzipped to reveal the fleece underneath streaked with blood. He looked so tired, his hair straggly and wet, drooping in front of droopier eyelids. He looked to have taken a serious blow to the front of his head as well, some dried blood still caked in his wrinkles. Even with all of it, he was able to smile as they locked eyes over his daughter's shoulder.

The floor stopped moving beneath Maddie's feet and she stood in the kitchen and stared on.

"Oh my God," she said, trembling fingers pressing her mouth closed as if she believed in blasphemy.

Ella, still clinging onto Tony, turned around to face her; revealing the grinning countenance of an innocent.

Maddie surged forwards and threw her arms around them both, pressing her flushed cheek into Tony's stubble hard enough to bump his head into Ella's. She didn't react to it and neither did he, all three of them seemingly content to huddle together.

"You've hurt your head?" Maddie said as she leant back to try and assess the wound on his forehead. He shook his head and pulled her back in.

"It's nothing. Don't worry."

"Oh my God, I missed you so much. It's been so hard, it's been-"

"I missed you too."

Tony smelled as damp and as dirty as he looked, like the towel in their garage that was reserved for when Tank had decided to jump in the canal or go nosing around in cow shit. He smelled like tree bark, moss, and mulch.

They separated finally, Maddie and Ella's faces both tear-streaked and ruddy, while Tony stared blankly ahead at his eldest son, a slight grin tightening the skin against his cheekbones.

"Everyone is here," he said, the words little more than hollow breaths.

"Tony, where the hell have you been? Are you sure you're ok, you don't need to go to hospital?" Maddie said, turning over his hands to look for open wounds. "You could have internal injuries or something, from the crash. Can you remember the crash? Do you remember what happened?"

Tony looked up at her, that weak smile still present, and put his arm around her shoulder.

"You are so beautiful," he said.

"Tony, I'm serious," she said, taking hold of his arm. "Where have you been? Have you been outside all this time? You're so cold, how are you not shivering? You could have pneumonia or hypothermia."

Tony swallowed and looked to Ella, who was still perched on his lap. "Can I have a drink please, love?"

"Oh shit, course," she said, hopping off and scooting over to the sink. She took a glass off the draining board and switched on the tap and passed her finger through the stream a few times as it cooled.

"No," Tony said. "Not water... can I have some milk?"

"Milk?" Ella said. "Like cow's milk?"

He nodded. "Please."

"Ok," she said, raising an eyebrow at Maddie.

She shut off the tap and scooted over to the fridge and filled the glass. It seemed as if all of her maternal authority had disappeared the second Tony had returned. She was simply a child now, grateful to be waiting on her dad.

"Tony?" Maddie said, shaking his arm again. "What happened?"

He looked at her for a moment, his grey eyes rheumy under the glare of the spotlights overhead, as if they'd never known a light so bright.

"It's hard to tell," he said. "I don't remember a crash, or even being in a car."

"What about being with Al? Do you remember the daytime?" Maddie said.

He shook his head. "There are just these... images really. Snapshots."

"Like what?" came Ben's voice from behind them. He was still scowling, arms folded, like the bad cop at the back of the interrogation room.

Tony shrugged. "Wandering around the forest on my own. I suppose I didn't know where I was going. I was bleeding and hurt. When I couldn't walk anymore I curled up at the foot of this tree, this huge tree... and I rested my head on the roots, like it was like a bed made of these roots, almost, and the branches were so high and the sky was getting so dark. I was so tired, so I just... I was there for a while, I think, and then I just seemed to wake up. I got up and I started walking and eventually I found my way out. Out onto the road."

Everyone in the room, even a dishevelled-looking Helen at the end of the dining table, shuffled around uncomfortably as Tony stuttered through his meandering monologue, but the stolen looks shared between Maddie and Ben spoke of a greater understanding. A secret acceptance.

Had they not experienced the forest for themselves the day before, they might have thought that Tony was concussed or in shock, like the rest of the room most likely did.

But they knew better. They'd seen first-hand how time appeared to evaporate within that forest, five minutes swelling to over five hours for them. If Tony really had stumbled in there, delirious, and got lost for what seemed to him like the best part of a day, then surely that could have actually been more like four days on the outside. It was all starting to make sense.

Maddie stood and looked at Tony and brushed his hair back from his forehead with her scarred thumb; a reminder of the wound she'd sustained the last time she'd seen him. Back then, Tony going away for a few days was her biggest problem. Only four days had passed, and it already seemed as trivial as a squabble over pulled pigtails in the playground.

"I'm sorry, I just can't remember much else, it's so strange," he said. He began to sob. A strange, forlorn sound that Maddie hadn't heard since the morning Tony heard that his brother, Luca, had died.

"Oh Tony. Please. Come on, don't apologise," she said, hugging him again. "It's not your fault. I totally understand, I promise you. I understand. You're back now, that's all that matters."

Heavy footsteps thudded across the tiles towards them, and she heard Ben's voice and felt him pat his father on the shoulder.

"It's alright dad, you're back now."

Tony sniffed away the tears and smiled again, stroked Maddie's cheek.

"You're so beautiful, Maddie."

19

Maddie and her stepchildren sat alone in the kitchen, whispering like conspirators, careful to ensure that the volume of their discussion stayed lower than the sound of Tony showering upstairs. Helen had gone over to the Old Cottage, ostensibly to do the same, though Maddie had seen too many of her shame-filled hangovers to believe that cleanliness was the only reason she wanted to escape.

"Do you think he needs to go to the hospital?" Ella said, her eyes constantly flicking towards the bottom of the stairs, which were bathed in glow of the landing light.

"He says he's fine," said Luke.

"I heard him," said Ella. "But I heard all that other stuff he said as well. He's like... he seems like he's lost the plot."

"It can happen," Ben said. "I've seen it happen to lads when they've been injured before. The confusion, the shock. It's exactly what you'd expect."

He looked over at Maddie. While she sensed he was telling the truth, she knew that's not what he actually thought. She nodded towards the front door in an attempt to pull him out for a private conversation, but he shook his head.

"Do we need to tell the police?" said Luke. "I reckon they'll-"

"We can't," said Maddie. "Not yet. We need to find out what happened, whether your dad could get in trouble. Leaving the scene is a crime isn't it?"

Ben nodded.

"I think so yeah. The last thing he needs is them getting involved now and they haven't been much help so far. We'll call them when he's ready, but I don't see why there's any rush as long as he's ok."

Without explanation, Ella stood and began drifting towards the hall.

"El, where are you-"

"Dad? Are you alright?" she said, her voice raised over the thundering of the shower.

Although Ella was all but blocking the doorway, Maddie was certain she saw the landing light flicker as if someone had rushed past it, like a blackbird swooping in front of the sun. Ella looked back towards her in apparent confusion, and they all listened as the bathroom door quietly closed.

. . .

Dusk was already bleeding through the skylights when they all sat down together for an early breakfast, though the burning spotlights stayed on alongside them. Helen was back from the Old Cottage, her still-wet hair scraped back from her face, though she seemed to be keeping her distance from Maddie, preferring instead to sit next to Ben at the quiet end of the dinner table.

Ella brought over a tower of toast, a large pan of baked beans, two trays of hash browns, and a half-empty tub of Vitalite. Luke had been forced to cook the animal products – bacon and eggs – himself, but it was a sacrifice that everyone in the room, bar Ella, was grateful for. He brought over the still-sizzling pan like a hunter-gatherer returning to camp with a fresh kill.

Tony shovelled the food into his mouth like a man who'd had been lost in a forest for four days, his head craned over the plate so as not to offer a morsel to the kitchen floor. To Maddie, he looked barely human in his gluttony, grunting like a feral animal that had smelled opportunity and snuck in through an open kitchen window. The rest of them shared wide-eyed glances as they thought about beginning their own meals, knives and forks poised in the air as if they'd all forgotten how to use them.

Despite this, Maddie began to feel more and more comfortable as the meal went on. She felt like she was chalking up a tally as the minutes passed, each mark counting towards the return to some kind of normality. She even started to believe that it wasn't a dream. That the seemingly impossible had actually happened. Cryptic speeches and questionable table manners aside, her husband was alive and well, and back safely with his family.

Strangely, the smell that had clung to Tony was undeterred by the shower and change of clothes. Even from where Maddie sat next to him at the dinner table, a plate full of steaming food in front of her, the odour of bark and mud and rotten leaves was impossible to ignore.

"Do you want to come over to the other cottage after we've eaten?" she said. "It's the one you and Al were supposed to stay at. It's not ideal, but it's quiet. You can have a lie down, just try... you know, see if you can get your head around everything?"

He looked up, tomato sauce glistening in the corners of his mouth, and considered it for a second while he chewed. He began to nod gently.

"Yeah," he said. "Yeah, ok. Are you going to come with me?"

Maddie let out a nervous laugh. He sounded like a toddler frightened of going to the dentist.

"Course, yeah," she said. "Course I will."

"What are you wanting to do El?" Luke said, his mouth full of bacon. "Do you want to hang around or..."

"Can we not all just go back now? Back to yours?" Ella said to Maddie.

"I'm not sure, really. We might still have to take your dad to speak to the police, depending on what happens... no rush though," she said, laying her hand on Tony's back.

Maddie sensed that Helen was staring at her, though her eyes darted back to the table as Maddie turned to face her. Helen started to play with her food with her fork, the knife lying unused beside the plate.

"Are you alright?" Maddie said.

"Me?"

"Yeah, you look a bit... I dunno." Maddie was reluctant to put her on the spot in front of everyone, but the tension was plain to see.

"I'm fine," Helen said, trying to smile. "Well, better than fine. I just can't believe it, it's so... I'm just really happy for you all. Happy it's all worked out."

"Shall we have a toast?" said Luke, picking up his cup of coffee and offering it forwards. The rest of the table followed suit, though it took a second for Tony to drag himself away from his food. He picked up his drink and completed the circle in the centre of the table. "To all of us for getting through this together. To family. Cheers."

Steaming cups and glasses of orange and glasses of water all clinked together and they drank in silence, the larks outside already tuning up for their dawn chorus.

. . .

Maddie and Tony walked arm-in-arm across the courtyard towards the Old Cottage, Helen trailing behind like a recalci-trant toddler. The click and amber glow from the MINI startled Maddie, and she turned to see her friend throwing her jacket on the back seat.

"You going now?" Maddie said. "It's not even 6am?"

"Yeah, it's fine. Woken up properly after all that coffee," she said, smiling weakly. "Should be back home before the traffic hits."

Maddie unlatched herself from Tony and left him on the doorstep.

"Are you sure you don't want to stay, even just for the day?" she said.

"Honestly, no. It's best if I get out of your way."

"You sure? If this is about last night then-"

"It's not that, I promise."

They stared into each other's eyes for a few seconds, then

218

Maddie pulled Helen in and embraced her. The smell of her perfume combined with the white orchid in her conditioner was sweet relief from Tony's ever-present musk.

"I love you so much," she said, her eyes still screwed tight.

"You too," Helen said. "I'm so sorry you had to go through all this."

"Don't say that, please. God knows where I'd be now without you. You've been so amazing."

They parted, then Helen crunched over to the car and opened the driver's door. Just as she was about to get in, she jerked to a halt at the sound of Tony's voice.

"Thank you, Helen," he said. "For looking after Maddie and for... well, everything. You're a good friend. We won't forget it."

Helen forced a nervous smile, though Maddie couldn't tell if it was out of humility or the general awkwardness of the situation. She nodded, stooped inside the car, then turned back for one final look.

"Maddie?" she said, her hand resting on the door handle.

Maddie said nothing, arching her eyebrows in expectation.

"Let me know when you're back and I'll come and see you, ok?"

"Definitely," Maddie said with a smile. "Drive safe. Let me know when you get back alright."

As Maddie walked back towards the cottage, her eyes locked on Tony's smiling face, her gaze drifted above his head to the bare wooden panel where the horseshoe used to be.

"Are you ok?" Tony said. He followed her eyes to the panel, then looked back at her in confusion. "What is it?"

"It's nothing," she said, attempting to smile. "Come on, let's get inside."

20

Tony stood and stared out of the bedroom window into the back garden, apparently oblivious to Maddie's huffs and puffs as she made the bed. Each time she finished tucking in a corner of the quilt or replacing a throw pillow, she glanced up to check on him, half-expecting him to have vanished again. From start to finish, he never moved so much as an inch.

When she was happy that the room was back in some kind of order, she perched on the edge of the bed and looked at him silhouetted against the powder pale morning light.

"Can you really not remember anything?"

He turned to face her, leant back against the window seat with his arms folded. She still couldn't see anything of his face, only shadow.

"I told you everything I could, Maddie. I'm just as confused as you are. I can't even remember this crash everyone's talking about."

"Well you were in one... at least I think you were. The police found Al in the wreckage of your car, right next to the woods. We went there yesterday – me and Ben – we even went inside the forest..."

She stopped short of admitting that they'd been subject to the same disorientating time-dilation as him, albeit on a smaller scale. Five minutes into five hours. He was confused enough as it was, she thought.

"And?"

"Well, it was... just like everything else here. Cold and dark and... fucking creepy."

Tony stifled a laugh. "But you didn't see anything? Any sign of..."

Maddie shook her head, her ponytail swishing from side to side, brushing her shoulders. It was the best she could do. A movement wasn't a lie. It couldn't be. A lie had to be a sentence, or at least a word.

"Do you really think that's where I've been? All this time?" Tony said.

"It makes sense to me. If you've hit your head or something... that could be why you're forgetting, why you're confused. That's why you need to go to hospital, so they can-"

"I don't need to go to hospital," he said. "I'm absolutely fine...

fit as a butcher's dog."

"Ok... well what do you want to do then?"

"We should stay here," he said, moving to come and sit next to her on the bed. It was a relief for Maddie to finally see his face, the face she'd been dreaming about, even if it was just one side of it for now.

"We've both been through a lot," he said with a weary sigh. "The best thing will be for us to just stay here, relax. Try and recover. The kids can go back to what they were doing, and we can concentrate on each other. So, I can make it up to you."

"Ah, so you remember *that*, do you? I did wonder..."

He smiled and turned to face her, took hold of her hands. His touch was cold and clammy.

"I could have never imagined that someone as perfect as you would want to marry me, have children with me. You're beautiful, Maddie, inside and out. I know you've felt neglected, that you've been so stressed because of... Well, you should never be that upset, especially not because of the person you love. It's not fair. I promise you, I will never do that to you again. When I was out there, under those trees, it felt like forever. When I thought I'd never get to see your face, to touch you-"

"Tony, please," she said, pulling her hand away and hiding it in the sleeve of her jumper. "You don't have to say all this... I'm

223

just glad that you're-"

"I'm not just saying it," he said. "I've not stopped thinking about you. It just seems like this is a second chance, for me... For us. When I walked out of that kitchen the other day it was one of the biggest mistakes I've ever made. And I've got plenty to choose from."

A burst of laughter shook a few tears from Maddie's eyelashes.

Tony took hold of her wrist. "I want to give you everything that I should have given you before. Everything you deserve."

Tony leant in, aiming for her lips, but Maddie jerked away, placing her hand gently on his chest.

"What's wrong?" he said.

"I'm sorry... I don't want to upset you or anything... I don't quite feel right. I think I'm just, I dunno, exhausted. You must be too."

She slid her hand up to his neck, making the initial touch of deterrence into one of affection.

"We should get some rest. Then we can talk later, I promise. I'm sorry... I'm so happy that you're back, I don't want you to think-"

She half-stood and kissed his forehead, then plopped back onto the bed.

"I don't want you to think I'm not happy, ok? I am. I promise I am."

. . .

Maddie was awoken by the shrill cry of the landline, the sound peeling around the silent cottage as loud as church bells.

Maddie shrugged Tony's lumpen arm off of her waist and skipped out of the room and downstairs, snatched the plastic handset from its receiver.

"Hello?"

"Morning Mrs Degrassi. Inspector Clark."

She froze, the phone suddenly as heavy as a house brick in her faltering grip. She was so thirsty; all she could think of was trying to stretch the phone over to the kitchen and putting her mouth directly underneath the tap and lapping at it like a hamster at its water bottle. She licked her lips and attempted to speak, though she only managed half a syllable before Clark interrupted.

"Apologies for the wake-up call," he said.

The carriage clock on the mantlepiece told her it was almost nine in the morning.

"Don't worry, it's nothing serious," he said. "But I've got some news for you."

"News?"

Tony reached the bottom of the stairs and hobbled over to lean on the chair arm in front of her. He looked on with his brow furrowed and his mouth partly agape, doing his best to decipher the crackles and pops of Clark's voice.

"Yes, finally. We've been at Nevill Hall Hospital all night, my colleague and I," he said. "Your friend Mr Rowlands... well, they've woken him up."

"Al? Is he ok?"

"More than ok, as it happens," he said. "He was practically whistling when we arrived. A few bumps and a couple of breaks but, other than that... He'll be out of there in no time."

Maddie tried her best to feel some kind of relief, or to sound that way at least, but all she could do was look at Tony and imagine what Clark would say if he knew. Was what they were doing illegal? Was Tony technically a fugitive?

"Has he said anything about the crash? Or about Tony?" she said.

"Unfortunately, not Tony, no... but he says the reason the vehicle came off the road was because a young girl was stood right in the middle of the road."

Maddie shuddered. She would have expected that Clark's monotone voice could make anything sound unremarkable, but even the mention of the little girl was enough to bring that pallid face flashing into her brain. Cold, emaciated limbs hanging like threads from the sleeves of her dress.

Clark paused, sighed heavily down the phone.

"Look, Mrs Degrassi, I really shouldn't be telling you this but I'm starting to get a bit... concerned."

"What, erm," she flashed Tony a nervous smile, a transparent attempt to appear unfazed. "What do you mean?"

"Well, we weren't obliged to say it at the time, but when we found Mr Rowlands in the vehicle – your husband's vehicle – he was belted in as the driver, not the passenger. We've never been a hundred percent sure of whether your husband was even in there at the time of the crash. Now all this about memory loss and this little girl all the way up there... all seems a bit far-fetched, doesn't it."

"Why are you telling me this?"

"Because, Mrs Degrassi," he said, lowering his voice. "There's press all over the place now, all trying to get their grubby hands on something. Something to do with the Facebook page your stepdaughter started, Ella is it? Anyway, I just wanted to be the one to let you know before you see anything that... I just don't want you to be under any illusions. I don't want you to have... false hope."

"You think that..." she stuttered, trying her best to keep

her responses as unreadable as possible. "Sorry, I don't understand?"

"What I mean is that – given the searches we've made, the interviews we've conducted – we're starting to run out of viable explanations as to where your husband could have gone after the crash without us knowing. It stands to reason that he was never in there to begin with. Obviously, Mr Rowlands will be left to recuperate, but once he's fit to be interviewed properly…"

"So, he's a suspect? You think he knows something?"

"I wouldn't like to say anything for certain, at this point, particularly to you. I just wanted you to know that we were still exploring every possible scenario… and if Mr Rowlands does know something, you can rest assured that we will too, soon enough."

21

After hanging up the call, Maddie drifted over to the sofa. She sat down and tucked her feet up underneath her legs and leant against the arm rest and stared vacantly at the log burner, its open door like the gaping mouth of some great, cast iron toad.

"What is it?" Tony said, his fingers slithering over her shoulders.

"I think... that they think you're dead," she said. "Sounds like they think it's something to do with Al."

"Dead? Where have they got that from?"

She parroted Clark's words in reply; her eyes still unblinking as she peered into the abyssal bowels of the burner. It groaned and creaked as the wind picked up outside, loose screws rattling in the hinges.

"You're going to have to call the police," she said. "You need to explain everything. Even if you are in trouble, it's not going to be murder is it. Al could be in serious-"

"I will," he said. He leant over and kissed the crown of her head and started kneading her shoulders. A waft of that stale outdoor smell came with him. "I'll call them. Tomorrow. I promise. Let's just have a day to ourselves first, before all the madness starts again."

"Tony, they're talking about questioning him, arresting him maybe... One call from you and it's all cleared up. I don't-"

Tony let go of her shoulders and came around to sit on the sofa.

"Look, if he's as banged up as they say he is, he won't be in handcuffs any time soon, will he? It'll all be fine, I promise. Come on... why don't we go back to bed for a bit?"

Maddie ignored him, still staring straight ahead.

"Maddie, what's the matter? You know I'm not actually dead, right?"

"I know you're not," she said, a slight snap to her words. "I think I assumed that you'd have some kind of explanation, you know what I mean? Like all of these weird things that have been happening... I just thought, when you came back, they'd go away. But they aren't going away. It's getting even weirder."

"There's nothing weird about any of it," Tony said, adding a patronising snort.

She thought again of telling him about the woods. About the little girl and the stone and the watcher, the strange garret only a few feet away from where they sat. Maybe one of those would qualify as 'weird' for him.

"It's all just a big misunderstanding," he said. "I'm feeling fine. We're all gonna be fine. I'll get everything cleared up tomorrow and then we can all get on with our lives. We can start making plans–"

He reached over to rest his hand on her leg.

"Tony, will you stop it? This is serious. You haven't got a clue."

She stood up and squeezed in between the sofa arm and the wall to put on her trainers at the front door. Tony simply looked on in confusion, like a child who'd just had their ice cream cone taken away after two licks.

"Where are you going?" he said.

"I'm going to get Ben. You obviously think I'm overreacting, so you can hear it from him. Come on. We're gonna go and get him, and he'll tell you. Then I'm gonna show you what's in there."

She pointed to the door in the corner.

"I don't care if the kids know about it all now," she opened the door and showed him through. "Come on."

Eventually Tony stood and came over to her, then picked up his muddied walking boots shoved the loose laces inside and slid them on.

As soon as Maddie was satisfied that he was willing to comply, she marched outside and headed for the New Cottage. Its front door was already open, and Luke was loading luggage and shopping bags into the boot of his car.

"What's going on?" Maddie said, her voice cannoning around the courtyard.

Luke looked around and smiled at her, then slammed the boot shut and walked over.

"We're gonna get off," he said, thumb-pointing at his car. "Me and El, anyway. Ben said he'd stay and see if you needed a lift... I've only got two seats in there."

"What are you going for? I don't-"

"Alright dad," Luke said, looking past Maddie. "How you feeling?"

"Like a new man," he said. "Power nap's done the trick I reckon. You getting off?"

"Yeah," Luke said, glancing at Maddie for a second, then back to Tony. "We all had a chat after you'd gone... decided we'd leave you to it. Have you figured out what you're gonna do about a car?"

"I... don't know actually," said Tony, rubbing at his forehead. "Maddie?"

"I don't know what your insurance is," she said. "You sort it yourself, don't you."

"Oh... ok. Don't worry anyway. We'll work something out, mucker."

The final word sounded unnatural coming out of Tony's mouth, despite the fact that it was what he always called his son. It was as if he was unsure how to pronounce it. Luke smirked at him.

"No worries."

"Morning," Ella said as she emerged, her bag slung over one shoulder. "We were just gonna come over. Has Luke told you?"

Maddie and Tony both bobbed their heads.

"He tell you about Al? There's stuff all over the Facebook page... and on Twitter-"

"The police called before," Maddie said. "That's why I was coming over here, actually, to see if-"

"You need to go to the police, dad," Ella said.

"I am," he said. "I'm just gonna have a day to get my head around everything, then I'll call them tomorrow."

"Dad, they think Al's murdered you."

"I've told him," Maddie said. "He says he won't go today."

Luke puffed out his cheeks.

"It's his call, at the end of the day, Maddie. One day's not gonna make a difference."

"Where's Ben?" Maddie said. Luke nodded towards the open door of the New Cottage.

"I'm gonna go and get him."

"Whatever," Ella mumbled.

The three of them were already hugging and saying their goodbyes before Maddie had even entered the building. She could hear the fading sound of Ella's voice as she entered the building, joking with her dad that he still smelled like he'd just come back from a festival.

Maddie shut the door, then edged into the kitchen. It was the stillest it had ever been. She ducked her head into the sitting room and said Ben's name, and the silence made her shudder.

She continued shouting his name as she headed upstairs.

"Ben? Ben?"

"Maddie?"

"Ben? Where are you?"

"Just in here," he said, his voice booming out from the bedroom at the top of the stairs.

The door creaked as Maddie entered. Ben was in the middle of taking his clothes out of the wardrobe and folding them next to his duffel bag, ready to be loaded in. He was fully dressed, complete with jacket and boots, as if he was on his way out as well.

"Luke said you were staying?" Maddie said.

He looked back at the wardrobe and shrugged. "For a bit yeah. Was gonna make sure you and dad were sorted with a car and that first."

He straightened up and walked over to her.

"You ok?"

"Not really, no," she said. "I don't get why everyone's acting like this is over all of a sudden, just because your dad's back."

"Well... that is the main thing isn't it?"

"Yeah, course," she said. "But it still doesn't explain every-thing does it? I think we need to tell them. About everything... the forest, the girl... and we should show them that room."

Ben sighed, itched at the stubble on his head. "I'm not sure what good it'd do to be honest. The more I think about it, we could have been in the forest for a while... and I know the room's weird, but it's not like there was–"

"What are you talking about?"

"You know what I mean, Maddie. With all of the stress we were under at the time, lack of sleep and everything. Maybe we just read too much into it. I know I panicked. You said yourself, it's just a room."

"I know what I said."

Maddie closed her eyes and massaged her temples, her teeth clenching in frustration. She was tired, that was undeniable, but to suggest that lack of sleep or even stress could conjure up the things she'd experienced over the past few days, to her, was madness.

"So, is that it?" she said, eventually snapping back out of her silent meditation. "We're just gonna pretend none of this has happened? Go back home and that's it? You can fly back off to Cyprus. Could be another story for the dinner table, couldn't it; 'remember when dad went missing'? Everyone can have a good laugh..."

"Maddie, you know it's not like that," he said. "We all talked about it and decided it was best to-"

"Ben, I need you here," she said, her eyes wide and sincere. "Please. Something still feels off. I can't say what, exactly, but... I just know there's something going on. It's even weirder now."

"What are you on about?"

"I haven't got a clue. There's just... something."

"What, like you think he's lying?"

"No," she said, her face contorting as she attempted to force the words out. "I know when your dad's lying, I know when he's hiding something. I know if he's stressed about something, or depressed..."

"Well if he's not lying or hiding something, then what's the problem?"

"Well, that's what I'm trying to say..."

She paused, looked briefly over her shoulder to ensure no one was eavesdropping at the foot of the stairs. Even though it was clear, she stepped forward and pushed the door closed behind her.

"I can't tell what he's hiding because I don't think he's... Ah fuck me, I can't even say it."

She clasped her hands together on top of her head and strode into one corner of the room, trying to burn off the frustration.

"What is it Maddie? Come on, you're not making any sense."

"Fuck," she said, closing her eyes again. She growled in frustration, then took a deep breath and hurled herself into confessing the very thoughts she'd spent the last few hours trying to suppress. "I can't read him. I can't tell because... I don't think it's him. It doesn't feel like it's him. The things he says, the *smell* of him, even. It's just... none of it's the same."

She opened her eyes to see Ben staring directly at her, only a few feet away. He'd moved close and was studying her with mixture of confusion and unease, as if she'd miraculously transformed into a surrealist painting. His silence smothered her, so much so that she felt compelled to say it again just to shock him into action.

"I know how it sounds, believe me," she said with a shrug. "I know it's mad, but that man downstairs, whoever he is... He's just so different, I can't even describe how, but I'm sure. It's like he's some-"

Ben swore and walked over to the window, most likely looking down on Tony, Ella, and Luke on the driveway. He muttered something else, then interlaced his own fingers at the back of his head and leant back and sighed up at the ceiling.

"I can't do this anymore," he said eventually.

"What do you mean? Do what?"

"This. You. I've given you the benefit of the doubt from day one. And I don't just mean all this stuff; I mean day fucking one."

He held up his index finger at her, the slight shake to it belying his anger.

"Keep your voice down," she said, closing the distance between them again.

"No, Maddie. Listen," he said. "I've always given you the benefit of the doubt. Even with that Boxing Day stuff and everything else-"

"You're blaming me for Boxing Day?"

"I'm not blaming you! I'm just telling you that I've always kept my mouth shut, no matter what, because I thought, deep down, you were a good person. I've always thought that. Despite you and my dad and my mum and all of that, I still felt like you were a good person. I always thought you were too – I dunno – too normal for us. I even used to feel bad that you had to deal with all our shit. I felt so bad for you that-"

"Why are you telling me this? What are you-"

"I'm telling you, Maddie, because I've had enough."

The muffled slam of a car boot interrupted them briefly, long enough for them to realise that they'd ended up within inches of each other. Maddie could feel the heat of his breath as their chests heaved out of time, a wordless call and response. His eyes were fixed on hers, so intense that she had to force herself to look away.

"I'm going," she heard him whisper.

Maddie turned to face the wooden dresser that was pushed against the far wall. It had three drawers on either side, which supported a thin tabletop and a brass-framed triple mirror. Although it appeared to be made of solid wood, closer inspection revealed that it was more likely flat-pack MDF, probably Ikea. Much like the rest of the New Cottage, its simplicity gave the impression of timelessness, of luxury. In truth it was cheap, rickety, and – after a short period of utility – destined for the tip.

Ben's reflection in the third panel of the mirror was little more than a flash of a black jacket as he loaded his clothes into the bag and zipped it up and slung it over his shoulder. She listened to his footsteps pound over the floorboards, then the door handle rattle as he threw it open. All Maddie could do was look into the mirror at the space he'd vacated, unable to fathom the pain of looking into his eyes one more time before he left. She flinched slightly at the unexpected sound of his voice.

"You need to stop all this Maddie. You need to face up to it, face up to the truth. Just because something isn't perfect, doesn't mean you need to throw it away. Maybe it just needs work, you know? If you're always chasing the next thing... it's no good. For you, or for anyone else. Just try to be happy with what you have now. Your husband's back Maddie. It's over. All of it."

Maddie felt searing heat as tears traced their way over her cheeks, pooling on her fingers where they were pressed over her lips. She could barely see the mirror now, barely hear him through the rumbling in her ears.

"I'm flying back tomorrow night," he said. "Tell dad to call me if you need anything before then. Otherwise... take care."

22

Maddie sat on the bed for a while after Ben left. Once the tears had ceased, she was content to stare at the incessant grey outside, mesmerised by the swirling, endless nothingness of the Brecon sky. It seemed to be so intent on smothering her now that it was practically pressing itself up against the windows like a thick fog. The wind rushed madly around the courtyard, shrieking its frustration at failing to sway the New Cottage with as much ease as it tormented the old one.

Maddie listened while Ben and his family exchanged brief goodbyes. The sound of him loading up his car and driving away was almost drowned out by Luke, Ella, and Tony's increasingly jovial conversation. Maddie wondered what they could possibly be laughing about at a time like this, though they can't have been half as disquieted by Ben's departure as she was.

After all, he was just a sullen, serious older brother to his siblings and a distant, doleful son to his father. To Maddie, in this moment of absolute helplessness, he was supposed to be so much more. He was supposed to be everything to her; a confidant, a conspirator, a protector. Instead he had chosen to abandon his belief in her when she needed it more than ever.

He had abandoned her, just like her father did. Just like her mother did before that. Now, once again, Maddie was alone and afraid.

23 - November 1996

Maddie awoke with a gasp, shaken from her dreams by a distant clattering. Thanks to the dull morning light bleeding through her curtains, she could just make out the silver box of her television set, the lines of the tiny corner desk that supported it. She screwed her eyes shut, then popped them open again. This time she was even able to read the names of the boy band posters on her wall and make out the pearly grins and dead eyes of the spiky haired icons that graced them.

She sat up and checked her bedroom door, then double doors on her wardrobe; all of which were firmly sealed. Another sound, glass bottles whistling as they rolled over concrete, caused her head to whip instinctively around to the window.

She swung her legs out of bed and dropped down onto the carpet, padded over and parted the curtains with freezing fingers, first the layer of polka dots, then the plain white net.

The scene outside was still, though everything was glistening with the rain that must have fallen in bucketloads while she slept.

She scanned from left to right, and her attention was immediately drawn to the alley behind the terrace, sandwiched between the back-yard walls of the next row of houses. In the pale pink glow of a fading streetlight, she saw a figure leaning unsteadily against a row of black wheelie bins. His denim jacket was wet through, his scraggly ginger hair hanging in ropes from his swaying head.

Maddie glanced back into the room, at the white face of the alarm clock next to her bed. She couldn't be sure in the gloom, but it looked to be a lot closer to breakfast than it was to the time her father had left on the pretence of 'a couple of pints' the previous evening.

He'd cut this ritual back to twice or three times a week since her mother had finally gone through with her threats and left him. Unfortunately, he'd ventured out on this particular jaunt on a Sunday evening, meaning Maddie would have to start getting ready for school in the next hour or so, come what may.

She peeped through the curtains once again to see him still in the same place, though he'd whipped his hair back from his face and was staring up at the rapidly lightening sky. He looked almost messianic, with his beard and his long hair and the glow of the streetlight above, his white shirt open to the sternum.

After breaking from his brief reverie, he slumped forwards,

245

back into his customary hunched position, and shambled towards the gate to the concrete box that was their back yard.

Halfway through his second step, his right boot gave way against the rain-slick cobble stones and he plunged forwards and down, his whiskey blunted reactions too slow to save his face from slapping straight into the cold floor. Maddie winced, recoiling away from the curtains with a clipped shriek.

She stood there for a second staring at the pink and white curtains, the net just visible between them, feeling that crunch into the stone over and over again. She considered jumping back into bed, pretending it hadn't happened, but she knew it would be useless. That had never worked when she was trying to drown out the screaming from downstairs and it wasn't going to help her now.

Her fingers trembling, she separated the curtains again and pushed her head back through. Her father was in the middle of heaving himself back to his feet, strings of blood dangling from his nose and mouth. He pushed the cobbles away with one final effort, then stood and spat and touched his mouth. He wobbled on the spot for a few seconds as he assessed the slick red mess on the palm of his hand, then carried on towards the back gate.

. . .

By the time Maddie had pulled on her dressing gown and slippers and thundered down the stairs, her father was in the kitchen slumped against the back door, blood now soaking the front of his shirt. She edged over and crouched in front of him, moved his sodden hair to one side.

"Daddy," she whispered. "Daddy are you awake?"

"Oh, there she is. Morning treasure," he said, his eyes still closed. "Ah, did I wake you up again?"

"Daddy, you need to let me help you, please... you've fallen. You've hurt you nose, and your mouth."

He blinked a few times, eventually heaving his eyelids open long enough to meet her gaze.

"There you are," he said. "You're the most beautiful girl in the world, I swear. I was telling them all again tonight. God, look at you. What time is it?"

"Come on, come and sit down in your chair and I'll get some water and a cloth."

Maddie hauled him up and led him into the sitting room by his bloody hand, then went back into the kitchen and dragged one of the plastic dining chairs over to the sink. She clambered up and filled the bowl with warm water and washing up liquid, swirling it around with her fingers to encourage the bubbles along. Satisfied, she stepped down and replaced the chair, then carried the bowl into the living room, her spindly forearms straining under the weight.

She helped her father take off his jacket, then his shirt, and took them into the kitchen and dropped them in front of the washing machine. By the time she returned to the living room with a clean cloth, he had fallen back asleep. The blood was beginning to coagulate in his beard and his chest hair, making him look like a lion halfway through feasting on a fallen zebra.

He flickered in and out of consciousness as she cleaned him up, occasionally wincing when she reached a particularly sensitive spot. His nose was already swelling, and the water revealed a series of angry looking gouges around his mouth, most likely from his lips being crushed between teeth and cobblestones.

"Jesus, girl, what would I do if I didn't have you, eh?" he said, scraping his hair behind his ears.

"Well, you have got me," Maddie said as she wrung out the bloody cloth one last time. The water was murky and crimson, and even the remaining bubbles had taken on a sickly orange hue.

"Are you alright, love?" he said.

"I'm fine. Just tired... Glad you came home."

"Do you know, when you were first born, I could never get to sleep in my own bed without you. Supposed to be the other way around isn't it," he slurred. "I just used to sit by your cot and watch you, all night long, until I fell asleep on the carpet. I was terrified. I thought, this baby – *my* little baby – she's so perfect, so beautiful. Your mother said I was a madman, but I knew I had to keep my eye on you. If I didn't... well I was sure the faeries would come and try to take you away. Take you back to their lands and leave another in your place. A changeling. My old mam always used to say they'd want babies just like you. Only the most beautiful, perfect ones. Golden hair and blue eyes... eyelashes long as a peacock's feathers."

Maddie stifled a laugh and he beamed back at her; his teeth streaked with the fresh blood that was still oozing from the open cuts. Her stomach lurched at the sight of them, so she stared at his feet instead. She heard him sigh, then he slumped back into the chair, probably looking up at the swirls of plaster that covered the ceiling.

"I can't watch you forever though, Maddie," he said. "You have to remember that. You have to make sure that once you're grown up and I'm not around anymore... you have to make sure you get a good man to protect you. A good man... not like me. A good, safe home. Not a shabby old dump like this place; a real-life castle. You have to promise me that. Will you do that... for me?"

She was fixated on his feet, the big toe on his right foot protruding from a hole in his thick woollen socks. He wriggled his feet slightly as he pushed himself further into the chair.

Maddie looked up to reply, but he was already snoring again. She stood and touched his knee, then picked up the bowl and went into the kitchen to clean up the rest of the mess.

24 - Now

Luke, Ella, and Tony were all still waiting on the gravel when Maddie emerged from the New Cottage, looks of relief rippling between them, as if they expected her to have stayed in there indefinitely.

"Everything ok?" said Tony as she approached.

"Fine."

As she looked at him, the sound of her confession to Ben reverberated in her ears. When she heard it like this, as he must have heard it, the whole fragile notion began to disintegrate like dandelion seeds in a gust of wind. Was she really so damaged – so ungrateful – that she could invent a suspicion like that? Could something as mundane as stress really convince her that the man standing in front of her was some kind of imposter? In the open air, in front of them and their awkward smiles, it seemed beyond impossible.

"Right, well we'll get off then," said Luke. "Leave you to it."

He leant over to take hold of Tony, hands clapping on each other's backs, then dutifully approached Maddie and gave her the shallow, respectful equivalent. Ella's effort was even more fleeting, closer to the kind of arm squeeze she might give someone as she brushed past them in a busy club; a facsimile of a hug.

Tony pulled Maddie into his side as they waved his children off, Luke's Audi spitting gravel as it roared out of the drive. They stood in silence for a moment, staring at the open gate, their arms still cradling one another. Once again, Maddie caught the smell of the damp forest floor from where she huddled under Tony's arm. She closed her eyes and tried to push the uncertainty from her mind, focusing on feel of the wind as it whipped stray hairs against her cheek.

Even as they crunched their way back towards the Old Cottage, she was embattled by unsettling images. The gate where she had seen the watcher that first night, the bare wooden panel above the door where the horseshoe had been. Then inside; the door to the workshop, the thought of the cramped room above it covered in strange markings. The bed, the statue, the leather surgical bag. All of it seemed to be rising up around her, like a tidal wave, more than capable of engulfing her if she continued to ignore it any longer.

She turned to face Tony, who was loitering in the kitchen. He looked as if he knew the next round of interrogation was about to begin.

"You're going to ask me about the crash again, aren't you?"

he said with a sigh.

Maddie glanced down at his mud-caked shoes for a moment, then forced herself to meet his expectant gaze.

He shook his head and gave a feeble smile.

"Go on then, officer," he said, holding his hands up in mock surrender. "But I've already told you everything I know."

Maddie edged closer until she was stopped by the oak-topped island that separated them. She drummed her fingers on the wood as she thought.

"Why don't we go down there? See if it helps, you know, jog your memory?"

"Down where?"

"To the crash site," Maddie said, as if she was suggesting a trip to the pub. "We went there the other day, me and Ben... it's not that far. I bet there's an even quicker way if we go over the fields. I've still got the pin on my maps, I think."

"I don't know Maddie," Tony said with a nervous chuckle. "I'm not sure it'd help, to be honest. Besides, we've got the place to ourselves here. We can rest, you know, just focus on getting ready for tomorrow."

"I know, and we can still do all of that. Tonight. This way, we can get out and get some fresh air, some exercise. It'll be good for both of us."

"I'm not sure Maddie, I'm not feeling-"

"I thought you said you were fine?" Maddie said. "'Fit as a butcher's dog', you told me."

Tony smiled wryly. He puffed out his cheeks and looked up at the ceiling, taking his time to respond. Maddie had seen it a hundred times before. She felt her stomach flutter as he leant forward and clapped his hand over her restless fingers and looked into her eyes.

"Ok," he said. "If you think it might help, then... yeah, ok. Let's go. Come on"

25

The hike took them down from Stone's Reach over close-cropped fields, beneath colossal, grey skies. Chunks of cloud, like levitating icebergs, were gridlocked as far as the eye could see, casting shadows that scuttled fearfully across the expanse. Every so often, the sun would burst through to dapple the faces of the distant hills. Farm animals, suspicious, kept their distance.

The longer they went on, the more ordinary everything started to feel. Old routines even began to appear. Tony held gates open for her, like he always did. He helped her over stiles. Maddie made sure they stuck to the route she'd mapped out meticulously in advance. Occasionally she found herself slipping into other habits; like daydreaming about what food she would order if they reached a country pub, or what wine she'd choose when they got back to their B&B. Then Tony would say something strange, or gesture in an unfamiliar way, and the reality of the situation would come thundering towards her like a landslide.

This was not man and wife out for a Sunday stroll. It was a

woman, plagued by suspicion, leading her broken husband to the scene of his greatest trauma. Or worse; it was encouraging a dangerous impostor to follow her to the most secluded place she'd ever seen.

. . .

They reached the crash site just before 2pm, both Maddie and Tony now zipped inside the waterproof coats they'd fumbled on during an ambush of rain. Although the downpour only lasted a few minutes, it was intense enough to ensure that they'd spend the rest of the day soaked to the bone.

Aside from the streams of water surging down both sides of the road, the entire scene was just as Maddie had left it; the undergrowth still sunken where the Range Rover had gone ploughing into it, shredded debris still piled in the field behind. Tony stood and stared at the cavity where his car, his friend, and possibly even himself had crossed from this world into a one of unspeakable pain. Maddie stood behind him and laid her hand gently on his shoulder.

"You alright?" she said.

He nodded without turning, then reached up and patted her hand. Tony's fingers were even colder and wetter than hers. She pulled her hand away, almost instinctively, though she made sure to give him another reassuring touch on the arm before she walked over to the other side of the road.

While seeing the crash site for the first time must surely

have been a visceral experience for Tony, Maddie was so accustomed to it by this point that it became almost trivial. It was the forest that called out to her, beckoning her to return.

She stepped off the road, then began to edge closer, the sodden grass squeaking under her boots, licking at her ankles. Although the little girl was nowhere to be seen, Maddie could still remember the exact spot where she stood, her strange appearance. Now, staring from the grey light into the darkness, Maddie could almost see her again, like a visual echo. Her cold, bare arms, the paleness of her skin. It was like looking at an old photograph, bleached by time and overexposed, not quite enough detail to pass for anything else but a ghost.

"Sorry," said Tony from behind her. "Lost track of time."

Maddie scowled at his choice of words, still disturbed by the way that five minutes had become five hours for her last time she stepped inside those woods. He can't have meant it, she thought. She shook it off and turned around to face him. The stiff hood on his jacket was pulled so far forward that his face was partly obscured, droplets of rain shaking free of its peak every time he moved.

"Don't worry," Maddie said. "We're in no rush. You ok?"

"Yeah, fine. Just so strange to see it."

"Has it helped? Brought anything back?"

"Not really. Still seems like it happened to someone else, you know what I mean?"

Maddie tried to smile.

"Is that it?" Tony said, nodding towards the forest. "That where I was?"

"Who knows," Maddie said. "I had a look in there yesterday and couldn't see any sign. Police and fire searched in there right after the crash too..."

Tony scratched at his beard and forced an awkward cough.

"Do you want to go and have a look?" said Tony.

"It's up to you. Do you think it will help?"

"Well, we've come all the way here."

"Ok. Come on, you can get through the fence just over here."

They trudged down the hill and ducked under the wooden fence. Maddie checked the time on her phone again – *14:08* – then crept past the first line of pine trees. Both of them stared up at the canopy as they walked, like awe-struck tourists stepping into the atrium of some vast green cathedral.

Even the cawing and chirping from the previous day had stilled in the passing of the rain. All that could be heard, for miles it seemed, was the slow drip of water as it meandered from branch to needle to forest floor. Maddie looked back to see that Tony, for some reason, was smiling.

"What is it?" Maddie said.

"Nothing, just... strange to be back. I didn't realise it was so-"

"So what?"

Tony shrugged. "I dunno really. Peaceful."

Maddie ignored him and looked away; her face screwed up beneath her hood. She moved further inside the cover of the trees, over towards the hidden circle of bracken where the pink stone had been. The whole area was exactly as she had left it, though the strange object was nowhere to be seen. Maddie swore under her breath and hunched over, swiping sodden bracken aside with her sleeves as she searched.

"What's wrong? What are you looking for? Have you drop-"

"Nothing," she said. "Doesn't matter now anyway... it's not here."

"What's not-"

"Nothing. It doesn't matter."

Maddie tried to strain her lips into a reassuring smile, but it came off more like a smirk. Despite the insincerity, it was still enough to satisfy Tony.

"Alright," he said with a shrug. It was still hard to see him, his nose and chin the only parts of his face protruding from the shadows cast by the peak of his hood.

Maddie looked deeper into the forest. "So," she said. "Is it helping at all, being here? You remember anything?"

"A little bit, maybe," he said. Maddie sighed.

"No, no, it is helping," he continued, as if to reassure her that her efforts had not been in vain. "It's just hard, that's all. I don't really know much more than what I told you, really. Walking around, then finding that tree and lying down for a bit. It was really strange at first... I had all these stories going through my head, the ones that Al had told me on the drive up here. It was a bit like-"

"Stories about what?"

"About here. This forest... the legends and the history of it. He said everyone around here knows about it. The people at the cottage not tell you?"

"No," Maddie said. "Nothing."

He waited for a beat, apparently waiting for her to object, then wiped the rain from his face and continued.

"Well, obviously I didn't buy it at the time, but he said there's a bunch of stories about the things that are meant to live here. Called the gwyllion."

"What's that, like an animal or some-"

"No," he laughed, cutting her off. "No, not an animal. They're like these... mountain spirits or witches or whatever, you know. You can see them here at night or sometimes in the day, if it's misty. They're like these ugly old women who try and lead travellers astray or frighten them off. Do all sorts of horrible things to people. Then there's the-"

"You say Al told you all this?"

Tony nodded. "Yeah, I don't know what he was getting at. He just knew everything about it. I was just taking the piss at the time, but he was dead serious. It was like he's-"

"What about children?" Maddie said.

"Children?"

"Yeah... are they supposed to have children, these things? Could there be younger ones walking around here too? As well as the old women?"

Tony snorted again, though this time it seemed to be more out of unease than condescension.

"It's just a story Maddie," he said slowly. "Reminded me of all that stuff your dad used to say to you, faeries and spirits and all that."

Maddie kept her eyes fixed on his long enough to make him

realise she meant what she was saying.

"Al didn't mention anything about kids, no. There could be, I suppose, but... yeah. He didn't say so. Why do you ask, anyway?"

Maddie just huffed and stepped back towards the spot where the stone had been. The flattened grass left in its wake was like a ghostly insult echoing through time. He followed her and held her from behind.

"Do you like it?"

"Like what?" she said, bristling at the question.

"Here. In the forest. Aren't you glad we came?"

"Not really," she said, stepping out of his arms and turning to face him. "As far as I'm concerned, it's just like any other forest you've ever dragged me through, only this time there's no drink at the end of it."

"Ok then," Tony chuckled. "Well, I'm sure we can find a pub or something on the way back."

Despite herself, Maddie laughed too. The closest thing they'd seen to civilisation on the entire trek was a stone shepherd's hut that had all but collapsed and the odd feeding trough.

"I don't remember seeing one," she said.

"True... well, my lady, we shall to make do with what we have."

Maddie scowled. "What are you on about?"

"How about I treat you when we get back?"

"Treat me to what?"

"Call me Chef Degrassi," he said, placing an open hand across his chest and bowing his head.

"Tony, are you fucking-"

"I mean it," he said, dropping the faux upper-class accent. "I'll cook. Ella's left that big bag of stuff, I'm sure I can sort something out. Do you remember that Aglio e Olio we had in Florence that time... in that little hole in the wall place?"

Maddie grinned, but was able to hold her tongue.

"Yeah, you remember," he said. "It was kind of like a cellar, almost. We'd heard about from the guy at the hotel, but we couldn't find it. There were all those scooters parked everywhere, all down the alleys and that, but no people. Was like a ghost town. Then we heard that music playing, and we knocked on that little, wooden door and there it was. Do you remember?"

This time Maddie failed to suppress her smile altogether. To see Tony's face illuminate as he told the story was like being thrust straight back onto those cobbled streets. It was intoxicating. He was himself again, and she was back in that very same moment with him. The pair of them wandering, hand in hand, the smells of wood-fired pizza and garlic and drifting through the summer air. The sound of ice cold Vermentino sloshing into clinking tumblers, the feel of it cooling her heat-chapped lips as she slumped into her seat and drank deeply.

Maddie looked up at him, mirrored his smile, then leant forward and rested her head on his rain-slick chest.

"That does sound amazing," she said. After a few seconds of silence, she looked up at him. "I wish we were there now."

26

Although the walk back up to Stone's Reach had been a lot harder than the downhill stroll to reach the woods, the promise of hot food and plenty of wine was enough to drive Maddie's tired limbs through the pain and biting rain.

Despite the reason for – and context of – their hike, conversation on the return leg had been relatively light, mostly Maddie quizzing Tony for more specific memories like the one he'd brought up in the forest. Anything to convince her that the man trailing behind her was, in fact, her husband.

Even so, the strange things that he'd said prior to his Florence story continued to prickle Maddie each time silence began to fill the space between them; his unsettling comments about the gwyllion, his odd behaviour at the crash site, his bemusing happiness afterwards.

To further add to Maddie's confusion, it turned out that she and Tony had emerged from the forest only a few minutes after they'd entered, *14:13*. No missing hours, not disorientating darkness. No sign of the mysterious girl. Again, that intrusion of normality was almost jarring alongside wave after wave of weirdness.

One step towards suspicion, then two steps back. It was like trying to hold onto two Tanks at once. Gradually being torn apart as each disobedient beast pulled in the opposite direction, both of them deaf to her cries of submission.

. . .

After dinner, they retired to the small corner bedroom that was starting to feel like home to Maddie. Despite the good food and pleasant conversation the two of them had enjoyed downstairs, Maddie chose to sit as far away from her husband as the cramped room would allow; her curled up on the armchair where Ben had sat 'on stag' the previous night, Tony sat on one side of the bed, his foot dangling down onto the floor like a 1930's Hollywood actor. They sipped petrol station wine from stoneware mugs. Although Tony had been noticeably ravenous again at dinner, his customary appetite for alcohol looked to have taken a serious dive from the way he continued to nurse his one and only drink of the evening.

Maddie, on the other hand, had decided to keep herself suitably well oiled. She'd shelved her initial plan of avoiding drink in order to keep her wits about her in favour of a tried and tested technique; drinking as a form of self-medication. This time, the malady she was trying her best to drown was a powerful pairing of fear and mistrust. So far, the alcohol was doing its job.

"I know I keep asking," said Tony. "But are you sure you're ok? You've been different since the kids left. Like you're always thinking away."

"Sorry," Maddie said, her wine-weary gaze barely making it over the rim of her mug. "Just a lot to get your head around isn't it... we've still not sorted a car for tomorrow, for a start."

"Day just got away from us, didn't it."

"You are still going, right? To the police?"

"Course I am," he said, putting his cup on the side table and leaning forwards. "I'll go first thing. Can just call a cab or something. Hopefully the courtesy car should be sorted after that."

Maddie took another sip. Tony let out an involuntary half-sigh, though she could tell he was doing his best to avoid any potential arguments before they appeared. He stood and walked around to the foot of the bed and leant against it.

"How's your thumb, by the way?"

Maddie scowled.

"What do you mean?"

"When you cut it, the other day. As I was leaving."

"Oh," she said, turning her hand over to inspect the paper-

266

thin scab. "It's fine. Was nothing really. I didn't think you'd be able to remember. You know, after... everything."

It was his turn to furrow his brow, though he was careful to keep his tone neutral.

"Course I remember," he said. "Was horrible leaving you like that. I thought about it all the way down here."

"How come you didn't message me then?" she said, keeping her eyes fixed as she took another mouthful of her wine. "Worried myself sick."

Visions of Tony and his Gothenburg girl flashed through her mind.

"Well," Tony said, popping out his bottom lip. "I... well there wasn't really any..."

He slapped both palms onto his thighs and puffed out his cheeks.

"Honestly, I don't know," he said. "I should have. I'm sorry to tell you this, Madeline, but your husband is a dick."

His choice of words was jarring, as was the use of her full name. Half of her wanted to laugh at his self-deprecation, out of character as it was, and the other prickled with suspicion at the way he referred to himself in the third person. He must have sensed this, as he fell back into sincerity again.

"I'm so sorry for all of this," he said. "It's all my fault."

"Don't start with all that," Maddie said, her words beginning to bump into one another like drunks at a bar queue. "You had to do what you had to do. Al's your friend and he needed you here."

"But you needed me too. At home. And I should have realised that. Honestly, Maddie, I'm so sorry. I just want to... I need to use this as a wake-up call, you know. To be a better husband, a better dad."

"You're a good dad," she said. "And they're good kids."

"They are," he said, a smile blooming on his face. "It was so nice to see all the family together again. I really miss that, you know. The sound of a full house. Kids just... being kids. I'm sorry you've never, you know... It must be really hard to want all that and have to give it up... To marry me, of all people."

"What do you mean?"

"Well, because of the way I felt about kids, you had to lie to me and – even worse – you had to lie to yourself. You've always wanted a baby, deep down, I know you have, and you'd be an amazing mum. I've been so unfair, and so selfish, to not even consider how you felt. I really am sorry, Maddie."

Maddie gripped the mug in both hands and stared at Tony's feet. He was wearing his favourite socks; the Oliver Sweeney ones with a geometric print in orange, yellow, and black. They always reminded Maddie of the carpet from the hotel in *The Shining.* The one that the little boy rode over on his trike – *roll and thunk, roll and thunk* – until he came face to face with the ghosts of the old caretaker's daughters.

She had always complained to Tony about the similarity, as if it was somehow his fault.

"Maddie?"

"Sorry," she said, meeting his gaze again. "I just... I've spent the last few days thinking you might never come home... now you're here and you're talking about all this. I dunno, it's a lot to take in."

"Course," he said. He pushed himself away from the bed and came to kneel in front of her. "And I know it's maybe not the time to be talking about it, but I really want you to experience it. I've never been more certain of anything in my life. Obviously, there's no rush... but I really do want this, with you."

He put his hand on her knee and she, despite her misgivings, felt compelled to cover it with hers. She smiled to hold back the tears that were welling in the corners of her eyes and kissed him. After a heartbeat, Tony pulled away.

"I mean it, Maddie."

"I know you do."

She leant back in and kissed him again, this time sweeping

his lips apart with her tongue. Although she could discern the alcohol fumes and the hum of garlic, there was something else there too, something unfamiliar. It was a taste similar to that strange smell Tony hadn't been able to wash off since he returned. That earthy, woody musk. She drew him closer, almost in spite of the taste, determined to lose herself in the kiss, to feel something like normality again.

They continued to rediscover each other's bodies; Tony's hand sliding from her knee to her hip, easing her slowly off the chair towards him, Maddie scrunching the hair at the nape of his neck. They stood together, neither one of them breaking from the other's lips. Hands fumbled at belts and buttons and zips, noses snagged on shirts as they were yanked over heads, both of them clumsy like teenagers.

Tony hooked his thumbs inside Maddie's waistband and pulled her leggings down and wrestled them over her ankles. He stood, kicking out of his jeans as he did so, and slapped his palms back onto her naked waist.

Although feel of his hands against her skin was familiar, the way they moved was not. Instead of grabbing her shoulders and spinning her around to face the bed, as he usually would, he slipped his hands down to the backs of her thighs and hoisted her up into the air. Startled, she looped her arms around his neck and gripped his hips with her thighs and kissed him so deep that she felt as if she could devour him.

27

Maddie awoke with a smile on her face. It was an easy smile, a natural one. A breed apart from the expressions she'd been forced to contort her face into over the last few days in an attempt to seem like she was coping. It was even different to the kind of smiles she'd adopted in months gone by to convince her friends that she was still living the dream she'd always coveted, back when her whole life was a lie. Now, in this bed, she found herself smiling because she wanted to smile.

The night with Tony had been unlike anything she'd ever experienced, with him or anyone else. It was like all of the things he'd said, all of the promises he'd made, had somehow been transformed into physical action. His deepest regrets made flesh. The way he touched her, moved her, the way he listened to her body. It was almost as if he was making up for the countless nights he'd grunted his satisfaction, then rolled off and gone straight to sleep.

As she began to stir, Maddie could sense that the morning

sun was burning through the curtains, beckoning her to leave the blissful nest into which she'd just awoken with light and warmth and promises of rejuvenation. Irreverent of these meagre offerings, she rolled away from the window towards Tony's side of the bed and began feeling for his bare feet with hers. When she could find nothing more than cold sheets and fresh air, she batted the covers away and sat up to find her husband missing once again.

She arched her back into a stretch and surveyed the room, wrinkling her nose at the musty odour that hung in the air; like muddy boots drying in the porch, or the grey chocolate inside a long-forgotten advent calendar.

"Tony?" she said, though it was little more than a croak. She cleared her throat and tried again. "Tony?"

The silence that followed was enough to tempt her from the bed. She swung her legs out from under the covers and drove her feet into the vile carpet, then straightened up and tried to tame her hair back into its ponytail. As she raked her fingers from front to back, one of them snagged on a tangle of hair too tight to be teased out. It wasn't a natural knot, almost like the beginnings of a plait. She wondered if she'd somehow done it in her sleep.

"What the fuck?"

She scrunched up her face in confusion, her eyes still half-closed. After a few seconds of tugging, she was forced to work at it with both fingers, eventually having to untie it like a stubborn shoelace.

Once the strange plait was untied, Maddie padded over to pull the curtains open, inviting the sun to burst inside the room. The sky was open wide, endless and sapphire blue. The clouds that had dogged her since her arrival were nowhere to be seen. She shielded herself from the brightness with one hand, then turned away and went to make sure that the bathroom was empty. Satisfied, she pulled on socks, leggings, and her baggy hooded jumper and opened the door with a rattle of its handle and stepped out into the hallway.

There was no sound from downstairs. No kettle boiling, no food cooking on the stove. No radio. No television. Maddie took hold of the wooden bannister and began edging her way down, one carpeted creaking step at a time. She was already craning her neck to survey the ground floor well before she reached the bottom, but there was no sign of her husband.

Instead, sat in the living area in front of the log burner, were two women, both dressed in the same plain summer dresses, which were delicately embroidered with coloured patterns. Although Maddie didn't recognise the elderly woman sat in the armchair, the bright red hair cascading over the back of the sofa could only have belonged to Ginny.

They both turned to look at Maddie as the final step squeaked under her weight, smiles automatically spreading over their wizened faces.

"There you are," Ginny said, her voice soft and airy. "We were starting to think you'd be up there all day. Do you want a drink? Some tea?"

The old woman, whose thick accent was immediately familiar to Maddie, squawked towards the kitchen, waving her hand impatiently.

"That's right," she said. "Make us all a brew Gwilym, for goodness sake."

Maddie's gaze snapped towards the sink, where Wil – dressed similarly to Ginny and the old woman – was blasting the tap into the top of the kettle.

"It's Wil, nan, how many bloody times..." he muttered under his breath.

He looked so much older out of his greasy jeans and his obscene t-shirt. Maddie even noticed a few strands of grey sprouting from amongst his dark beard and mop of hair. After he'd filled the kettle, he lit the stove with a few clicks of a disposable cigarette lighter and placed the kettle on top, then turned and folded his arms and leant against the cupboards. As if he didn't look anachronistic enough in his embroidered linen shirt and trousers, he then fished his phone from one of his baggy pockets and began scrolling on it as if he was waiting for a bus.

Maddie, still open mouthed, looked back over at the women.

"Oh, Maddie," Ginny said as she stood and hurried towards

her. She pulled her in for a brief, one-sided hug, then led her over to the sofa. Maddie stared blankly at the other woman as she passed, who was still grinning hard enough to crease a few new wrinkles into her leathery skin.

As well as the loose dress, the woman wore a long-sleeved shirt and tights underneath, both in the same natural colour, and a red ribbon in her hair. Much like Ginny, her wrists and neck were heavy with copper, gold, and gemstones. She wore only one earring – a miniature version of a Native American dreamcatcher – from which hung a single feather that shimmered blue and gold in the beams of sunlight. Her silver hair was long and ratty, and had been allowed to cascade freely over her shoulders and down her back.

Ginny eased Maddie into the corner of the sofa and sat down next to her. The kettle was bubbling away like distant thunder in the kitchen, though everyone assembled was content to sit in silence and stare at Maddie. She felt as if she'd just won a competition or had somehow turned into a celebrity overnight. She adjusted herself to face Ginny.

"What..." she managed eventually. "What are you doing here? Where's Tony? Have you seen him?"

"Oh love," said the old woman. "You poor thing. You must be so confused... been through so much already, haven't you."

"What are you doing... who are you?"

"We spoke on the phone, love, don't you remember? My

name's Branwen. Course you were all over the shop at the time, I imagine. It was when you phoned me up when your Tony first went missing, you remember? This is my cottage, you see. And the one over the way there. You met my grandson too, of course."

She glanced over to him and mimicked his distinctive drawl, while flicking air quotes out in front of her: "Wil."

"Nan, that's my name," he said, looking up from his phone. "Why are you making a big thing-"

"Oh, I'm only messing, boy," she said with a snort. "Trying to lighten the mood."

"I'm sorry, what mood? What are you... ok, so you're the woman from Red Dragon," said Maddie, nodding to herself. "But what are you, like... what's the problem? Is there something wrong? Why are you all dressed so... I don't..."

She stopped and turned to Ginny. "Ginny, what's going on? I don't understand why you're... why you're all here? Can you just-"

"Ok, it's alright," said Ginny, tapping Maddie on the knee. She took a deep breath and continued like a nervous supply teacher addressing an unfamiliar class. "Right, well there's a few different versions... well, not versions... There's kind of a long story and a slightly shorter story, or we could-"

"Ginny," said Maddie, more insistent this time. "I don't care

276

about hearing stories, I just want to know where Tony is. Why are you even here? Have the police taken him or something? Where's Al?"

"All these questions are getting us nowhere, love," said the old woman. "Best way to do this is for us to talk and you to listen, alright?"

"The fuck is this bullshit?" Maddie said to herself. "Who even are you? I'm calling Tony. I'm calling the police."

Maddie got up and shuffled between the wall and the sofa again, just like she had when she'd fled Tony the previous morning. This time, Wil was there to stop her. He stuffed his phone back into his pocket and stepped in between Maddie and the landline, his palms held up apologetically.

"I'm sorry babes, I can't let you do that," he said.

"Don't you fucking speak to me like that, you pervert," Maddie said, looking over to the living room in disbelief. "Get out of my way."

She attempted to walk around Wil, but he moved back into her path and reached forwards to take hold of her wrists.

"Don't fucking touch me either, you creep," said Maddie, snatching her hands into her chest and stepping backwards. "What the hell is going on here? Are you all mad or something?"

She turned back to Ginny and strode forward until she was only inches from her face.

"Where is my fucking husband?" she said through gritted teeth.

Ginny continued to try and placate her, though the breathy tone she'd adopted only made Maddie more incensed. Without thinking, Maddie snatched a handful of bright red hair and pulled Ginny towards her, then shrieked into her ear.

"Where is he?"

She heard a clattering sound from the kitchen, then the sound of Wil's voice.

"Jesus Christ... Fuck this."

The next thing Maddie felt was something like rough material being pulled over her face. Everything went black, and a clump of Ginny's hair came away in her fist as she was jerked backwards into the kitchen. Maddie struggled against Wil's invisible hands for a few seconds, though it seemed as if there were ten of him.

"Gwilym what are you doing?" said the old woman, shouting over Ginny's cries.

Maddie and Wil rolled over the cold stone floor and suddenly all his weight was on top of her, crushing her. She could smell the sweat, the sickly sweet cannabis smoke, as they continued

278

to tussle.

Maddie managed to free her arm and, after swiping at fresh air for a few seconds, the nails on her left hand dug into flesh, then into something softer than flesh. She began to burrow deeper, screaming as she did so, but was eventually torn away. Warm blood trickled down her fingers as her hand was slammed to the floor. Wil was shrieking.

Maddie tried to sit up, but the first blow was enough of a shock to paralyse her, to freeze her limbs solid. It clearly wasn't enough for Wil. She continued to feel his fists falling on her like hammers until she couldn't feel anything at all.

28

"Oh my God, you could have killed her, you... you animal!"

"I've never seen anything like it. What have you-"

"She nearly gouged my fucking eye out; can you not see that? Look at it. Ow don't fucking touch it, Jesus Christ! Fucking hell-"

"If someone... If they find out because of this... my goodness, can you imagine? If all of this is ruined because of your... because of this-"

"Don't you dare call him anything, he's a good boy. He's just-"

"I'll call him what I want; he's a b-bloody... nutcase! Did you not see that? Did you not-"

"Can you two fucking shut up and help me please? Where's the sink? I can't see a bloody thing. Nan, please?"

"Over here, come on you daft apeth. Over there, go on. Just

get the water on it, get some water on it. There you go."

"Oh shit-"

"The bloody kettle, take that kettle off now before we all-"

"I can't see! Where is it? Jesus, Nan."

"Oh, I'll do it then. Move, move out of the way, go on-"

"Branwen? Branwen, I think she's waking up. Oh God, I think she's waking up."

. . .

It sounded like there was a football stadium full of people arguing as Maddie swayed back into consciousness. The kettle was screeching louder than Wil had done when she'd dug her nails into his eye. As she moved her head around, Maddie could see pinpricks of golden light through the bag, but nothing more. It was some kind of potato sack, like the kind you'd use to race on a school sports day, but smaller. It smelled like that too, like soil and dirt. She could feel it sticking to her lips and nose as she wheezed, sticking to the blood.

She tried to stand, to wrench her hands from where they rested at her sides, but she was bound in place. It felt like she was sat on a hard, wooden chair. Maddie guessed it was the ornately patterned one that had stood unused behind the front door, like an old-style rocking chair with four feet instead of runners.

"Ginny," Maddie said, her voice muffled. "Ginny? I'm sorry, I... please just tell me what's going on, please."

"Look, Maddie," came Ginny's voice, even more feeble than usual. She was close, directly in front of Maddie. "Look, I'm so sorry this has happened... it wasn't supposed to be like this at all, not at all. I'm... I'm going to take this bag off, ok? But you have to try and calm down, ok? I know this is really hard... really stressful for you, but we can't risk having to hurt you again, alright? It's really, really not an option. Is that ok? Do you understand?"

Maddie nodded, and in a few seconds the living room was revealed to her again. Ginny and the old woman were both leant against the back of the sofa, assessing her with frowns on their faces. She assumed that Wil was the one who'd removed her hood, and by the sounds of his constant moaning, he was probably happier to stay out of sight.

"How are you feeling love?" said the old woman to Maddie. "Gosh, he's caught you with one there, look at that. Come here, Gwilym, give us that over here."

"Nan, I'm using it," he said. "Look at the state of this."

"Ah, you'll live. I only need it for a second, come here."

The old woman disappeared, then appeared again at Maddie's side with a damp, bloodied tea towel. She dabbed at Maddie's lips and chin, then at each nostril in turn, gently sopping up the blood. Although every touch of the towel came with

282

miniature eruptions of pain, she was at least relieved to have the mess cleaned off her face.

"There you are, that'll do."

The old woman straightened up and handed the towel back to Will.

"Heaven help you if anyone turns up now," she said, tutting. "My goodness, what a beauty you are. Look at that face. They said you were a looker but... I never."

Maddie squinted up at her. "Who are you?" she said. "What is all this?"

"Well," the old woman said, heading back over to lean next to Ginny on the sofa. "Do you actually want to hear it this time? We can't have you getting all wound up like that again, you know. I wouldn't have thought you had it in you, to look at you. You've messed my grandson up for a good while, that's for sure."

"He deserved it," Maddie said, touching the open wound on her lip with her tongue.

She looked down to see where her hands were bound, but they were hidden behind the back of the chair. It felt too smooth and sharp against her wrists to be rope. After working at them for a while, she was reminded of the zip ties that Tony insisted it was necessary to keep in her cutlery drawer. Sleek, black, brutal; like leeches digging their teeth into her skin.

Between the zip ties and the sack, Maddie began to suspect that the three of them had come prepared to restrain her. She wondered what else they had brought, whether they'd used any of them already, then thought of the doctor's bag in the garret.

"As I said, my name's Branwen, and-"

"Where is Tony?" she said for what felt like the thousandth time.

The old woman sighed.

"I don't want to upset you any more than you already are, love, but-"

"Hold on, are you sure?" said Ginny. "I'm not sure this is the right time for-"

The old woman smiled and silenced Ginny's protests with a gentle hand on her arm.

"It's ok, love. Now's as good a time as any." The old woman walked towards Maddie and crouched in front of her. "Like I said, I don't want to upset you, but you need to understand that your husband is no longer with us."

Maddie stared into the old woman's eyes, looking for some kind of cruel glimmer, but she could see only sincerity. Her smile too, was unwavering. She was the very epitome of the concerned grandmother, kneeling at the feet of her most cherished grandchild.

"I promise you, this is the truth, love. Your husband... he's become a part of something that's incredibly special, incredibly important. He's had to be-"

"What the fuck... are you talking about?" said Maddie, tears tickling her cheeks as they fell.

"He's gone, Maddie," said Ginny. "Tony's gone. I'm so sorry."

"What? How can you know that?"

"Because," Ginny's voice faltered as she failed to suppress her own tears. "Because Al was with him when... well, when they-"

Ginny swallowed and closed her eyes, attempting to compose herself. Just like the old woman, this didn't seem to Maddie to be some kind of act. She was distraught.

"Look," Ginny said. "We've all played our part in this, but it was just that Tony had to be the one to-"

"Tony was here last night," Maddie said. "Are you fucking mad? He was here. I slept in a bed with him last night, with my husband. It wasn't just me; Helen saw him, his children saw him. Call them, ask them. This is all... none of this makes sense."

"Look, Madeline," the old woman said.

"Maddie."

"Sorry, either way... I told you this would be hard to get your head around, but you have to realise what we're saying to you before we can go on with this. That... person − the one who stayed here last night − he was not your husband."

Maddie's eyes darted towards Ginny. She was sniffling into her handkerchief and looking out of the window. It was as if she couldn't even watch.

"This is insane," Maddie said. "You're all insane."

She was expressionless, as if all the tension that had been building up since Tony's return was finally allowed to drain away. "You're some kind of fucking... Welsh, hillbilly con artists and you've roped her in for... I don't know what. Do you want Tony's money or something? You want the house, the cars... what? You know the police are looking at Al, right? You listening Ginny? Whatever part you've got in this fucking bullshit; the police know. They know you're up to something."

"The police want Aled for the disappearance," said the old woman, her voice measured. "Everyone with a telly knows that. But it will all come to nothing. Of course, the crash complicated things, but ultimately there's no evidence. You have to understand that the group we're a part of, the goal we're all working towards... it's a lot bigger that just us. Bigger than the police, the press even. We have friends in every possible corner. Besides, Aled didn't technically do anything wrong, not legally anyway; he just took Tony where he needed

286

to be and made sure he stayed there."

"Tony was here, you stupid old bitch," said Maddie, like she was reading the insults off a list. "Are you all fucking deaf?"

"Now watch your tone, young lady," the old woman said. "Look, I'm trying to be as diligent as possible here, but... if you continue to disrespect me and my family, then it won't be long before I ditch the bedside manner, alright?"

"Fuck's sake," Maddie said. She bowed her head and tried to wrench her hands free of the zip ties. She growled wordlessly as she struggled, spit and blood dripping onto her thighs as she rocked back and forth. The old woman stayed where she was, content to watch her thrashing around until her limbs were drained of energy once more.

"He was here," Maddie said as she panted. "I saw him, I spoke to him, I touched him-"

"You lay with him too," the old woman hissed.

Maddie's mouth hung open as she breathed deeply, silence filling the room like a thick fog. She leant back into her seat to meet the woman's expectant gaze. She smiled again, but this time it didn't reach as far as her wrinkled eyes. This time the spite was there, plain to see.

"We know everything, Madeline, and we know because he told us... as he was leaving this morning. Back to his own home. You may well see him again, one day, but as I tried to explain already; he is not your husband. You need to understand... the man you married, Anthony Degrassi, walked into that forest on Friday and he never came out. The very fact that you saw that person, the person who looked like him, in this house... it's proof that your husband is dead. There is no way that person could exist in this world if that wasn't the case. I'm sorry, but the man you know is dead."

29

Maddie forced herself to look down at her blood and spit-spattered thighs. It was the only way she could avoid the old woman's face.

The words she had uttered so calmly were still ricocheting around in Maddie's head, shredding the last few strands of sanity she had left. She knew, instinctively, that the old woman was telling the truth. In a way, she'd been interrogating herself as much as she'd been interrogating them. Using these intruders as the cork board for the pins of suspicion she already had. The very suspicions she'd begun confessing to Ben the previous day.

Somewhere, deep in her subconscious, Maddie had always known that the man who had returned from the wilderness was not her husband. Even when, after being fed wine and stories of their past life together, she gave in to his advances, she had still known something wasn't right. It wasn't his gaunt appearance or his strange eating habits or his awkwardness or the way he'd made love to her. It was the smell. That odour of the forest floor, of mud and mulch and moss.

He could never wash the smell away or cover it up was because it wasn't on him to begin with. It had been coming from inside him. From whoever had been wearing his skin.

"Who was it?" said Maddie, her body still hunched forwards in the chair.

"Who was what, Maddie?" said Ginny, her pumps shuffling along the floor towards the chair.

"The... whoever, whatever it was. In my bed last night. In this house. Who was it?"

Maddie looked up to see the two women wordlessly passing the buck back and forth, before the old woman sighed and stepped forwards once again. Ginny came to stand beside her, then they both sat on the stone floor in front of Maddie like expectant children waiting for a story.

"You have been chosen, Madeline," said the old woman. "Selected to play a very important part in something bigger than you, or even I, can possibly comprehend. Last night, upstairs in that very bed, you became the vessel for his most royal seed."

"What the fuck are you talking about?" Maddie said, unable to stop herself from smirking.

"That's right Maddie," said Ginny, eagerly nodding her head. "You've always been destined to be a mother, and now you finally will be. And to the most special child any of us will ever know. It's such an honour."

"Such an honour," echoed the old woman, seizing on Ginny's momentum. "That's what we were trying to say before this all got out of hand. You are so lucky. Growing inside you is the direct heir to the throne. Half of this world, and half of the other. He will be a Prince, born on the day of Imbolg. Welcome in the court of the Horned God himself. On his eighteenth birthday he is destined to ride-"

Maddie laughed again, though the silence into which it burst was cold enough to chill her blood. They were deadly serious, looking almost upset by her contempt. Maddie tried to flick the stray hairs out of her face, sniff away the blood that was running into her mouth, but she was useless without her hands. Ginny rocked forwards onto her knees and obliged, tucking Maddie's hair behind her ear and wiping her nose clean with her thumb. She smiled weakly as she sat back down, wiping the blood onto the stone floor.

Maddie stared smear of blood for a few seconds, then up at the old woman, at the ornate embroidery on her dress. Although the designs differed in their specifics, both her and Ginny's had a swan on either side of their collar, facing one another, and two red dragons doing the same below that. A seven-pointed star, just like the one drawn on the floor of the garret, could be seen just above the waist on both dresses, as well as indecipherable symbols dotted along the hem. The longer

Maddie looked, the more the outfits seemed like some kind of uniform.

"So," Maddie said, still indignant. "If I'm pregnant, then what does that make you two? The midwives?"

"Not quite," the old woman said with a shy chuckle. "Not at my age. You never know though, maybe Virginia here." She gestured to Ginny. "Right now, we're more like... student nurses, I'd say. We're here to look after you until the time comes."

"The time?"

"The birth," said the old woman. "But don't worry, the right people will be here by then. The ones who can help us deliver the little Prince."

"To be honest with you, Maddie, it's more surgeons than a midwives, if you-"

"Virginia, leave off with that. She doesn't need any more worry than she already has, look at the poor thing. All that can wait as she comes around to it all. Have I shown you the birthing room yet?"

Ginny smiled and shook her head, Maddie scowled uselessly at her. So many of Ginny's mannerisms had become childlike since that day at the hospital, like she had become giddy about the whole thing.

"Come on then, come and have a look and see what we've done. Gwilym? You watch our special mummy, will you? Make sure she's alright, you know... No more nonsense out of you, either."

The two women went over to the door in the corner of the room and disappeared into the annex, chattering excitedly as they went, Branwen apologising for the mess. Maddie tried to look back over her shoulder for Wil, but there was no movement. Instead, she heard a chair squeak as it was dragged from the kitchen, then the loud clap of it being dropped onto the floor behind her.

She could smell him before he spoke, his breath was warm and damp on the back of her neck.

"You've proper fucked me up, you know that?"

Maddie looked straight ahead at the log burner, attempting to zone out from whatever was about to come next.

"Calm down, don't worry," he said, patting her on the shoulder. "I'm not going to do anything stupid. I'm surprised I hit you in the first place, to be honest. I'm a right pussy really. My Nan knows it, that's why she's left me with you... even after all that. She knows I don't have the bollocks to do anything."

His lips touched her ear lobe. "I fucking want to though."

She heard the chair squeak as he sat back and laughed to himself.

Every muscle in Maddie's body was taught, her fists clenched, straining against the zip ties. She tried to squirm out of the ones around her ankles, to use the smoothness of her leggings, but it was no use.

"Fuck me, this is sore," he whispered to himself. "Fucking bastard."

"Was it you?" Maddie said, thinking of anything she could to keep him too busy to indulge himself.

"Was what me? Pretending to be your husband? Jesus fucking Christ, I wish. Oh my God, don't."

He sniggered.

"No. The one who's been watching me, all this time. Out there. At the end of the drive, and the next night... in the garden. Was that you?"

He puffed out his cheeks. Maddie's chair rocked forwards and he leant his foot against the back of it.

"I have absolutely no idea what you're on about babes."

"I told you not to call–"

"I've not set eyes on you since I left here that first night. Not until today. If you ask me, I'd say that it was probably your Prince Charming. Sizing you up, maybe. I can't fucking believe you let that fucking thing have a piece of you, Jesus. You wouldn't have if you'd seen him, believe me. What he really looks like."

He let out an exaggerated shudder, wobbled his lips from side to side like a cartoon character.

"Gives me the creeps just thinking about it," he said, his voice still drenched in mock revulsion.

Maddie heard him stand and his footsteps shuffle over the stone. He drifted into her eyeline, eventually crouching until his face was level with hers.

She tried to look past him, to focus on something behind him; a single stone in the wall, the top of the chimney. It was useless, and within seconds her gaze was drawn to his injuries.

He carried three scratches that ran from his forehead down to his right cheek, all of which passed straight over his eyelid. The eye itself looked to be intact but the white of it was red and angry looking. Broken blood vessels looked to be bursting from edge of his iris like solar flares, his cornea like the molten surface of the sun. Thick, almost black, blood was leaking from the corner of his eye, making him look like one of those weeping Madonna statues that occasionally popped up in the news.

From the spiteful expression he was wearing, Wil appeared to have gotten over his initial shock. Now he was simply focussed on wreaking vengeance.

Maddie looked down at her legs again, just to look at anything but his smirk.

"I wanna show you something," he said, disappearing back into the kitchen.

She heard the sound of a rucksack unclipping, then the zip, then rustling and clinking.

"My Nan asked me to come here and help with everything today," he said, grunting with effort as he fought something out of the bag. "Mostly, I'm here as security, you see. Keep an eye – fucking hell... an eye," he laughed. "Well, it *is* one eye now isn't it... anyway, to make sure you knew who was in charge, and anyone else for that matter."

The noise stopped and he reappeared with a large metal implement in his hands. Maddie flinched as he passed, his giddy smile proof that he had been craving such a reaction.

"What the fuck is that?"

The weapon was around three feet long, two points branching out from a short handle. The first, slightly longer, point was like a curved sword blade, flat and sharp-edged, while the other was a right-angled spike. The whole thing was ancient and scabbed with rust, though the brown lace that had been wound around the handle looked to have been a more recent DIY job.

"I know, right," Wil said, turning it over in his hands. "It's called a Welsh hook. They used to stick them on poles back when we were fighting you lot in the medieval times, you know, like a spear?"

He jabbed it forward into the air, as if to demonstrate the technique.

"This is just the top bit, really. Cool innit."

"Why have you got that?"

"It was my dad's," he said, looking at the weapon as if he was leafing through a family photo album. "He used to collect all sorts of shit like this. Weapons and tools... coins and that. Ended up getting into detecting after he retired, you see. You can get loads of good stuff if you know where to look."

Maddie leant forward to draw his attention away from it.

"I mean why have you got it here?" she said.

"Oh," he laughed. "I see. She told me to bring something... just in case anyone showed up, you know. So, I did. It's heavy, feel this."

He stretched the weapon out and rested the blade side on her shoulder. Although her hoody provided some padding against its weight, it was clear that it had the potential to do serious damage. She attempted to shrug it off, but he held it in place, his grin widening.

"Would your dad be proud of you, using it for this? Using it to scare a woman tied to a chair?"

Wil's smile disappeared and he removed the weapon and stood it up against the back of the sofa.

"I was only messing with you," he said defensively. "I just had to show you who's boss. Wish I'd have shown it to you before you-"

He poked at his eye again, as if to remind himself of the pain, then whipped his hand away and growled.

"Fucking hell man," he said. "I can't believe you did that. They said you'd be happy when they told you. Said we'd all sit down and have a brew and just... get on with it."

"Get on with what?" Maddie said. "Being your hostage for the next nine months, so I give birth to some fucking... I can't even say it. They're fucking mental, Wil, can you not see that? Surely you're not into all this like they are?"

"Into what?"

"All this fucking... Horny God, baby Prince, fucking... hubble bubble bullshit?"

"Horned God," Wil snorted. "And yeah, I am, as it happens. I know I look like your average numpty, but I do care about some stuff. All of this is really important to me, you know. Being part of something like this; it's a big deal in our group, in

298

my family too. My Nan and my Mum and Dad always brought me along to meetings and stuff, ever since I was a little lad. This might all be new to you, but I've been hearing about this my whole life, about you even. Been going on for generations, all this. Was like meeting a celebrity when I first came up to let you in here, like meeting the fucking queen. They always said he would want the most beautiful woman on the whole island, and they weren't fucking wrong were they. Look at you. Bloody hell. Rare as rocking horse shit!"

Maddie grimaced as he ran a stubby finger along her jawline, though it didn't deter him from going all the way along, resting on her chin for a few seconds before she pulled it away.

"Plus, it's a good opportunity for me too, for the future," he said. "You know what they say: you've got to do your own growing, no matter how tall your grandfather was."

Maddie tilted her head back and sighed loudly. Her opening strategy was dead in its crib and she was still tied to a chair with an armed lunatic for a guard. If she could just get Wil out of the way, she was sure she could overpower Ginny and the old woman, if necessary. She stared at the oak beams overhead, hoping to be struck by falling inspiration, but all she could think about was Wil's hideous weapon, the pain it could inflict with a single swing.

"Wil can you just untie me please? I promise, I'm not going anywhere. I've got no car, I don't even know where I am. Please?"

"Oh yeah and then you run off and I'm fucked," he said with a snigger. "I've seen you in those pants, I bet you're running every bloody day. You'd leave me for dead."

If you give me the chance, you're fucking right, she thought.

She'd always exercised to stay in some kind of shape, to offset the drinking and the takeaways, but her marriage to Tony, and subsequent early retirement, had allowed her to make working out one of her many part-time jobs. As a result, she'd sculpted a body she could be proud of, and had the fitness to match it.

Her face and head were still throbbing after Wil's barrage of punches, but her lean strength had been more than a match for his raw, doughy power, not to mention that he was wheezing after less than a minute of exertion. All she needed was one chance to use it to her advantage. If she could get her hands on the Welsh hook, so much the better.

Ginny and the old woman came back through the door, chattering over one another about the merits of the grotesque garret as if they were friends returning from a day out shopping.

Maddie snarled at them in turn.

"My goodness, Gwilym, what on earth is that?" said the old woman, stabbing her wrinkly finger towards the weapon.

"It's my Welsh hook, isn't it," he said. "It's one of dad's."

"When I said bring something I meant a cricket bat or some-thing, not a bloody-"

"It's horrible," said Ginny, her hand over her mouth.

"I wasn't gonna do any harm with it," said Wil. "It's a psychological deterrent."

"I don't care what it is, put it away. Put it in the van."

"Ah, come off it, Nan."

"Just get rid, alright?"

"Ok, bloody hell," he said, walking over to where it leant against the sofa.

He had only just hoisted it into his arms when he stopped dead, transfixed on the window to the left of the front door. He stood there, staring outside as hard as he'd stare at a blackboard full of algebra.

"You've got to be fucking kidding," he said, his voice barely audible.

"What's wrong?" said Ginny.

"Oh shit," he said, plopping the weapon onto the sofa and rushing to shut the curtains. "Shut those Nan, shut the curtains."

She rushed past Maddie and did as she was told, swearing to herself as she did so.

"What is it?" said Ginny. She went over to stand behind Wil be he shooed her away.

"No, no, get back," he said.

"Wil, what is it? Get off me."

He began shepherding her away from the window, back towards the back of the room.

"It's a car," he said.

"What car?"

"A fucking car, I dunno."

"The police?" Ginny said.

"No, it's like a rental car. Fucking Skoda shit heap or some-thing. There you are, stay there... just stay there a minute. Fuck. What are we doing with her?"

He pointed at Maddie.

The old woman was still peeping through a gap in the curtains.

"Nan?"

"Sorry, sorry. Sugar. Right... get those ties off her and get her in the boiler room, we'll sort whoever this is."

Wil went for the cutlery drawer, clinked around until he found a suitable blade, then hurried over to Maddie.

"Help!" Maddie screamed. "Help, in here! Hel-"

Wil dropped the knife to the ground and rammed his chubby fingers up against her mouth. She could taste the sweat on his palms.

"Good lord."

The old woman retrieved the bag from the counter and pulled it over Maddie's head, synched it tight at the back of her neck. It squeezed the breath out of her, squeezed her silent. Wil snatched his hand out from underneath and clamped it back over the bag. Maddie felt the zip ties popping off as they were cut one at a time, then two new ones being added; one around her wrists and one just above her knees.

Maddie heard the old woman's voice, muffled by hessian and the sound of rushing blood.

"Get her in there and keep her quiet. No funny business. Go!"

30

Maddie's feet shuffled hopelessly across the stone as she was hauled off the chair and frog marched towards the door at the back of the room. It was hard enough to walk with her knees bound together, but her legs were so numb and heavy that they felt like they belonged to someone else. She tried to pull her hands in front of her for balance, but they were tied together behind her back.

Ginny, Wil, and the old woman were all hissing orders at one another as they rushed around the room, no doubt attempting to hide anything incriminating before their uninvited guest made it to the front door.

Maddie was shoved into a wall and held there as the latch rattled, then bundled into the cold air of the annex. They stumbled around for a few seconds, locked in some kind of grim waltz as Wil tried to find a suitable hiding place in the darkness. What a sight they must have been, Maddie thought; her with a sack for a head and him a one-eyed maypole dancer, tangled and swaying like the couple of clubbers too drunk to realise the music has stopped and the lights have been switched on.

Presumably to keep things simple, Wil pushed Maddie back the way they had come and pressed her up against the door and clamped his hand over her mouth, over the bag. Their breathing began to slow in tandem, though Maddie tried her best to keep hers shallow, so as not to inhale too much of Wil's sickening musk. The longer they stayed in this clinch, the more the smell of his sweat and weed and mothball clothes paled in comparison to his rotten breath. Like a fresh pile of Tank's shit. She gagged in the damp miasma of the sack, gritted her teeth in order to keep her stomach acid where it was.

"Ok, ok open it," she heard the old woman mutter.

Maddie strained to hear over the sound of Wil's panting, eventually discerning what she assumed to be a man's voice.

"Hiya... sorry, I thought... My name's Ben Degrassi. Is my dad here, Tony? And his wife?"

"Ben, how are you? I'm Ginny, Al's wife... This is my mum."

"Oh, right... Ginny, yeah sorry. I was just a bit confused; I was expecting my dad-"

"Course, yeah I bet you were," Ginny affected a playful giggle. "Yeah he's just gone to hospital to see Al, see how he is, you know."

"Ok, I see. No worries, is Maddie about?"

"She is, yeah, but she's upstairs in bed at the moment. Not feeling very well, you see. She's come down with something overnight. Probably with all the stress and everything, not surprising really is it. That's why we're here actually, just checking in on her, really."

There was a long silence, though Maddie could practically hear the cogs in Ben's brain from the next room. The murmurs of conversation started again, presumably with Ben questioning Ginny further, but Maddie was too concerned with her own problems to listen to exactly what was said.

Instead, she focussed on her sweaty captor. If she could just get away from him, even for a second, she knew she could shout loud enough for Ben to hear her through the thin wooden panelling. Maybe there would even be enough room to shunt Wil into the shelves that she knew were piled up only a few feet behind them. That amount of noise would be impossible for the women to explain away.

"Don't. Bother," Wil said as Maddie began to squirm. He was so close that his lips would have been touching her earlobe, were it not for the bag.

Maddie attempted to find an inch of space inside his bear hug and, as she moved from one side to the other, noticed something that wasn't there a few seconds ago. She paused, then readjusted herself and felt it again; the pressure of his stubby cock in the small of her back. It was nothing particularly impressive, but she could tell it was rock hard through his cotton breeches. He let out an involuntary moan as she backed herself into him, testing the waters.

As if sensing her thoughts, he pulled her tighter into him.

"I've told you. Pack it in," he said through gritted teeth. "You can still have this baby with no fucking teeth, you hear me?"

She hunched forwards and lifted her hands up and grazed the tip of his cock with her fingers.

"Oi," he said, shoving her into the door. "That's enough!"

She felt his limbs loosen as he realised his mistake. The door rattle would have to have been audible from where Ben was standing, it had to be. There was no way he'd ignore it.

"Shit," he whispered.

A commotion began to bubble up in the main house, and Maddie felt Wil's grasp lighten even more. Now was the time.

She pressed her right foot against the door then pushed up and away as hard as she could, shoving her backside into Wil's crotch at the same time. His arms were still firmly around her torso as they stumbled back, so she reset herself and swung both legs up and pushed at the door again, this time propelling them both backwards.

They stumbled and thumped into twisted metal, screws and

bolts and coils of wire all clattering to the stone floor, then fell backwards after them. The bag was thrown from Maddie's head as she slammed on top of Wil, though there was barely anything to see in the gloom of the workshop.

For what felt like an eternity, she stared at the boards above them, imagining the weird markings etched on the other side. The grotesque horned statue up there, the way it leered over the mattress. The surgical bag. Her birthing suite to-be.

"Ben!"

She screamed his name as loud as her battered lungs would allow, then hauled herself up and tried again.

"Ben! Help! Ben! In he-"

She felt the earth move as Wil writhed around underneath her, groaning and swearing and shoving at her ribs.

"Get off me, you stupid bitch!"

She was thrown sideways, the floor appearing from nowhere to knock the wind from her once again. She felt the air move as he stormed past her, then a blinding golden rectangle burst into the darkness.

As the light poured in through the open door, so did the noise; the old woman shrieking, the bass of Ben's voice, firm and measured, below it. Ginny's eerie silence. Wil screamed as he bowled into the Old Cottage.

"Get off her… Don't you fucking touch her."

"Gwilym!"

The door swung shut and the cacophony was muffled again.

Maddie rolled onto her back and rocked like an upended tortoise, trying to hook her arms around her feet like she'd seen devious prisoners do in action movies. It was easier for her than some of them made it look, and she was up and hopping forwards within seconds. She wrenched the door open, her hands and knees still bound together, and fell forwards into the living room of the cottage.

Ben was stood just inside the open front door, one of the varnished walking sticks clutched in his fist, while the old woman lay unconscious at his feet, a small knife loose in her gnarled fingers. His eyes met Maddie's for a second, before Wil stole his attention by lunging for the Welsh hook that was still on the sofa.

"Come on then," Wil said as he drew the weapon behind his head like a baseball bat.

They flinched and feinted at each other for a few seconds, then Wil made the first real move, flailing wildly at Ben's head with the blade side. Ben pulled his head away from path of the swing, then dove into the space it left behind, lifting Wil from his feet with a crunching rugby tackle. Ginny, who was stood speechless in the kitchen, screamed as the Welsh hook and walking stick both clattered to the floor, the two tangled men not far behind.

Maddie pushed herself off of her hands and knees and hobbled towards Ginny.

"Ginny," she said, attempting to distract her from the violence. "Please, help me."

She was shaking her bound hands at Ginny by way of explanation, to no avail. With the rest of her face fixed like an oil painting, Ginny looked at Maddie then back at the men on the floor.

Wil had managed to find himself on top of Ben and was trying to crush his Adam's apple with his forearm, both men spitting as they shouted empty orders into one another's deaf ears. As Wil's advantage grew, Maddie saw Ben's left hand fumbling around in his jacket pocket, the one that she knew contained his lock knife.

"Ginny, wake up," Maddie said, her voice cracking. "That knife there, give it to me, please... Someone's gonna get hurt, come on!"

Ginny's gaze drifted over to the knife next to the old woman, but she seemed uninspired by the suggestion. It was a short blade, a coring knife perhaps, but it would definitely do the job just as it had before. Maddie swore in frustration, barged past the red-haired woman towards it, then snatched it up with both hands and sawed at the tie around her knees until it popped away onto the floor.

The growling from the men increased as feet scrabbled, and hands swiped each other away to try and gain some kind of advantage. Maddie noticed Ben's knife was now out and gripped firmly in his left hand, though Wil had hold of his wrist and was bashing it into the floor.

Maddie put her knife down on the floor, then picked it up again with a reverse grip, twisting her wrists around until she was in a position to dig the blade into the zip tie. With another pop she was free, her arms afflicted by the same numbness and confused detachment as her legs had been.

She put the knife down and hurdled the old woman, who had begun to stir, and ran around behind Wil and hooked her arms under his and attempted to lever him away.

She could see Ben's face over Wil's shoulder, the heat emanating from them both as they strained every muscle to try and overpower one another. A vein was pulsating in the middle of Ben's forehead as he continued to fight, though Wil's weight advantage was clearly starting make a difference. He was crushing him.

Maddie decided to change tactics, moving around to the side and thrusting her knee into Wil's ribs. He let out a roar as the blow connected, slumping off Ben towards the sofa. Although she hadn't planned on it, Maddie tumbled over with him. They rolled around together and somehow, yet again, he came out on top. After a second or two, Ben's hulking form appeared behind him, his forearm sliding around Wil's throat like a boa constrictor.

Wil scrambled to prize the chokehold away, but Ben was too strong and too angry. Maddie, still trapped underneath both men, looked to her side and saw Ben's knife on the floor. She snatched it up and punched it into Wil's stomach, then wrenched it out and punched it in again. His shrieks were more like gargles, thanks to the firm arm around his neck, but Maddie had left thoughts of mercy far behind.

She remembered his cruel words, the feel of the blade on her shoulder as he tormented her. The smell of his breath and the feel of his cock and the threats he'd made. And she stabbed and stabbed and screamed into his reddening face.

"Stop," screamed the old woman as she appeared behind Ben, blood trickling from a wound on the side of her head. "You're killing him, you're killing him, stop it!"

She disappeared again, and Ben hauled Wil's lifeless body off to one side. Maddie winced as his face slapped down onto the floor. The sound was familiar, like an echo from a past life. The vivid memory of her father being unable to save his face from slamming into the wet stone, drunk instead of dead.

Ben stared down at Maddie, exhausted, and eased the knife from her bloodied, trembling fingers. They both stared at one another but just as Ben was about to speak, the old woman came flying back into view with the Welsh hook high above her head.

Ben did his best to stand and block the swing with his arm, but the rusted blade bit deep into the bone. He grunted and blood spurted all over the old woman's face, both of them falling to the floor. As Maddie pushed herself up, Ginny drifted over from the kitchen and slowly bent to pick up the coring knife.

"Ginny, no," Maddie said, leaping to her feet. "Ginny, please, it's not worth it. This is all-"

Maddie's eyed darted back over to see the old woman with her hands still firmly around the weapon that was buried in Ben's upper arm. She was attempting to wrench it away but was only able to wobble it, causing Ben to roar in agony with every movement.

"Go, Maddie," he said over the din. "Get out!"

Maddie turned back towards Ginny, who was still fixed in place with the coring knife dangling from her fingers, apparently still mesmerised by the violence she was witnessing.

"Ginny, stay there... don't move, it's alright."

Maddie looked over at Wil's blood-soaked body. The wounds in his stomach were seeping onto the stone floor and his tongue was lolling from his frozen lips. She moved closer, her languid movements in stark contrast to the frantic brawl on the other side of the room.

As Maddie eyed Wil's body, two different objects vied for her attention; the bloodied knife next to his twitching body, and the keys to his Hilux that had fallen out of his pocket in the melee. Ben was still shouting for Maddie to leave as he thrashed at the blade still stuck in his arm, and each time he did so, the keys called out to her.

Just then, at the edge of her vision, Maddie saw Ginny begin to move towards the struggle, springing Maddie into action. She scooped Ben's knife up out of Wil's pooling blood and lunged forward, swinging the blade from right to left and roaring like a lioness protecting her cubs from a hyena.

"I said stay there! Give me that!"

Maddie snatched the coring knife from Ginny's weak grip and turned, a blade in each fist, and fell on top of the old woman. She punched one into her dress just below the shoulder blade, and the other at the nape of her neck. The force knocked her down with a pained wail, the momentum finally wrenching the Welsh hook from Ben's arm.

He sat up and swung a wide, arcing punch at the old woman as she fell, catching her squarely in the side of her head. He swore and clapped his hand against his arm where it was cascading with blood.

Maddie helped him stand, her eyes fixed on Ginny to make sure that her surprise attack on the old woman was the final one. The whole room had become choked by a haze of violence, engulfed by the smell of blood and sweat and Wil's freshly shat linen trousers.

Maddie allowed Ben to lean against her as they moved towards the front door, which was still wide open, motes of dust swirling in the golden rays of morning, glowing like fireflies.

Maddie grimaced as she fished the keys from Ben's jeans pocket, each one of his pained grunts forcing her tears closer towards freedom. They began to find a rhythm as they staggered closer to the door, then Maddie stopped and turned to ensure Ginny was still frozen in place, and she still was. The shock of having bodies on either side of her was creating some kind of invisible barrier; a grotesque forcefield.

Maddie scowled at her one last time, then turned back and led Ben into the blinding warmth outside.

31

The rental car roared as they sped from the driveway and lurched down the hill, Ben panting on the back seat as he attempted to staunch the spurting blood from his arm. She heard him biting at his shirt, tearing strips away to use as a makeshift tourniquet.

Maddie felt so numb, so disembodied, that it was like the car was trying to run away from her. All she could do was hold on and attempt to point it in the vague direction of the hospital.

She overshot the first corner, the junction at the bottom of the hill, by well over a car's length, eventually finding the brake with a quivering foot and screeching to a halt in the middle of the lane. She half-screamed, half-cried in relief, and threw the car back into gear and let it take off again, rumbling and sputtering as it went.

Perhaps due to a lack of options, Maddie found herself on the road that she and Helen had taken on the way in. This time there was nothing but cold mountain air between her and the ravine below, though she was barely lucid enough to notice it.

The blood on her hands looked black against her gleaming white skin, as did the smears and spatters on her face; the latter startling her each time she made the mistake of glancing up at the rear-view mirror.

The sun, high and bright in the crystalline sky, was diffusing through the windows and filming everything in a layer of gold. Each time she passed a clutch of trees, the light disappeared for a second, plunging the car into darkness and uncertainty, before the reassuring daylight flooded back inside again.

All she could do was look ahead at the road, at the way the front of the car seemed to gobble up its markings one after the other.

Every so often she would feel the horror bubbling in the pit of her stomach, then rising higher and higher, up through her chest, until she was forced to exorcise it in an eye-watering, vein-bulging scream. Sometimes it was a babbling rant or a flurry of obscenities, others it was a single, wordless yell. Occasionally, she would aim one at a passing driver, particularly if they'd flashed their lights at her or been forced to swerve out of the way.

The longer they went on, winding their way out of the mountains, Maddie began to picture the old woman and Ginny, both soaked in red, coming after her in Wil's battered Hilux. She imagined them hanging out of the windows with their weapons swinging in the air, like gladiators from a chariot, drunk on blood and rage and strange faith. Was the old woman dead? she thought. If so, it was likely she had two deaths on her hands already with a third bleeding out by the minute.

"It's not far now," Maddie lied. "We'll be there soon, just hang on. Just try and stay awake."

. . .

Despite Maddie's best efforts at ploughing into walls and buildings on the way, they arrived in one piece; screeching to a stop directly outside the hospital's tiny A&E entrance, so close that Ben only had to stumble a few metres before he collided with a pair of unsuspecting paramedics walking back to their ambulance.

Maddie – with only a few cuts and bruises to show for the bursts of violence she'd endured – had been advised to admit herself as a non-emergency, just as a precaution. Once through to the waiting room, she headed straight for the toilet to face herself in the mirror for the first time since taking a man's life.

Her hair was a mess, still kinked at the side from the strange knot she'd awoken with, blood and sweat and dirt caking it together in locks. Her face was streaked with red too, though it had faded to watercolour around her eyes and cheeks where tears had washed it away. She filled the sink and bent over and soaked her hands and face, scrubbing herself with wad after wad of blue paper towels. It felt like sandpaper against her pampered skin.

Once the majority of the blood was gone, she looked one last time into the mirror, into her tired, shellshocked eyes, then took a deep breath in through her nostrils and burst back into the waiting room.

Perhaps due to the early hour, the two blocks of blue plastic chairs were almost empty. Maddie sat at the front of the right-hand block, directly opposite a smooth-faced boy dressed in flannel, denim, and work boots; most likely a young farmer, she thought. His head was bowed, his expression sullen. The older woman sat next to him, also dressed for working outdoors, occasionally turned to adjust the makeshift tea towel sling that cradled the boy's broken arm.

"Jesus! It's fine mum... just bloody leave it, will you?"

His accent was thick. It reminded Maddie of Wil's. She looked down at the lines in her hands, imagining the blood that had filled them like crimson tributaries only a few minutes earlier. His gurgled screams echoed in her ears as she continued to stare. He would never say anything, ever again, and it was all because of her. She wasn't sure if she was glad about that, or not.

"Madeline Degrassi?" came a gentle voice from over her shoulder.

Maddie stood and gave the nurse a shallow wave, her lips unwillingly twitching into an awkward smile, like a shorting circuit, as she walked. She followed the nurse into a window-less room and sat on a chair in the far corner, her back to the mint green wall. A fluorescent strip light hummed impatiently overhead, while shoes and wheels and voices swept past the open doorway like rush hour traffic.

The nurse sat down and cleared her throat, her eyes never leaving her clipboard.

"So," she said, dabbing the nib of her pen on her tongue. "The doctor will be in to see you shortly, but I'll just have to double check a few details first, ok?"

Maddie nodded.

"Ok... so, your name is?"

"Madeline... Madeline Degrassi."

"Good. And the home address?"

"105 Styal Road. Wilmslow."

"Ok, and do you have a contact nu-"

"It's there," Maddie said through gritted teeth. She jabbed her finger at the yellow file on the nurse's lap. "Look, I've answered all of this already. Can you please just tell me whether my... whether the man I came in with is ok? The man with the arm wound?"

The nurse stopped writing, looked up, and put on her best smile. "Oh yes," she said. "Another Degrassi, isn't it?"

"Ben."

"That's right, Ben."

"I know it's right... Is he ok?"

"Well, obviously we're not a hundred percent sure down here, but I think he's still in surgery at the moment. We should be able to let you know more soon."

Maddie sighed and caught a glimpse of her grimacing face in the full-length mirror on the opposite wall.

"Sorry," Maddie said. "It's been a long day already."

"I understand," the nurse said. "What I'll do is take-"

A knock on the door frame cut her off. It was short woman in her early thirties dressed in crisp, royal blue scrubs and a pair of stethoscopes slung around her dainty neck.

"Ah, no worries," said the nurse. "This is Dr Jha, she'll be looking after you from now on."

"Good morning," the doctor said, patting her thanks on the nurse's shoulder as she crept out of the room. "Is it morning still?"

She checked her Apple watch as she sat down in the nurse's place and beamed a wide, red-lipped smile in Maddie's direction.

"It doesn't matter. How are you feeling today?"

The doctor's pleasant disposition was jarring after dealing with nothing but form fillers and box tickers up until this point.

'I'm, erm... ok, I guess. Do you know how-"

"Mr Degrassi?" the doctor said, arching her perfectly manicured eyebrows. "He's stable, for now. He's still in surgery but they've managed to stop the bleeding. Very nasty injury by all accounts."

"Yeah," Maddie said vacantly. "Was a nasty thing that did it."

"Hmmm, I bet. Ok, good," said the doctor. Maddie caught the scent of some floral perfume as the doctor flipped open the chart that was rested on her lap. "So, I think I'd like to see if I can get you booked in for a CT scan as soon as possible, just to make sure that bump on the head is no more serious than it looks. Before that I'd like to have a look and see if we can catalogue these other injuries, ok?"

Maddie nodded.

"Good," the doctor smiled again, then stood and pulled the door closed and took a small torch from the top pocket of her scrubs.

Maddie did as she was told. Looking up, then down, then to the right, then saying 'ah', then letting the doctor listen to her chest and take her pulse.

"So, you were attacked, is that correct?" the doctor said as she worked.

"Yes," she whispered.

"And is there anywhere that hurts other than these injuries on your head and face?"

Maddie stayed silent as she ran through each scuffle in turn.

"My back's pretty tender," she said eventually. "And the back of my neck. I went to the floor a couple of times. Stone floor."

"Ok," said the doctor. "Any blurred vision? Blackouts? Memory loss?"

"No. I don't think so."

"Good. Anywhere else?"

"My arms, kind of. My elbows," Maddie paused and let out a sheepish laugh. "Just everywhere really. It all happened really fast."

"Bless you," the doctor said. "Well if it's ok with you, I'd like to take a look just to see if there's any bruising already, or any bleeding. Is that ok?"

"Course, shall I?" Maddie took a handful of her hoodie.

"Yes, please," the doctor said. She walked over to the small cabinet next to the door and took out a box of surgical gloves and fished a pair from the hole in the top. "There's a screen over there if you'd like to-"

"It's fine," Maddie said. She stood and walked over to the padded table against the far wall. Her limbs creaked as she wrestled her hoody over her head, adrenaline-numbed impacts making themselves known for the first time. She swore under her breath, sucking air through her clenched teeth.

Once she was stripped down to her underwear, the doctor came over and began prodding at her injuries.

"Does that hurt?"

"Yeah."

"Ok, and here?"

"Ow! Yes."

"Sorry," said the doctor with a chuckle. "I'll leave that alone for now. How about here?"

"That's fine."

"That's great, can you turn around for me?"

Maddie turned to face the sickly coloured wall.

"Wow, ok," the doctor said, her voice more animated that before. It was as if her 'real person' voice had somehow been allowed to push past her 'doctor voice' by accident.

"What is it?" Maddie said, attempting to look over her own shoulder at her back. "Is it bad?"

"No, no" the doctor said, apparently noting Maddie's surprise. "Sorry, no, it's ok. You look ok actually. I just wasn't expecting all of that."

"All of what?" Maddie said.

"Your tattoos... or, sorry, is it henna? They're very..."

Maddie looked into the doctor's eyes for a second, then into the full-length mirror in the corner. She stepped to the side, so her whole body was visible in the reflection.

From the nape of her neck, down to the small of her back, was a mess of black symbols. They varied in size; from crosses and angular runes no wider than a penny, to larger, more intricate sigils. There must have been at least fifty individual shapes, all inked onto her skin in perfect detail.

The whole piece seemed to be arranged in some kind of spiral pattern, with everything emanating from a plate-sized symbol in between her shoulder blades that looked just like the huge seven-pointed star that had been scrawled on the floor of the garret at Stone's Reach. The longer Maddie looked, the more she began to recognise other symbols from there;

almost as if they had been drawn by the same hand.

Her mouth fell open of its own accord. She wanted to scream, to run into the shower and scrub her back with wire until anything that he – that it – had touched was no more. She could practically feel the brush strokes on her skin, the wetness of the ink.

She barged past the doctor and lunged towards the wastepaper bin, slapping down onto her hands and knees just in time to fill it.

32

The visitors to the ward came in waves, lugging everything from tablets and newspapers to shopping bags full of meal deals and stacks of takeaway pizza boxes. Sullen spouses and tearful parents and oblivious children cackling.

Somehow, Ben managed to sleep through all of it. Maddie was forced to sit and absorb it – the worry and the sadness and the frustration – crammed into the same kind of tired armchair that Ginny had occupied as she watched over her ailing husband, gemstones cluttering the cabinets and talismans jingling at her throat and wrists.

Ginny. How could she have been so brainwashed? Maddie thought. She simply couldn't reconcile the gentle bohemian she once knew with the kind of person who would sanction kidnapping and perhaps even murder in the service of some insane folk religion. Now, only a few hours after the fact, it was beginning to seem like some kind of nightmare too surreal to be true. Even from a logistical point of view, Maddie was struggling understand how Ginny could have facilitated such a grotesque arrangement with her husband still laid up in hospital.

This hospital, she thought suddenly. "He's still here," she whispered.

Maddie reached over and squeezed Ben's wrist, then stood and burst through the curtains onto the ward. She wasn't certain that her brain, which felt little more than dead weight by this point, would be able recognise enough to lead her tired limbs back to Al's ward, but she resolved to walk until something sparked in her memory.

In reality, it all rushed back quicker than she could have hoped. She realised she was already on the third floor, so it took only one stretch of corridor and two sets of double doors, and she was back on the ward with its moss-green linoleum floors and mint green walls and screaming fluorescent lights. The echoing voices and cloying odours of bleach and sanitiser.

She followed the sound of conversation until she reached the nurses station, where a plump young woman sat transfixed by her computer screen. Instead of stopping as she had a few days before, Maddie simply looked ahead and walked straight past.

"Excuse me," came a voice from behind her. It was the lean, straw-haired nurse that had tried to stop her from seeing Al the last time, just emerging from the set of double doors to Maddie's left.

Maddie jerked to a halt, her fists balled at her sides, and strained her lips into the thinnest of smiles.

"Hello."

"I'm sorry," the nurse said, looking anything but. "Mr Rowlands is busy right now. You'll have to come back later."

"He's awake?"

"Yes, he's awake, but you can't-"

Maddie dropped the charade and breezed past the nurse, who began scurrying to catch up with her.

"Hold on, miss... Listen to me you can't go in there-"

Maddie felt bony fingers coil around her right arm just below the armpit.

"Miss, I'm talking to-"

Maddie spun around to meet the nurse's steely gaze and, instead of freezing – as she surely would have the last time they met – she simply grabbed hold of the woman's wrist and twisted it forwards until the rest of her stumbled after it. Maddie adjusted her body and, using the nurse's momentum, stepped sideways and swept the woman's legs out from under her, sending her clattering to the floor along with her clipboard and stethoscope. The nurse shrieked as her hands slapped into the linoleum, but Maddie barely broke stride, carrying on to the blue ward up ahead, Room Four.

She burst into the room, outraged voices still reverberating at her back, and was confronted by the frowning faces of three uniformed police officers. They had clearly been in conversation with Al – who was sat up in bed now, grinning from ear-to-ear – but must have emerged from behind the curtain at the sound of the commotion in the corridor.

"Mrs Degrassi?" said the eldest of the three men. Although it was difficult to tell, given how loudly her pulse was thundering in her ears, she recognised his dreary voice as being that of Inspector Clark.

Maddie swallowed dryly. "Are you arresting him?" she said, pointing a trembling finger towards Al.

"We're not at liberty to discuss the investigation here, Mrs Degrassi, I'm sure you're well-"

"This piece of *shit* killed my husband," Maddie yelled, foamy spittle flying from her lips.

"Alright now, that's enough," said Clark, holding his open hands out in front of his body. "Just try and calm down, ok?"

Just then the blonde nurse and a short woman dressed in suit trousers and a dark cardigan bashed through the double doors behind Maddie.

"Calm down?" Maddie said, still pointing. "He's a murderer!

He's part of a fucking cult... why are you.... Get away from me."

Every step away from Clark and the other officers was one towards the two women in the doorway. She was trapped, and she knew it, but the sight of Al's grinning face was too much to bear.

She growled and hurled herself forwards, spinning away from the first set of hands and practically sprinting towards the bed. She was so close, only a few feet away from being able to drive her thumbs into Al's glistening eyeballs, when a meaty pair of arms wrapped around her waist and wrenched her backwards.

"No," she shrieked. "Get off me, that piece of shit killed my-"

"It's alright Maddie," came Al's watery voice from somewhere outside of the scuffle. It almost sounded like he was laughing. "It's all over now, you should be happy. You've done so well; everyone has done so well. You should be-"

"Mr Rowlands, please," said Clark, grunting as he joined in to stop Maddie's legs from flailing. "Come on, let's get her out of here."

Maddie's wild eyes searched the spinning room for Al as she was hoisted up and carried towards the door, keys jangling and clothes ruffling and men whispering curses and she continued to thrash.

"Get the fuck off me!"

She heard the doors boom open and, just as she was being carried through them, the sound of Al's voice, shouting now.

"You're going to be a great mother to him Maddie, you'll see. You'll see why we had to do all of this. It's all for him. You'll see."

His voice faded along with the fluorescent lights and the buzzing activity, until all Maddie could hear was her own fevered breaths and thumping heartbeats.

. . .

Maddie was allowed onto her feet and led, silent but for her gnashing teeth, down a long and dingy hallway. The *clop clop clop* of what sounded like a hundred pairs of dress shoes was echoing all around her, disorientating her. She occasionally thrashed from side to side, though it wasn't much use. All she could do was jab her useless feet into the gloss of the tiled floor, the soles of her trainers chirping each time they were wrenched away from it.

"What are you doing with me?" She said in between struggles. "Where are you taking me? Clark? Clark! You're one of them, aren't you? One of those fucking freaks. Please, listen to me," she pleaded with the man who was dragging her by her right arm. "Please, he's part of all of this too. They're mad. They're murderers. They're gonna try and take me away."

"Please, just try and remain calm, Mrs Degrassi," said Clark. "We're just going for a chat, alright? I'm not taking you anywhere, please just stop-"

"Fucking liar," Maddie snarled. "I'm not going back there...
You *can't* do this."

The clopping seemed to echo louder with every step, closing in around her like the rising tide. Just as she was about to scream again, to try and shout the noise away, they smashed through a fire door and into the blinding light of day.

Maddie tried shield her eyes as Clark and the other two men herded her into a cramped alleyway that was hemmed in on both sides by gas canisters and industrial-sized rubbish bins. Cigarette ends were swirling in the puddles of rainwater beneath her frantic feet. Finally, they released her and shepherded her towards the far wall, the men behind her all breathing sighs of relief as she went.

"It's alright lads," Clark said, panting. "Just give us a minute. It's fine honestly, she's alright now."

The two policemen eyed Maddie with suspicion, then glanced back at Clark, raising their eyebrows at him as if he was asking them to lock him in a tiger's cage. Eventually they relented and edged back inside the hospital.

Maddie leant against the rough brickwork, her chest still heaving from the struggle.

"Alright," Clark said. "I'm not going to hurt you, do you understand? I'm not arresting you and I'm not taking you anywhere, you have my word. I just want to talk, that's all."

Maddie couldn't help but snigger in between gasping for air. "Do you even know what's going on? Look at the state of me. Tony's dead. His son, Ben, is in a hospital bed. He could have died. People did die."

"I know," he said, though it was almost inaudible.

"You what? What do you mean you know?"

Clark looked at her sheepishly, then took off his hat and clutched it in both hands. "I've been made aware of what happened at Stone's Reach."

"Are you serious? By who? Have you arrested them?"

He sighed and looked up at the sliver of sky visible between the two roofs high above. Maddie's stomach lurched.

"Please do not tell me you're a part of this."

"No," he said solemnly. "It's not that. It's... Look, my concern here is for your wellbeing, which it always has been since-"

"You're a policeman, shouldn't your concern be the law?"

Clark closed his eyes and breathed deeply. It was as if the thought of dealing justice in these circumstances was some-how causing him physical pain.

"Mrs Degrassi," he said. "I'm sure, by now, you've realised that things work a bit differently down here. The interests that are at work, it's... there are a lot of difference parties. This isn't just a few local people, It's... you can't even imagine the-"

"I've heard all about it," Maddie said, shaking her head in indignation. "The whole story. From that fucking mad old bitch, whoever she was. She was full of it. You really telling me that you're the police and you're still at the mercy of this... fucking-"

"Mrs Degrassi, please," he shushed. "Keep your voice down. This isn't the time to be-"

"Jesus," Maddie pushed off the wall and walked away from him, puddle water seeping into her trainers. "You do realise this is impossible to get away with, right?"

"I'm sorry?"

"Tony's kids have seen... well, him, as far as they're concerned. Ella, his daughter, she made this Facebook group, and announced he was back. Thousands of people saw it. You said yourself, the media were interested in the case. I don't..."

Clark's eyes dropped again.

"I understand this is a lot for you to take in," he said eventually. "But I can assure you that you're in no danger. Now that you're... well, now that all of this is has happened; you, the rest of your husband's family... none of you are in any danger. There'll be no repercussions for the, how shall we say, 'mishaps' at Stone's Reach. That's all by the by, as far as the higher ups are concerned. Just a hiccup, in the grand scheme of things. You can't make an omelette without breaking a few eggs, and all that."

He tried a cheery laugh, but it was beyond him and the situation.

"You have my word, Mrs Degrassi. Whether you believe me or not, I'm still here, if you need me to be... but − please − don't make this any worse than it already is. You can't change what's happened, and no amount of shouting about it or attacking people in hospital beds will make any difference. No one will believe you, I promise you. All the concern for your husband and the story, all the outrage and the questions... It will all fade away eventually. It always does. They'll all get distracted by something else and it will be as if it never happened. I've seen it all happen before."

"You've let it happen; you mean. My husband is dead. That woman and her grandson − fucking mad as they were − are dead. And for what?"

"Look, Mrs Degrassi," Clark said. Maddie looked up as she heard the door creak open. "Whatever you feel like you want to do to Mr Rowlands, it's not going to happen. There are officers on his ward now and, once he's out of here, they'll make sure you can't get anywhere near him. The best thing you can do now is go home and be with your family, try and move on from all this."

He looked down at his shoes for a second, then tried to force a final smile. "All the best, Mrs Degrassi."

. . .

Back on Ben's ward, visiting time was coming to an end. Patients' friends and family members streamed past Maddie, their duties done for the day, heading back into the real world. Back to the environment they wrongly believed to be less depressing, and more hopeful, than this one.

The grimace Maddie had worn since Clark disappeared melted away when she pulled back the curtains to see Ben sat up in bed.

"Hey... You're awake," she said.

He tried to smile, though it was more of a wince. Maddie thought he looked tired, but the stoic gaze that rarely seemed to waver filled her with relief.

"How are you feeling?"

It was a stupid question; she knew that before he even mustered the energy to answer. The arm that had been eviscerated by Wil's heirloom Welsh hook was strapped across his chest, and his head was wrapped in thick layers of white dressing, dried blood blooming at his crown.

"I've been better," he said eventually. "But... I've been worse too, I suppose. How about you?"

Maddie sighed and slid back into her armchair without breaking from his steely gaze. She was struggling to come up with a sentence to adequately express the depths of despair she was feeling, the utter hopelessness of their situation.

"Where have you been?" he said, growing impatient.

Maddie leant forward, pulled the sleeves of her hoody back over her hands. She opened her mouth to speak but the words were still too twisted, too strange to allow into the room.

"What is it?" Ben said, shuffling around to face her.

"I spoke with the police," she said, omitting the fact that the conversation happened after a small-scale riot on one of the other wards. "Clark."

"And?"

She shook her head and sighed.

"What, so they're in on it?"

"No," she said. "But he did know what happened. He says there's nothing he can do. Says that's it, with your dad, with all of it. It was like it was no big deal. It was like... what must it have looked like up there, you know? At the cottage. Can you imagine? How can they just cover that up?"

Maddie had quieted her voice to a whisper, but she wasn't sure why. It was almost as if she was embarrassed to discuss Stone's Reach in public. Ben clenched his jaw, then looked up at the pockmarked tiles and fluorescent lights. It was the same kind of mannerism that Tony used to affect during an argument. That seething, calculating rage that erupted inside him without a sound.

"We saw him," he said. "Me, you, Ella, Luke. All of us saw him. Your mate, Helen too."

He tried to reach for the phone in his jacket at the foot of the bed, but the pain froze him in place almost instantly.

"Ben," Maddie said, pouncing from her seat to ease him back against the pillow. "Jesus, just stay still."

"We need to call someone," he said. "Need to do something. We can't just sit here–"

"We can," Maddie said, laying a hand on his chest as she stooped to look at him. "As much as I hate him for it, Clark's right. We've run around trying to sort this out from day one, all with no fucking clue what we were doing, and where's it gotten us? What's it done to this family already?"

Maddie's hand stayed flat to Ben's gown as he breathed deeply, following the rhythm like a buoy bobbing gently on the open sea. He was beginning to smell too much of the hospital, as if all the sterile, sickly odours were starting to seep into his skin, into his teeth and his bones. She must have wrinkled her nose slightly, as he pulled away and sat back into the pillow.

"So, what now?" he said.

"*You* just need to get better. For now, that's the best we can hope for."

33

The lock clicked behind Maddie as she slumped against the front door of the house – her house, now she supposed. The adrenaline was finally beginning to drain from her exhausted limbs and, as it did, aches and pains bloomed in her elbows and knees and wrists, her head throbbed alongside her bruised jaw and swollen lip. She looked up into the cavernous atrium, the last rays of light retreating through the glass to make way for night.

It had been two full days in the same sweat-soaked, blood-stained clothes, but her surface wounds had been nothing compared to Ben's. He'd endured two surgeries – one major, one minor – and been pumped with all manner of drugs. By the second day, he'd more or less demanded that they discharge him as soon as possible or he would leave on his own. This was a bluff, of course. In truth he'd been so shaky on his feet that, when they left, Maddie had been forced to support him every step of the way from his wheelchair to the waiting rental car.

Thankfully, Kelly had been happy to take her son in and act as his nurse. Although Maddie was fully aware that she owed Ben her life, she couldn't move past the aftermath of Stone's Reach enough to face looking after him. A pervasive nothingness throbbed inside her; like the pins and needles that follow searing pain of a stubbed toe. It was as if the whole series of events, and their violent climax, had left her numb inside and out. The thought that she would have to, at some point, care enough about anything to look after someone else was, to her, inconceivable.

After a few minutes on the floor of the hall, Maddie hauled herself up and walked into the kitchen and slapped her phone and keys down on the kitchen island.

She'd already showered multiple times at the hospital, scrubbing at the markings on her back like a flea-infested rodent, but she could almost feel that they were still there, if only as faint streaks of black paint by now.

She slid a bottle of red from the wine rack – Opus One, 1997 – then took a corkscrew from the drawer and padded upstairs to the bathroom.

Clouds of steam billowed from the bath as it filled, crawling up the walls and clinging onto the ceiling like ghostly spiders. Maddie looked up at them from her spot on the bathroom floor, watched them mingle and mesh and reform, then slowly drift back down into the water. It was like she was back in school, a child transfixed by an otherworldly science experiment.

She allowed her drooping eyes to drift away and looked down at the bottle of wine, now half empty. She took hold of the neck and brought it to her lips and took a long, deep pull, then set it down on the tiles next to a rubber-handled kitchen knife. To the casual spectator, its long, sweeping blade would have looked out of place on a bathroom floor, but Maddie was used to the sight of it by now.

Not long after she'd arrived back at the house, Maddie had decided that it made sense to carry a weapon with her from room to room, just in case. She was alone in the house, of course – she'd had the foresight to extend Tank's stay with Anna – but after everything that had happened at Stone's Reach, she found herself unable to trust in things as feeble as ten-foot gates or granite walls or security cameras. After all, those things had been made by humans and, as far as she knew, humans had not yet found a way to take someone else's skin and voice and memories and wear them like a fancy-dress costume. She had to be ready for anything, at all times, despite Clark's hollow reassurances.

She lurched to her feet as water began to trickle over the side of the bath, leaning forward and swatting the tap off with her second attempt. The water looked strange without any bubbles, almost dirty somehow.

She turned back around and picked up the wine and the knife and placed them on the rim of the bath, leaving an unused pregnancy test on the bathroom floor where she'd been toying with it.

It had been less than a week since she and Tony had slept together on his return from Gothenburg, and only a few days since her night with his uncanny surrogate at Stone's Reach. If either of them had impregnated her – if that was even possible – it would still be far too early to tell. Even so, the urge to satisfy her creeping curiosity was almost inescapable.

She walked over to bath, eased her dressing gown from her shoulders, swung her foot over the side, and lowered it into the scalding water. Even with the wine numbing her nerves, the pain was blinding, shooting all the way from the sole of her foot up to her kneecap. It burned higher as she plunged deeper, her temples already rumbling as she reached the bottom. Her lip twitched as her other foot breached the surface of the water, then again as she lowered in the rest of her body.

With every passing moment the urge to scream decreased, until eventually she was submerged up to her collarbone, wraiths of steam dancing before her blurring vision. She reached up and took the bottle of wine and had another long swig, the thick liquid dribbling from the corners of her mouth, then put it back on the side of the bath.

She looked at her thumb, at the way the wine ran down the thin scar on its side, then sucked it clean and closed her eyes, allowing herself to slip serenely beneath the water.

34

Maddie stood in the kitchen looking out at the garden, the house in total darkness but for the glow of the moon. The floor-to-ceiling glass was so clear that she felt as if she could step through it and onto the patio outside. She imagined walking over to the pond, the manicured lawn massaging her bare feet, and sitting at the ice-cold water's edge and dipping her toes in. She would be able to look up at the stars and see the cherry blossoms tumbling all around her, covering her like a blanket.

She began to wonder what it was that was causing her to yearn for these sensations. What had been awakened inside her? Was it truly the presence of her first child and, if so, was it really something other than human? Was that why she felt the pull of the natural world calling her out to embrace it?

If she'd read this kind of story in a magazine, she was sure she'd use words like 'crackpot' or 'mentalist' to describe the author. Even her father – the faerie warden in-chief himself – would surely have raised an eyebrow, given the plot twists of cross-breeding and all-powerful cult conspiracies. The whole thing was so outlandish, yet the violence it spawned was chillingly real, and still ringing in her ears.

The blood and the ink had been washed from her skin long before, but the flashbacks made her feel as though she was back at Stone's Reach, causing her to squeeze the knife's handle tightly as she stared out at nothing. She could practically smell that foul mixture of odours. She could taste the blood in her mouth, both hers and Wil's. She could see his face, grey and gormless and wild eyed as he lay dead. The screams, all of the voices clattering around in her head. All of it was still so loud.

The door buzzer rang, calling her away from the window. Once she confirmed on the monitor that Helen was alone, she set her knife down on the kitchen worktop and stood by the door, willing it to open.

"Oh my God, Maddie," Helen said as she entered. "Are you alright?"

She burst in, leaving the door open behind, and Maddie fell, exhausted, into her friend's arms.

Helen helped her over to the large L-shaped sofa in Tony's Lodge and laid Maddie down, though she had to wander around turning on lamps before she could join her. Maddie curled up in the corner and let her tears flow as Helen rubbed her back and listened and whispered her consolations.

"You're gonna think I'm mad," Maddie said after the strongest of her crying had subsided. "It's... none of it makes any sense."

"You know I won't do that," said Helen.

Maddie sat up and crossed her legs, then took a deep breath.

"It's Tony," she said, her voice quivering. "He's... he's gone, again. I mean, he never... Oh God I can't even say it, fucking hell, why is this so-"

She wiped tears from her cheeks with the sleeve of her jumper and breathed deeply again.

"What I'm trying to say is: it wasn't Tony who... when we came over to the house that day, when you'd stayed over there... that wasn't... fuck, why can't I say it?"

"It's ok," Helen said. "I know."

Maddie stopped dabbing at her eyes and looked at Helen.

"You know... what?"

"Everything," she smiled. "I know everything."

Maddie looked around the room for someone to help her make sense of her friend's cryptic words, but she found only darkness. She glanced back at Helen but was unable to bear the sincerity in her friend's eyes.

"I don't... what do you mean? How can you... how can you know that?"

"Look, babe, I know you've been through a lot – more than a lot – in the past few days, but I need to tell you this and I just hope that you're not going to lose your head... ok?"

"Lose my head?"

"Yeah," Helen said. "It's gonna be a lot for you to take in and I just need you to promise me you'll try and be calm and just trust me that everything's gonna be ok."

"Helen, what the-"

"Just please, promise me."

"What could you possibly say that could be any worse than what I've been through already?"

"Please."

Maddie froze. All she wanted was for Helen to spit it out, whatever it was, regardless of the consequences. She had it right from the start, Maddie thought; the waiting really is the worst part.

"Ok... I promise," Maddie said.

"Good."

It was Helen's turn to gather her thoughts.

"So," she said. "The reason I know about what happened with Tony is because, not long before you called, I had a call from Sister Branwen."

"Oh... my fucking God," Maddie stood and walked away with her hands on her head. "You're taking the piss, Jesus fu... you have got to be fucking joking. Sister Branwen?"

"Maddie, please, you said you'd listen."

"I've lost it. I've lost my mind. It's hereditary. This can't actually be real. It can't be happening. I must be-"

"Stop it, please. You promised."

Maddie's disbelief burst into fiery rage at the sound of Helen's pleas. She turned on her heels and rushed back towards the sofa, leaning in to hold her face as close to Helen's as her exhausted limbs would allow.

"Do not – *do not* – tell me you are part of this," she said, her voice splintering. "Do not fucking sit here and tell me you knew they were going to kill my husband!"

"Maddie, it's not like that at all. It's an amazi-"

"Shut your fucking mouth, shut up!"

Maddie caught her with three furious slaps to the back of Helen's head, mussing her perfectly straightened hair into a brown tangle.

"Did you know they were going to kill him? Answer me!"

Helen dropped her head away from Maddie's fury and buried her face in her hands.

"Look at me, look at," Maddie grabbed her chin and wrenched her head up again. "Look at me and fucking tell me you knew. You knew they were gonna do it. Do you know they tried to kill Ben too? That they tried to kill me?"

Helen struggled from Maddie's grasp and fled to the other side of the wide oak coffee table.

"They'd never hurt you, Maddie, not on purpose. I would have never agreed to any of this if I thought-"

"How long have you known?"

"About what?"

"About me. About my part in this... fucking deluded bullshit. How long ago did they brainwash you?"

"They don't brainwash people, Maddie. They only choose the perfect people for the job. They didn't choose me first, they chose you. They've been planning this for so long and everything had to go just right. It was Al who found you. Saw you on Tony's Facebook, saw how beautiful you were. How perfect you were. It was just good luck that I started talking to them. It was through the groups, do you remember? When my mum was ill and we were trying to find some-"

"Jesus Christ," Maddie said, sniggering. "Those hippies you were speaking to online... Promising you a miracle? Fucking parasites."

Maddie fell back onto on the sofa and cradled her face in her hands.

"It's textbook," she said through the gaps in her fingers. "A vulnerable, gullible, stupid little rich girl... and they brainwashed you. And you fucking believed them. And now my husband is *dead*!"

Maddie screamed the last word so hard that her vision became blurred with darting silver fish. It was as if she was looking at Helen from beneath the surface of a swimming pool.

"They told us: any great endeavour requires some sacrifice," Helen said quietly.

"Shut up!" Maddie said, lunging forward and hurling a stone candle holder towards Helen's head.

She ducked and it thudded into the wall, taking a chunk of plaster with it. Maddie clenched her fists and stared wildly over the table at Helen; her stance solid, ready to continue the attack if necessary. She looked like a tribesman just aching for the naïve missionary to land on his undiscovered shore.

"If you say one more word of that... shit, I swear to God I'll kill you. I will get my knife from the kitchen and I will fucking kill you. Get out."

"Maddie, if we just-"

"Get out," Maddie shrieked. "Get out of my fucking house!"

Helen's lip began to shake, her eyes darting around aimlessly. She pressed her fingers to her lips, and eventually nodded her resignation.

"Ok," she said.

Maddie slumped back onto the sofa and watched her leave, her eyes still burning with hatred. The urge to pick up the candle holder and follow her into the atrium and beat her to death was excruciating, impossible to ignore. It was drilling into the back of her skull. Pulsating, taunting her to give in. She resisted.

"Maddie," came Helen's whisper-thin voice.

Maddie turned to face her, a disbelieving smirk on her face.

"I'm sorry," Helen said. "I totally understand you're upset, but I have to..."

She started walking back into the room with her head bowed, her hands clasped in front of her. Maddie stood.

"I thought I told you-"

"I've said I'm sorry, and I really am. I just have to... give you something."

Helen started fumbling around in her coat pocket as she backed away, holding her free hand out to keep Maddie at bay. Her expression was panicked and pleading, the whites of her eyes like beaming crescent moons. After a few more seconds of rummaging, she snatched her hand out of her pocket and unfurled her fist to present Maddie with a small velvet purse, pulled closed by a thin piece of bootlace.

"Please don't throw it at me," Helen said, still childlike in her timidity. "It's very precious."

Maddie took it and couldn't help but frown at its surprising weight. She gave the lace a tug and the purse yawned open, exposing the smooth, faintly pink object within.

Helen took a few steps back as Maddie removed the stone with her thumb and forefinger and dropped the purse to the floor. She stepped back into the Lodge, then held the stone up towards the lamp. It shimmered as she turned it over, millions of tiny internal refractions erupting like microscopic pink volcanoes. It almost looked as if it was breathing in the light, feeding off it.

Maddie looked back at Helen, who had managed to sneak all the way back to the front door.

"It was a gift," she said. "The little girl you saw... she's real. She's one of them, of the... she wanted you to have it, for the child. That's why she put it down, for you, but you scared her away. They're scared of us; they don't trust us. Sister Branwen told us all about it... but it'll be good, you know, for the baby. It's special."

"How do you... Where did you get this?"

"I told you, it's a present. For you. That little girl, she heard about what you were doing... with the baby, and the prophecy. She likes you. That's why she scared Brother Aled off the road. She felt bad for you, but... she wanted you to have the stone too. For health and happiness. You should keep it with you."

Maddie turned back towards the light again. There wasn't a doubt in her mind that it was the same stone she'd seen in the forest that day; the day where time seemed to rush past them like a gust of wind. After all, it wasn't the kind of object that could be easily mistaken. Its colour shifted as Maddie inspected it. She looked away as the door clunked open and Helen backed out.

"I'm gonna be around for you Maddie," she said. "Always. For both of you. I'm gonna be around to make sure everything's ok, when you need me. I love you."

35

The Degrassi family invites you to celebrate the life of
ANTHONY SALVATORE DEGRASSI
At the home of Madeline Degrassi – 105 Styal Road, Wilmslow
10:30am | 11th July 2019
In lieu of flowers, the family asks for donations to the Brecon
Mountain Rescue Team

After the cars had filled the driveway, they began to park out on the street. People in solemn suits and dark dresses filed in through the open gates, their heads bowed like pilgrims entering a sacred city.

As Maddie looked upon the rows of cars in black, white, and gun metal grey, she felt thankful. After all, many of those in attendance had garages full of luminous vehicles to choose from – fluorescent Italian speed machines, ostentatious American muscle cars – for Maddie, their respect was almost palatable in this gesture alone.

While the white-hot rays of morning struggled to brighten proceedings, the high garden walls and overhanging slabs of cloud combined to keep everyone, for the most part, in the shade.

Maddie was stood on the drive at the front of the house with Ben, Luke, and Ella lined up at her side. All of them were dressed in black, though Ben hadn't felt the need to shield his eyes with dark sunglasses like the rest of them had. They waited patiently as each group of guests made their way down the row with hugs, kisses, and platitudes in abundance. Occasionally, a few of the more confident or familiar mourners – usually other women – would place a gentle hand on Maddie's bump, or squeeze her reassuringly on the shoulder as they related their own pregnancy related anecdotes.

Anticipating that the lawn would be soft thanks to the morning dew and the mist that crawled out of the pond, Maddie had arranged for a temporary decking to be constructed at the water's edge to hold rows of white wooden chairs. She could see people admiring the pond and the cherry tree as they took their seat. Some tapped their partners on the shoulder to point out a darting koi beneath the surface of the water or the blooming rosebushes that lined the far wall.

Despite the strangers in her garden, Maddie felt that it was one of the most peaceful mornings she'd ever spent in it. No sweaty jogging or errand running or dogs shitting on the grass. Just the fresh air on her face and the reverent silence of collective grief.

Once everyone was seated and her stepchildren had left her side, Maddie walked to the front of the decking and stood behind a sleek wooden lectern. She removed a folded piece of paper from the inner pocket of her long, black trench coat, unfolded it noisily and smoothed it out. Once her hands were free, she instinctively rested one on her stomach.

She took a few shallow, flickering breaths and glanced to her left, at the large and ornately framed portrait of her late husband.

While she had originally decided that the monochrome photograph would give Tony an air of dignity, she now realised that it also served to show up the wrinkles that had come to line his face towards the end of his life. The dark rings under his eyes and the creases at the corners of his smiling mouth. He looked old, even if he did look happy.

Maddie tore her eyes away from his, then straightened the sunglasses on her nose and began, her voice no stronger than the fluttering of a butterfly's wing.

"First, I'd like to thank all of you for coming today. Apparently, you don't usually invite people to funerals, but I suppose that's not what this is. Things are still-" she paused to exhale, her breath causing the paper to crackle loudly as it moved.

She glanced up, muttering her apologies, and locked eyes with Ben. He nodded slowly, as if to reassure her in his own, solemn way. She sniffed and tried to continue.

"The main reason we wanted to invite you here – me and the kids – was to take the chance to get together and... remember Tony and, kind of, say goodbye to him in our own way. We may never get to see him again, so... I suppose, this is the right... the best thing we can do."

People shuffled in their chairs as Maddie shuffled her sheets of paper, a ripple of awkward coughs breaking the silence as it threatened to gather.

"So, yeah... Tony," she paused and dabbed at her nose with back of a gloved finger. "Even though he left us too soon, Tony was able to accomplish something in his life that very few people manage. He truly achieved his dreams. He built a successful company from the ground up, with the brother he loved so dearly by his side. He built a perfect family too, and a perfect home to put them in," Maddie turned to gesture towards the castle of granite and glass behind her, then at the pond and the cherry tree. "He was able to build this, to live in a place like this, because he worked hard for it. He earned it."

The sun began to peek over the back wall of the garden, warmth and golden light spilling over onto the shrubs and across the lawn towards them. It was so central in between the wall and the two banks of chairs that the whole thing looked like some kind of druid monument.

"Tony was a very special man," she continued, nodding her head. "He was also a very kind man. I'm sure this won't be the first time here for any of you. He loved to look after people and for everyone to enjoy themselves. He was never more at home than in a room full of friends, family, and laughter, preferably with a Jack and Coke in his hand."

Despite her monotone delivery, a small ripple of respectful laughter passed through the assembled guests. It was as hushed as it was short-lived, but it gave Maddie a beat to pause and wrench her face into a smile.

"Maybe, it was that kindness that's brought us all here today."

Maddie glanced up, expecting to see Ella and Luke, maybe even Kelly, jump up from their seats and tell her to stop, but the sea of black in front of her was as still as the rest of the garden. She felt a strange urge to walk out into the aisle and start prodding at people to make sure they were all still alive, to make sure the world hadn't stopped turning altogether.

"I'm sure all of you know that Tony's accident happened when he was on a trip in Wales, but what you might not know is that the only reason he was there was to support somebody else. He thought someone needed his help and, regardless of the impact on his own life, Tony dropped everything and went. His selflessness... well it most likely cost him his life, his family who he loved so much. If that isn't-" she paused and glanced up to see Ella leaning on Kelly, her face buried in her mother's shoulder. "If that isn't a hero... I don't know what is."

. . .

After Ben's austere eulogy and a full PA system rendition of

359

Champagne Supernova – Tony's signature karaoke song – the crowd ambled over to the kitchen's open bi-fold doors. A plentiful selection of food and drink had been spread across the worktops, while black-clad staff stood ready at the side with assorted hors d'oeuvres. Although it seemed strange to do so without considering Tony's preferences, Maddie had decided to hire their go-to catering company for the occasion. It was the same one that had catered many a birthday for them, as well as a pair of wedding anniversaries. The only two, she realised, that she and Tony would ever share.

This day signalled the end of a lot of other things too. The end of morning coffees on the patio, the end of watching the rain together as it bounced off the surface of the pond and drummed against the glass. It was the end of Maddie moping from living room to kitchen, glancing at the door monitor in hopes of seeing his car pull through the gates after a long trip.

Tony's death also meant the end, most likely, of Maddie living in his monstrous house. It had been iconic during the years they were together; slowly changing from a symbol of her aspirations, to the proof of her ascension. Now, it just felt like nothing more than a giant mausoleum. A monument to the perfect life she almost achieved and the husband she wanted to share it with.

While the rest of the guests were over at the kitchen, Maddie went over to the empty decking and sat on the front row of chairs and stared out at the water. After a few minutes of silence, she heard the chair next to her creak.

"Ah, bless you," said Kelly, resting a hand on Maddie's shoulder as she sat down. "How are you feeling?"

"Fine really. It's so... weird," Maddie said with a shallow smile, her eyes still entranced by the ripples of cherry blossom as they fluttered into the pond. She leant back in her chair, looked down at her bump, rested her hand on it, and smiled.

"Got another scan coming up soon. Classes too. Still loads of stuff to buy."

"That's good. Keeping busy," Kelly said. "But I meant what about *you*?"

"Me?" Maddie was taken aback, as if the question was totally absurd. "I'm ok really, I suppose... considering. There's so much to think about with the baby and Tony and everything. I've not really had time to think about me."

"Well make sure you do. I can tell you for a fact it's going to be tough. I was basically a single mum for Ben and Luke; the amount Tony was flitting all over the place, it's... well, it's fucking hard work, to tell you the truth."

They both forced out breathy laughs. Maddie kept her hand pressed on her stomach.

"Have you heard anything else?" Maddie said. "From the... you know, the investigator?"

Maddie checked over both shoulders for lingering guests or

nosy catering staff.

"It's the same story love," Kelly said. "No matter what he digs up, it never seems to go anywhere. That Clark is as clean as a whistle, apparently. As it stands, you can't provide evidence of the likelihood of death and neither can the Welsh police. Chances are they won't issue the Presumption of Death Order until you can do that, so... we're a bit stuck."

"Stuck?"

Kelly bit her lip.

"I'm sorry, Maddie, honestly I am... but there's no way I can represent you in this. Even to say you'd be fighting a losing battle is putting it mildly. You'd be asking for... just a world of shit, basically. You could even end up getting in trouble yourself."

She pulled Maddie towards her, engulfing her in a cloud of perfume and stale cigarette smoke.

"You just have to try and forget about it all for now... concentrate on you and the baby and nothing else."

Maddie nodded and nuzzled deeper into Kelly's coat, which was still damp from Ella's tears.

"I just feel so bad," Maddie said. "Like there's something else I should have done."

"Maddie," she said, her voice hushed. "Look, guilt will always fuck you up. It's brilliant at fucking you up. That's it's job. The problem is, that's *all* it can do. It never changes anything. You can't change the past by allowing the guilt to hang around with you, day in, day out, messing with your head. The only thing you can do is realise that it's doing nothing for you or anyone else and move on without it."

"Sorry, I," Maddie said as she sat up. "What do you mean?"

"I'm sorry, I just meant... I can feel it coming off you in waves, you know? I know it too well. You don't spend that many years with someone like Tony without knowing what guilt looks like."

Maddie leant as far away as she could and frowned, each word like a slab of marble as it fell from Kelly's lips.

"Whoever the father is, and whatever happened between the two of you... it's all ok now. Tony's never going to-"

"Tony *is* the father," Maddie said, her voice hardening. "The night before he left. There's no one else, there never has been. Why would you-"

Ben's face flashed into her mind and she almost had to spool through her memories to confirm that there had never been anything else between them other than that single Boxing Day kiss.

"It's Tony's," she said.

"Maddie, love," Kelly said, taking a handful of Maddie's knee. "Look, I totally get it, it's just... I know that it can't be, alright? But it's fine, I'm not judging you."

"What do you mean it can't be?"

"The baby," said Kelly, almost patronising her now. "It can't be his."

"How do you know that?"

Kelly sighed, then said: "Tony had a vasectomy years ago... did he not tell you?"

Maddie's jaw slackened and her stomach began to churn, like all of the baby's limbs were flailing at once at the mention of its name. Kelly continued, oblivious to Maddie's descent, though her voice was barely more than white noise now.

"God, he didn't tell you, did he, the old bugger. I would say I can't believe it, but I guess I can. Yeah... probably fifteen years ago now. He'd been umming and arring about it for ages then, one night, Ella must have been just three... She had this almighty tantrum and when he got back in bed he just said: 'right, that's it'. Went to get it done the next day. Said he never... Jesus, Maddie I'm so sorry. I didn't mean to... It's none of my business, only reason I mentioned it is because I didn't want you to feel bad for anything. Didn't want you to worry. Whoever the dad is, it doesn't matter now. All that matters is you... you and the baby."

Maddie turned away and looked blankly at the pond. All she could hear was the blood thundering in her ears, all she could see was Tony's face.

The breeze picked up, hurling the cherry blossom up into the air and across the garden. For an instant, Maddie caught that musty aroma one more time; the damp and the moss and the mulch.

Kelly stood up and smoothed her dress back down over her hips.

"Come on," she said, holding out a gloved hand. "I'm sorry, just forget I said anything. Come on, let's get inside and get you some food."

Maddie stood, almost automatically, then took Kelly's hand and started towards the house, both women's heels clopping against the decking. The closer they got to the doors, to the din of voices and the clatter of plates and cutlery, the more her stomach ached.

The baby growing inside of her was hungry again and, now, so was she.

Also by S. R. Durham

Prey

After falling into debt with a violent gangster, small time criminal Aaron visits his estranged grandparents' house with the intention to beg, borrow, or even steal in order to save himself and his mother.

The tables quickly turn, and Aaron finds himself taken captive by his imposing grandfather and transported to a secluded estate where the rich pay to hunt those who've made similarly unfortunate mistakes.

For the hunters, Aaron and his fellow captives are no longer human, they are merely prey.

To survive, they must become as ruthless as their predators.